CW01635217

LEAVE IT TO THE HANGMAN

THANE & MOSS MYSTERIES

BOOK 3

BILL KNOX

ZERTEX
CRIME

LEAVE IT TO THE HANGMAN

ISBN: 978-1-912767-81-6

Published worldwide by Zertex Media Ltd.
First published in 1960.
This edition published in 2024.

6

Copyright © 1958 by Bill Knox
The right of Bill Knox to be identified as the author of this work has been asserted in accordance with the Copyright, Design and Patents Act 1988.

All rights reserved. This book or any portion thereof may not be reproduced or used in any manner whatsoever without the express written permission of the publisher.

CHAPTER ONE

WITHIN THE GREY, soot-stained walls of the Justiciary Buildings, the fifth day of sitting was about to commence. Two red-coated trumpeters sounded a fanfare, and as the occupants of the crowded North Court rose to their feet, Lord Culzean, the presiding judge, came to the bench, the brilliant red and white of his robes contrasting sharply with the sombre black of waiting counsel.

In the hallway outside, the trumpeters tucked their instruments under their left arms and, medals jingling, walked away, their job done for another day.

Lord Culzean bowed a solemn greeting to counsel and jury, then slowly settled in his chair. Behind him, in its bracket on the wall, the gilt mace, symbol of the court's authority, glinted brightly in the morning sunlight. In the smaller chair placed to one side of the judge, a court shorthand writer opened his notebook at a fresh page.

Savouring the moment's leisure before the coming storm of words, he took time overheading it: 'John and Patrick Kilburn—Lord Culzean's summing-up.'

It was the final day of the trial. The judge's tired but still keen blue eyes took in the scene before him. Faces changed, but the roles remained the same, year in, year out.

The jury of fifteen—ballot had plucked six women and nine men from everyday life, decreed that they be kept from their homes and all normal contact until the case was completed, and had presented them with the power of life or death over two fellow beings.

At the counsel table, his task completed for the moment, the Hon. John Howard, advocate depute—the Scottish term for prosecutor—sat relaxed for the first time in almost a week. With his assistant, his had been the responsibility to present the Crown case, drawing from some forty witnesses, the jigsaw of evidence which built into the indictment against the Kilburn brothers.

It was a task peculiarly Scottish—for Scots law, so jealously guarded by its practitioners, allows no preliminary hearings, no opening statements by the Crown of the evidence to be presented. Only at the trial, and not until, does each fact come forth. And even then, it is by question and answer, each question having to conform to a rigorous code that ensures above all else that the prisoner's rights remain sacred.

On the other side of the counsel table, giving a brief twinkle of acknowledgement as his eyes met Lord Culzean's glance, Sir Mark Thomson, QC, Dean of the Faculty of Advocates, leaned back, his thumbs in the pockets of his black waistcoat. Sir Mark represented John Kilburn, and his final defence speech had taken three hours the previous afternoon—three long hours while the sunshine crept slowly round the dull cream of the court walls.

Not once had he faltered, not once had attention flagged as the tall, broad figure made his address to the jury. But even Sir Mark couldn't make bricks without straw.

Beside the Dean, his horsehair wig pushed well back on his head, Patrick Kilburn's counsel, Joseph Eting, QC, was penning close lines of writing on a pad of quarto paper.

Framing an appeal for his man already, thought Lord Culzean—and ready to amplify it as soon as I'm finished.

Joe Eting always believed in being prepared for the worst. He, too, had made the best of a bad job. The court had lost count of the number of times he had hammered home the point that 'Where doubt remains, that doubt must go to the benefit of the accused.'

His Lordship cleared his throat, a soft, low sound that stilled the murmur of voices from the public gallery more effectively than any court official's roar.

'Ladies and gentlemen of the jury...'

It was a necessarily long preamble. There were the three verdicts the jury could bring in on each charge, guilty, not guilty, and the Scots 'not proven.'

The latter was often unfortunately translated by the public as, 'We know you did it, but we're darned if we can make it stick.'

Lord Culzean was penetrating, meticulous, impartial—everything that his task required and more. In dry, sparse sentences, filleted of emotion, he led the jury through the contentions of Crown and defence, sketching the main points at issue, instructing firmly on law.

It was a brief, brutal story. John Kilburn and his son Patrick, had in a few short years, built up a large-scale smuggling racket out of Eire. They brought suitcase-loads of uncustomed watches, lighters, jewellery and worse over unguarded sections of the border into the Six Counties, lugged them aboard the Belfast- Glasgow boat which, like other Northern Ireland to mainland travelways, was free of Customs examination. Then, at the other end, distributed them on the first stages of their journey to a network of eager under-the-counter retailers. The profits for all concerned were high. So, of course, were the penalties for discovery.

But the Kilburns became more ambitious. They had friends and contacts on both sides of the water. Members of an illegal organisation in Ireland might feel the need for some explosives —and the Kilburns knew someone who could place his hands on quite a quantity, stolen from a North of England quarry magazine. Sometimes it might be guns, heading either way across the water according to demand. Or currency, either forbidden dollars or phoney pounds.

Gradually, the scene changed more and more often to the Channel ports when there was urgent traffic between France and England, then to other parts of Europe. In fact, they became underworld couriers supreme— and, whether their errand was dope or dynamite, as long as money was changing hands in the deal, the Kilburns were middlemen who took a handsome share for their risk.

It could only last so long. And, for the Kilburns, luck finally ran out.

One of their less important customers, caught fair and square by police as he was trying a rather clumsy mailbag theft at Manchester Exchange Station, decided to tell all he knew in an attempt to get out from under the shadow of the preventive detention sentence which was due by his record. He mentioned the Irish father and son, their courier service, and what he knew of their other activities. A very interested CID traced the Kilburns' history as running parallel with some awkward gaps in their files.

London, Belfast, Dublin—three of their apartment headquarters were empty and unused. But at the fourth, in Glasgow, there were signs of life.

The Kilburns, in fact, were just back from a quick trip to

Belfast. Trade was slack; they had contented themselves with a couple of hundred uncustomed watches, the traffic which had started them on their road to the major leagues.

It was an unhappy moment for Patrick Kilburn when he answered the doorbell that evening and two detectives marched in.

John Kilburn was sitting in an armchair in the living room, watching television, a cheese sandwich in one hand, a tumbler of Irish whiskey in the other. The detective sergeant produced a search warrant, coupled with a request that the Kilburns 'come down to the station for a few questions.'

John Kilburn got up from his chair, put down the sandwich, switched off the television set. Father and son exchanged a glance—and as John threw the tumbler of whiskey straight into the eyes of the sergeant, Patrick crashed against the second policeman. The Kilburns bolted from the room, heading for the door leading into the street.

Behind them, the sergeant was still stumbling about, blinded by the neat spirit.

Detective Constable John Newton, roaring like a bull, had picked himself up and was thundering after them. He reached the street door just as the Kilburns opened it.

What happened next was described in Newton's deposition, read in court by a fellow officer.

On the evening of March 28, DC Newton, dying with a bullet in his lung, had said he 'took' Patrick Kilburn in a waist-high tackle. They smashed against the doorpost, the policeman clinging on grimly. As they fought, the older Kilburn joined in. But, despite the rain of blows and kicks, Newton held on to his captive.

Then there was a single shot, the policeman collapsed, and the Kilburns, throwing the door wide, bolted again just as the sergeant, eyes still burning, appeared from the sitting room. The

Kilburns raced down the tile-walled tenement close and burst into the street, crashing head-on into a half-dozen passers-by.

In the sudden confusion one of the group, an elderly woman, was knocked sprawling—the automatic, fired by trigger pressure of a jarred arm, sent a bullet spanging off the concrete pavement, then itself clattered to the ground—the still half-blinded sergeant came out of the house shouting—and the Kilburns lunged forward, to be promptly grappled by the three men in the party.

Patrick Kilburn dropped on one knee, his right hand extending for the gun, then screamed in agony as a metal-tipped stiletto heel stamped down on his wrist as another woman joined in.

Eyes still smarting, the sergeant was still able to help stop the final struggles with his baton. Handcuffed through a railing, the Kilburns waited sullenly while more police, an ambulance, and a doctor were called.

But who fired the shot that killed DC Newton? The sergeant didn't know. The other witnesses weren't even sure who had dropped the gun in the street. Newton, in his dying deposition, had been unable to tell.

John and Patrick Kilburn's fingerprints were both found on the gun. The usual paraffin-wax test applied by police scientists immediately after the men were taken into custody showed traces of powder grains on each man's right hand. And both declined to go into the witness-box, or to make even a statement from the dock, during their trial.

It was, in fact, an open-and-shut case apart from that one point. Obviously, in law, they were jointly guilty of murder. Their conspiracy of silence on who fired the fatal shot seemed a long-term gamble at forcing the Crown to commute what were obviously going to be sentences of death for capital murder to life imprisonment, rather than be faced with the unpleasant task of hanging two men when one would suffice.

At not one of these things did Lord Culzean hint. When he concluded his charge, the jury of fifteen rose and filed out to consider their verdict—and were back within fifteen minutes with a firm 'guilty.'

John Kilburn, aged fifty-four, tired-eyed, grim-faced, and his son Patrick, thirty years of age, taller, slimmer in build than his father and less certain in demeanour, rose from their seats in the dock as Lord Culzean spoke.

'You have been found guilty by a jury of a most brutal and savage murder, and I cannot but agree with that verdict. In cases such as this there is, and can be, only one sentence.' He paused and felt in the narrow shelf beside him. His hand closed on the object he sought—the small, traditional black cap. 'John Kilburn and Patrick Kilburn, the sentence of this court is that you will be taken from this place to the prison of Barlinnie at Glasgow to be detained until the fifteenth day of May and on that day, within the said prison and between the hours of 8 and 10 a.m. suffer death by hanging.'

He swept the little black cap across his bewigged head as he added the final words: 'This pronounced for doom.' As he replaced the cap under the bench, the two men had already about-turned and were being swiftly taken down the steps from the dock to the cells below.

Lord Culzean quietly thanked his jury, then prepared to rise. Another year, and he would retire from the bench. Another year... he glanced at the black cap, back in its place again. He shut his eyes for a fraction of a second, stood up, bowed slowly, once to the jury, once to the counsel, once to the gold-chained city magistrates in the visitors' box. Suddenly he felt very tired. In half an hour he would be back in court again, ready for the next case of the sitting.

In the days that followed, the Kilburns waited in separate cells in the prison death-block, still maintaining stubborn silence on who fired the murder shot.

Should they both hang?

Arguments raged in every pub and club, but speculation ended dramatically just twenty-four hours before the execution date with a tersely worded Crown announcement that 'Following certain information volunteered by the prisoner John Kilburn, the sentence of death passed on Patrick Kilburn has been commuted to one of imprisonment for life.'

John Kilburn had confessed to firing the shot—even as the public executioner, newly arrived at the prison, was busy carrying out the final tests of the gallows, using weighted sacks, the measurements of which had been mathematically calculated to a formula balancing the physical build of his two potential customers.

Patrick Kilburn was told of his reprieve when he returned from a brief, escorted walk in the otherwise empty exercise yard. A sudden fit of trembling shook his body. For a moment, he seemed to be struggling to find words. Then he turned away and stood staring silently at the dull grey sky visible through the high-set barred window of his cell. He did not turn round until the cell was once more empty of all but his normal prison officer guards.

Just after 8 a.m. the following day, the public executioner entered John Kilburn's cell.

With practised ease, he pinioned the prisoner's arms gently but firmly behind his back and, with two prison officers, led him from the cell the few quick yards to the execution chamber, stopping him with his feet over an inconspicuous chalk mark on the floor—the division line of the trap.

His assistant placed a strap round John Kilburn's legs then, while the condemned man, stiff, erect, still seemed bewildered by his new, terrible surroundings, a white cap was placed over Kilburn's head, the noose was placed round his neck, with the knot drawn tight under the left jaw. A lever was pulled, the trap fell open in its hinges, the thread holding the coiled rope at near-ceiling height snapped with the falling weight.

The public executioner glanced at his watch. Just under a minute since he entered that cell, and it was all over.

At almost the same moment, Patrick Kilburn was sick in his cell.

CHAPTER TWO

DETECTIVE CHIEF INSPECTOR COLIN THANE, head of Glasgow Millside CID, laid down the corner-clipped file of report sheets he had been studying. Once again, he read the letter with the 'HM Prisons' heading. Then, shoving back his chair, he strode out of his office and into the smaller room just down the station corridor.

'Phil,' he said. 'We're heading North on a wee job. Remember the Kilburns?'

Detective Inspector Moss abandoned the comic strip section of his morning paper, took another sip from his cup of tea, and nodded. 'Five years ago, isn't it? The case was in this division, just before we were transferred to the area.'

Thane gave a yawn. He had been in bed for only three hours the previous night, thanks to an inconsiderate safe-blower.

'Five years it is. They hanged the father after he confessed, and the son had corroborated. The son had his sentence reduced and is doing "life." He is in that new open prison near Perth. Now this has turned up.' He passed over the letter. 'According to this report from the prison governor, Kilburn had a threatening note in his mail two weeks ago. It was postmarked Glasgow, was unsigned and simply said—'

Moss whistled aloud. 'I've reached that part. "You have stolen five years. Now you will be killed, and the reckoning will be paid." Does Kilburn know who sent this?'

'That's it.' Thane, leaning against the nearest wall, went on, "Plenty of notes like that are found when prison staff are checking incoming mail, as you know. This one didn't get past the governor's office, so Kilburn knew nothing about it.

'But yesterday morning Kilburn demanded an interview with the governor first thing, and produced an identical note he found in his bunk. The fellow was in a state of panic and wanted to be taken off his outside work-party. Kilburn is a star-class prisoner and has a cushy number, tractor-driving with the prison farm gang. But he said he would be in danger there. He'd rather be locked in a cell all day after seeing that note.'

'Does Kilburn know who the note was from?' asked Moss, swirling his half-empty teacup.

'That's where we come in,' said Thane. 'The governor decided that the note through the post and the note found in prison appeared written by the same hand, and quizzed Kilburn. But all he could get out of the man was that this was definitely no joke as far as he was concerned. Well, the governor transferred Kilburn to a work squad in the prison gardens, and has told the "screw" in charge to keep an eye on him.

'The letter came from Glasgow, the Kilburns are an old Millside case, so someone at Headquarters looks around, decides that our division is as quiet as a home for retired gentry at the moment, and makes up his mind that we might as well work for our living.'

Moss sighed. 'There's a good boxing show on at St. Andrew's Hall tonight. I'd thought of going.'

'Maybe, Phil.' Thane glanced at his wristwatch. 'There's a train to Perth from Buchanan Street Station in half an hour. We can get lunch aboard, go straight on to the prison from Perth, find out what we can from the governor, pay our respects to the local force, and maybe get another train back about five. With luck, you might just make that boxing.

'I've got my own worries. Mary and I were going to take the kids to the zoo straight after school this afternoon. I'll need to scrub round that, which won't make her deliriously happy. This is the third arrangement in a row I've had to cancel.' He yawned again. 'I'll get a nap on the train North—that's one consolation.'

Leaving Moss still moodily swirling his teacup, Thane went back to his own room, lifted the phone, and asked for the scientific bureau at Police Headquarters. According to a memo attached to the governor's letter, handwriting experts were busy comparing the two notes sent to Kilburn.

It took only a matter of seconds for the connection, but with his free hand, Thane had already lit a cigarette, taken a pencil from his wallet pocket, and had commenced constructing an elaborate doodle on the desk blotting-pad.

Patience was an acquired discipline rather than a natural trait of the tall, dark-haired detective, in his mid-forties and carrying the first few pounds over what he used to joke of as his fighting weight.

He could admit to himself that more than a few of his cases had been solved by an impetuous rush along one of his sudden hunches rather than by the cold, machinelike method which he believed was the ultimate weapon in police investigation.

Phil Moss, a few years older than Thane, and exactly a quarter-inch over minimum police height, was outwardly a more relaxed, casual individual, but bottled-up nervous tension had left him with a grumbling ulcer and a somewhat grey outlook on his fellow humans.

If Moss had ever been asked—which he hadn't—he could have told Thane that it was that exact combination of beautifully balanced gambling guesswork and steel-ruled attention to detail that had resulted in his chief jumping by sheer ability over several heads in the promotion stakes. And a small battalion of dangerous men, removed from circulation for a substantial period of years, would have grudgingly agreed.

Thane was shading in the funnel of a small steamer which had unexpectedly emerged from his doodle when he was finally connected with the sergeant handwriting expert. The scientific bureau man had his report ready and waiting.

'The notes were written by the same hand all right,' he confirmed. 'No doubt about it. Adult style, moderately educated —you know, well enough formed during schooldays, but hasn't been used enough since to get down to the usual office worker's scrawl. The two notes are from the same notepad, the same type of notepad anyway, according to the check we ran on the paper. No joy with prints, however. One or two smudges, but not enough to give us anything to go on.'

Thane drew a billow of smoke from the ship's stack. 'Any chance of telling what time there was between the notes being written?' he asked.

'Have a heart,' came the indignant protest. 'We've used up our quota of miracles for this month.'

He thanked the sergeant, broke the connection, then flashed the Millside station switchboard and asked for a car to stand by to carry them to their train.

CHAPTER THREE

THE TRAIN JOURNEY through the sunbathed September countryside was the usual quick, monotonous run, with lunch occupying most of the distance. Phil Moss got through it with a slight slackening of his diet-sheet and a couple of bismuth tablets. A county car, a 3.4 Jaguar, was waiting just outside Perth Station, a stout man in prison service uniform standing beside the waiting police driver.

'Chief Officer Dunsyre,' he introduced himself. 'Governor asked me to come down—we've been having a busy morning. Someone took a potshot with a rifle at friend Kilburn just over two hours ago.'

The car was already in gear, pulling away from the station and heading through the town centre and the main road beyond to the prison.

The warder officer told the suddenly tensed detectives, 'Kilburn was working in the market garden about two hundred yards from the main block—we're an "open" place, as you know. He was hoeing a patch of turnips. There were another five men and an officer within a radius of about thirty yards. The first shot grazed him like this...'

He drew a swift line along his left lower ribs.

'Kilburn went down like a log—mixture of fright and shock, I suppose—and whoever it was tried a second shot. That bullet missed, though. It must have been a quick snapshot. Anyway, it smacked a neat hole through one of our wheelbarrows that was lying six feet behind Kilburn. The other men had started running over to him. When the second shot came, they caught onto what was happening, and dropped flat.

'But,' he said, refusing a cigarette and sucking instead at an empty pipe pulled from his tunic pocket, 'there were no more shots. The unknown marksman didn't seem to want to take the risk of hitting any of the other men in the market garden.'

The car was through the town now, and heading along a tree-lined country road, slowed by a lorry ahead carrying a high, overhanging load of golden-brown hay. Thane wound down the rear-door window, tossed his cigarette end out and, as the glowing stub bounced on the road, let the cool air come blowing in, pleasant in the car's warm interior.

'Where's Kilburn now?' he asked.

'In the sick bay. We don't rise to a full-scale hospital ward, but there's nothing seriously wrong with him.'

'How about Mr X?'

'Our friend with the rifle?' The prison officer shrugged. 'Well, it took a few minutes to get things organised. There was a bit of a panic on, frankly, and the guard didn't feel he could run off for help and leave the work party on its ownsome. But we turned out every man we could spare, and the governor phoned Perth police in the direct line. They had three carloads of men out in about fifteen minutes. Whoever it was that was shooting had got well away by that time, however.' He broke off, and, pointing ahead, said, 'Look, we're coming up to Warrander now —it's that big low building on your right.'

Warrander House had been, for over a hundred years, the seat of one of the best- known "county" families in Perthshire.

Then the laird had decided to swap its rambling, draughty expanse for the central-heated comforts of a town house in Edinburgh, and the Scottish Office had saved the mansion from the demolisher's hammer by taking it over as a prison-without-bars.

A prison officer on duty at its iron main gates, which were topped by a single strand of barbed wire, and the six-foot fence, also of interlaced barbed wire, running round the outer perimeter of the house and its immediately surrounding grounds—meant to keep outsiders from getting in as much as inmates from getting out—were the main immediate signs of Warrander House's new role.

They drove past half a dozen long, single-storey buildings, resembling wooden bunkhouses, and the car halted in the mansion courtyard. Two other cars were already there, one with a police driver standing by, the other, a light blue Standard with a row of pennants stuck to its rear window.

Moss grinned as, following Thane and the prison officer from the Jaguar and mounting the House steps, he caught the printed legend, 'Don't follow me—I'm lost,' on the nearest of the little flags.

'Doctor's car,' gestured their guide. 'He's the local GP, and takes care of most of our needs. Anything serious, we send the patient in by ambulance to Perth Prison or to one of the hospitals.'

The parquet flooring inside the entrance hall was still smooth and finely polished. The stairway, however, had no carpet and its wood had been stained a mahogany hue. The governor's office was on the first floor—an airy, high-ceilinged room with a large bay window giving a view down towards the River Tay, just discernible as a silver streak in the distance.

Governor Maxwell was a tall, bald man with an eagle beak of a nose, which, in conjunction with his pronounced stoop, had made more than one prisoner "on the mat" decide irreverently that he was like a vulture sitting with folded wings, ready to flap off through the air at a moment's notice. A three-inch scar running at an angle along one cheek and a missing earlobe showed where an unimpressed customer had once taken a swipe at him with a homemade chiv. As a result, the con had found that a broken jaw can be a very painful thing. But that was in the past.

The prison-without-bars was a very different place. Only men whose background and behaviour showed willingness and obedience could graduate to it from the normal cell-block jails and enjoy its freedoms and privileges.

Its ideal was one of the boldest experiments the prison service had ever tried, and the results in terms of a return of trust and a record of men going straight more than justified the existence of such places as Warrander House.

Thane had heard plenty about Governor Maxwell, all of it good, though this was their first meeting. He and Moss shook hands with the bald man, took the deep leather armchairs he waved them to, and waited.

With a slightly embarrassed smile, Maxwell leaned well back in his seat, and, palms together, fingertips touching his chin in an attitude of prayer, said, 'We're having a somewhat unusual day, as the chief officer would tell you. Where do you want to begin? Shall I have Kilburn brought along?'

'In a minute or two, sir,' replied Thane. 'Right now, I'd like to fill in a few background details. Do you mind if the inspector takes a note of points as we go along?'

'Fire away,' invited Maxwell. 'Incidentally, the local police should be back fairly soon—they're out with some of my men trying to find the spot these bullets came from. You can sort out the procedure end of it then, I suppose—won't be any trouble over that, I imagine. This seems to be a completely Glasgow affair, like so many other flare-ups these days.'

The detective's native pride was touched. 'Be fair,' he

protested with a smile. 'We don't have a monopoly in crime; it's just that we catch more "neds" at work than some other places do. Our cops don't spend their time guiding tourists round culture factories.' He turned to business. 'How long have you had Kilburn here, sir?'

Governor Maxwell flicked open a folder on his desk. 'I've got his file right here. He came exactly two months ago, after serving the first part of his time at Perth. As a long-term prisoner with a clean record of conduct since sentenced and no previous convictions, he was eligible for transfer. If he continues to behave, he should be out in another seven years.'

Any more potshots like today, and he may leave a lot sooner, feet first, thought Moss, as he noted the key points from the governor's report.

From the moment of his arrival, Kilburn had behaved as a model prisoner. Then, the previous morning, just after finding the note in his bed—each man had an individual cubicle in the bunkhouse huts—he had come before the governor in a white-faced state of fear.

'At first, he said he wanted a transfer to a job indoors. We have a few prisoners who work in the cookhouse or clean out the place, and others work in a small farm equipment repair shop round the back of the building. When I said I didn't think anything like that was called for, he begged me to send him back to Perth Prison.

'Well, I told him we weren't running a holiday camp, and that the best thing for him to do was to tell me all he knew.' The governor shrugged his shoulders. 'He said he couldn't tell me, but that he was afraid, and that his life was in danger. After that, I sent him packing, and passed the matter to the police.'

Phil Moss looked up from his notebook. 'You did transfer him from his normal work, I think?'

The governor looked a trifle uncomfortable. 'That's correct. Call it insurance. I wondered at first if it was just a put-up job to win him a better billet. He was on the farm gang, and they're doing some pretty heavy work just now reclaiming a new stretch of waste moorland about two miles from here. Just to be on the safe side, however, I switched him to the market garden squad.'

Neither detectives nor prison official had voiced their common thought. Did some relative of the detective murdered these five years ago feel that the law should have hanged both Kilburns—and that now was his chance to settle the account? It would be nasty if that turned out to be the case; nasty for all concerned.

The governor pursed his lips. 'The rest of the story, or as much of it as we'll know until the local police return, you know already. I'll get Kilburn now. The doctor said he just needed a spot of scientific bandaging.' He pressed a bell button on the desktop. There was a moment's delay, then a double knock on the office door.

Patrick Kilburn came in slowly, a burly prison officer just behind him. The prisoner's chocolate-brown battledress jacket hung unbuttoned. He wore neither shirt nor vest, and the edge of a white gauze pad dressing, taped to his left side, was just visible as he turned to face the governor's chair.

Thane took a long look at Kilburn.

The Kilburn case had been just a year before he and Moss were transferred to the Millside division, but Thane remembered a day he had spent in the High Court, listening to evidence in the case and studying the men in the dock.

Then the younger Kilburn, with a pencil-thin moustache, long sideboards, and small, frightened eyes, a sturdy figure in an expensively tailored suit, had seemed little different from a hundred other men whose photographs were in the Criminal Records Office files.

Five years in prison had fleshed the high-boned face and the muscular body with extra pounds. The starchy diet did that to them all. He was broader in the shoulder too, and that, with his long arms, made him seem smaller than his five foot seven.

One thing was still the same—the eyes were still frightened, darting round the room, staring out of the window.

'He won't get you here, Kilburn,' said Thane. As the prisoner's attention switched to him, the big detective asked quietly, 'He'll try again, won't he?'

Kilburn moistened his lips. 'They... he will. You've got to get me out of here. I've got rights. You can't stand back and let me be killed. I want to go back to a proper prison. I'll be safe there.'

Thane's manner changed. 'You said "they." Who are "they"? You know who's after you. Tell us, and we'll round them up.'

Kilburn looked down at the floor, silent.

The prison governor turned to the detectives. 'I told you—he just refuses to talk. Kilburn...' The prisoner looked up sulkily. '... someone tried to murder you today. Someone else could have been killed in that shooting. If you're not interested in your own safety, think of these other men.'

'To hell with the others,' Kilburn burst out. 'It's me that's in danger; no one else.' He took a sudden step forward, both hands gripped the edge of the governor's desk, and he almost shouted his demand again. 'Get me out of here.'

The prison officer escort jerked the man back. Kilburn didn't struggle. His frame seemed to go limp.

Quietly, sullenly, he asked, 'Can I go now?'

The governor nodded. The escort's grip tightened on one sleeve of the battledress, and Kilburn was led from the room.

'Well, we know one thing anyway,' said Thane as the door closed. 'Kilburn knows who is after him all right. And he must have a pretty powerful reason for wanting to keep quiet about it. How do you actually stand, sir, about this transfer he's asking for?'

'It can be done,' said the governor. 'A couple of phone calls and half-a-dozen forms filled in, and, under the circumstances, we could put him anywhere we wanted. You think we should move him?'

'Provided we can keep him out of danger, I'd rather see him sweat for a day or two,' replied the policeman. 'He may decide to tell us something that way.' He glanced at his watch. 'I'd like to have a chat with the local officers. Do you think we could go and find them?'

'Of course.' The governor rose. 'We can use that police car you came in. Detective Inspector Roy is in charge of the investigation.'

They found the Perthshire men on the fringe of a small, wooded copse half a mile away. Thane and Moss scrambled over a low dry stone dyke to be greeted by a large, beefy man wearing a dirty, white waterproof coat and a brown homburg hat.

'I heard you were on your way up,' greeted Detective Inspector Roy. 'Well, this is the place.' He broke off. 'Tommy, keep your great hooves away from that path till we check it for footprints.'

An embarrassed young constable, scarlet-faced, stepped gingerly back from the forbidden ground.

'Polis,' growled Roy. 'Some of them are that dam' stupid that it couldn't be true. Like I was saying, Mr Thane, this is where our marksman was waiting. We've found this.'

From one pocket of his raincoat, he pulled a small transparent envelope. Nestling in it was a single brass cartridge case. He turned the case over so that the base, with the punch of the firing-pin clearly visible, could be seen.

'It's a .300 rifle cartridge, recently fired.'

'A .300?' Thane whistled softly. 'That's a Canadian calibre, isn't it?'

Phil Moss interjected. 'Canadian Lee-Enfield,' he confirmed. 'I was in the Home Guard for a spell during the war.

We had them. They painted a red band round the gun so that we didn't try to use regular .303 ammunition with them. One or two didn't turn up when the Home Guard was demobbed.'

'Aye, that's right,' agreed the Perthshire detective. 'There's more than one deer-poacher with a .300 hidden in his loft these days.'

Together, they took a closer look at the sniper's lair, a flattened patch of grass and weed on their side of the rough stone wall, sheltered on the far-away side by a clump of shoulder-high bracken.

Detective Inspector Roy pointed over the wall. 'Down there, about six hundred yards away. See that turnip field? There's a couple of men working at the far end o' it now. Well, Kilburn was working about twenty yards in from this end when he was shot at. With a wall like this, you could stick a rifle through any o' the cracks between the stones and fire without being seen at all. An' take another look at the way the grass had been flattened. Notice anything?'

Thane turned, and studied the spot, now marked off by a streamer of white tape. He grunted suddenly and moved closer.

'Two of them?' he asked.

'Aye, that's how it looks,' said Roy, pointing to the spot. 'The grass is generally flattened, but if you look closely, there's two spots about a yard apart where the flattening is more clearly defined. Two people waited here, waited for quite a wee while, the way I see it. Then when Kilburn was as near to them as he was likely to be... bang.'

A constable—not the red-faced Tommy, but an older man—came over to them.

'We've followed that track, sir,' he reported. 'It goes about two hundred yards back, then joins a farm road. There's marks of coming and going, most of them pretty faint. We found one thing though, a footprint, or most of one anyway, in a soft patch of earth just a wee distance from the road. It was pointing back towards the road—she must have been in a hurry getting away, and not noticed.'

'She?' Thane and Moss spoke with one voice.

'Aye.' The constable gestured with his hands. 'It was just a wee bit size of a shoe. "Flatties" I think my wife calls them.'

It was an hour later. They were back in the governor's office, Thane, Moss, Inspector Roy, and Governor Maxwell. Chief Officer Dunsyre had seen that the eighty prisoners under his charge had been settled to their evening meal, with Kilburn having his food in the sick bay, where a prison officer was detailed to stand guard, and had also joined the conference. Thane had phoned Glasgow and told the Millside duty inspector that he would not be back till late that night, if at all that day.

A thick ham sandwich in one hand, a cup of tea perched on his chair-arm, Inspector Roy sketched his progress.

'So far, we've found one cartridge case and one bullet—the bullet that hit the wheelbarrow. It's pretty well flattened after punching through the metal, but the ballistic boys should get something from it. I think we can say, anyway, that the bullet was fired from that spot behind the dyke. We've got a plaster cast of that one print, almost definitely a woman's. We found the two indentations on the grass, and cigarette ash traces beside each. No stubs—they were careful about that. So, it looks as if we're after two people, one a woman. We've had a general alert put out, but I haven't much hope. They probably got away by car. They certainly couldn't walk far carrying a rifle without being noticed.'

'Couldn't they have hid the weapon?' asked the governor.

'We checked round about the area, sir,' said Roy. 'No sign of it. They could have dumped it farther along the road, of course.

My own belief is they'll still have it, ready to have another crack.'

Thane agreed. 'They'll probably be back once they learn Kilburn is still alive. But I think we can be sure of one thing. It's Kilburn, and Kilburn alone, who is in danger. Only two shots were fired. We're pretty certain that whoever was shooting saw the other prisoners running over, and didn't want to chance hitting anyone else by mistake.' He turned to Phil Moss, who was munching a dry tea-biscuit out of respect for his ulcer. Ham and marge sandwiches—thick, prison style—did the sufferer's acids no good whatever.

'Phil, you've been going over Kilburn's file. Any hint there as to what might be going on?'

Moss shook his head. 'Nothing. In fact, there's so much of nothing that something seems wrong about the whole affair. No visitors, no misdemeanours, no requests. On the face of it, he's a man doing his damnedest to behave and get out of prison in the shortest possible legal time.'

'He gets on all right with the other men,' agreed the chief officer. 'Keeps pretty much to himself; does what he's told.'

The telephone on the governor's desk gave a long ring. He picked it up, holding his other hand before him in a request for silence. The call lasted less than three minutes. When he replaced the telephone, he seemed happier.

'Well, we'll soon have Kilburn off these premises,' he informed the circle of men. 'That was the Home Department. I've been told to transfer him back to Perth as soon as it's convenient, until this business has been sorted out. They would hate to lose him and—' He stopped abruptly.

The clatter of smashing glass and the immediate sound of shouts was coming from near at hand. Thane was at his side as the governor dashed from the room, out into the corridor.

A blue-uniformed prison officer was running towards them.

'Someone tried to get Kilburn again,' he gasped. 'He went

over to the window of the sick bay, and a shot just missed him.'

Governor Maxwell led the way to the sick bay, a large airy room on the upper floor, containing three beds. Kilburn was crouched on the carpeted floor, one nervous hand-picking splinters of glass from his battledress. Two prison officers were already in the room, one cautiously peeping round the edge of the window frame, where only a few jagged sections of the pane remained.

'Nothing to be seen, sir,' he reported. 'Whoever it was must be using a telescopic sight.'

'Keep clear of the window just the same,' warned Inspector Roy. 'They may still be out there watching, and though it's Kilburn they are after, they might make an unfortunate mistake.'

Colin Thane was examining the wall opposite the window. 'Want the bullet?' he asked, taking out a broad-bladed knife, and preparing to dig into the plaster.

'Aye, but watch you don't scrape the metal—och, I'm sorry,' apologised Roy. 'You know the ropes as well as I do, and better. But I've got to keep an eye on some of my lads.'

'Forget it.' Thane carefully carved a wide hole in the plaster. The bullet was buried three inches deep, its nose flattened against the old stonework hidden under the thick coating. He coaxed it free and handed it to Roy.

'My bet is ballistics will match it with the bullet you got from the last attempt,' he said. 'Looks pretty much the same. Now, if we can work out where it came from...' He gazed out of the window. 'It came in at a slight left-hand angle, judging by the hole it bored. Let's see, that gives us a line just about to that house over there. Who lives in it?'

'No one,' said the prison governor. 'It's been empty for years. We use it as a store for some of the farm equipment. Want to go over?'

'No rush,' said Thane. 'Whoever it was is well away by now. Though if a couple of your men, Inspector...?'

'I'll fix that,' nodded Roy, striding from the room.

The Glasgow man turned to Kilburn, who had carefully crawled clear of the window and was now perched nervously on the edge of one of the sick bay beds.

'That's the second try, Kilburn,' said Thane. 'Want to talk about it yet?'

Kilburn just shook his head. 'Get me back into a proper prison,' he demanded. 'If they kill me, it'll be your responsibility.'

'Maybe,' said Thane. 'But you won't be around to see the fun if that happens, will you? And would you be so safe in prison? If this man and woman are so keen to get you, won't they find a way even there?'

'A woman too,' Kilburn whispered. 'God... she couldn't, she just couldn't. How do you know there's a woman in it, copper?'

'We found a nice footprint. Who is she? An ex-girlfriend?' asked Phil Moss, prodding some of the broken glass into a neat heap with his shoe.

'That's my business,' snarled Kilburn desperately. He rose to his feet, keeping out of range of the window. 'If you've any pity, Governor, you'll move me to Perth—not tomorrow, or the next day, but now.'

Out of the corner of his eye, Governor Maxwell saw Thane give a tiny shake of his head. 'We're doing what we can,' he told the man before him. 'No one's likely to try again tonight. By tomorrow we'll see how things are.' He turned to the prison officers. 'Keep him in the main block overnight, and away from windows,' he instructed.

Outside, in the corridor, Thane crooked finger and thumb in a sign of approval. 'Thanks. At this stage, we're pretty well in the dark. As I said before, if we let him sweat on it for a few hours, he may decide to co-operate.' He glanced at his watch. 'There isn't much more we can do here tonight. And there's one or two things I'd like to check on in Glasgow that may help us.

Can we get a run back to the station in—Oh, here's Inspector Roy. Can we borrow one of your cars to catch a train?'

Roy raised a surprised eyebrow. 'Are you not staying? I've just had a radio call from the patrol car I sent up to that storehouse. Nothing to be found. I thought we might have another go at Kilburn.'

Thane shook his head. 'Kilburn isn't talking yet. And I want to dig into his background at Headquarters. We built up quite a dossier on him and his father during the trial—there may be a lead lying somewhere there. Inspector Moss and I will come up by car in the morning, first thing.'

'Fair enough.' Roy nodded understandingly. 'Well, we'll keep a guard round the prison outskirts tonight, just in case. And maybe you can have some extra men on duty inside, Governor?'

Maxwell agreed. He had another idea in mind too, though he kept it to himself. Old Daddy Kenmay in the cookhouse, a likeable, talkative rogue doing five years for embezzlement, had a knack of knowing most things that were going on in the open prison—whether among the prisoners, or the staff. And Daddy Kenmay liked nothing better than a "wee chat with the governor"—it made him feel important, as befitted a former chief cashier. But Daddy would only talk if they were alone together, and if the governor, as usual, promised that his identity would never be revealed to a soul.

So, they went their separate ways—Thane and Moss dashing for their train, with Phil Moss wondering if he dare mention that boxing-match; Inspector Roy, with his bullets, shoe-cast, and cartridge case, and a puzzled indignation at the sniper who had entered his domain; the governor, with two prisoners on his mind—Kilburn, frightened and under guard, and the garrulous Daddy Kenmay.

Six hours later, the pot was to boil over. And the resultant mess was going to take an awful lot of mopping up.

CHAPTER FOUR

FIND a five-year-old grudge strong enough to make someone not only want, but try darned hard, to commit murder. A grudge that might have a woman involved in it somewhere.

Thane and Moss spent that night groping into the past, their only guide the police file on the Kilburn case. After two hours, Thane cursed wearily but efficiently, lit his sixth cigarette, and looked across the table at Phil Moss.

Warily, the inspector returned the gaze. He had just begun reading the pre-trial precognition sheets, a run-down of police evidence in the Kilburn murder, for the second time. A tiny corner of his mind was still mourning his lost boxing-match. But, like Thane, his entire attention was devoted to finding a lead, however slender.

'Still nothing?' asked Thane.

Moss shook his head at the big man opposite. 'Not a sausage. We rule out the family of the detective who was shot—and we have to now, especially after that check Sergeant MacLeod has been running on their movements—and the rest is a blank.'

'Aye.' Thane took another draw at his cigarette, felt the taste of the smoke flat on his palate, and stubbed it on his tin-lid ashtray. 'One funny thing struck me. Remember a point in his file at Warrander House—no visitors? Yet he's got a family according to this...' He tapped the blue folder before him. 'Mother, brother, two sisters. They're living over in Ulster, or they were five years ago.'

'Would they know anything about what went on?' asked Phil Moss. 'After all, father and son were in this alone as far as any of this evidence goes. I came across a couple of mentions of the brother—Liam, I think he's called. But he was supposed to be on the straight and narrow, a farmer or something.'

'That's true,' nodded Thane. 'Probably they were in the clear, or as near clear as you can be with a couple of crime couriers in the family. They knew where the money was coming from, you can bet your boots. And maybe they heard the odd thing which would help. Perhaps they'd talk if they knew someone was taking potshots at friend Patrick.'

'You'd think they would have visited him once or twice at least over the years,' mused Moss. 'Maybe they just decided to wash their hands of him.'

'Check on it, Phil,' ordered Thane. 'Get on to Barlinnie and Perth. See if you can get someone to dig into the records and make sure there have been no visitor passes issued to him. Barlinnie will have the pre-trial list as well—that might help. I don't know what particular good it will do, frankly, but it's always a start.' He pressed the bell-push beside him, flicking rapidly through the Kilburn file at the same time.

'Sir?' The uniform orderly had moved quickly, but was still conscious of the racing form sheet bulging inside his jacket, where it had been hurriedly thrust.

'Put out a teleprinter request to Belfast,' said Thane, stretching back in his chair and clasping his hands behind his head. 'I want a run-down on the family of John Kilburn, hanged for murder. Reported staying on a farm near—what's the place again—near Fordnacloy, five years ago.' Thane checked the file, scribbled the town name on a piece of scrap, and tossed it across the desk. 'Family's present whereabouts unknown. Say we'd be grateful for any Criminal Records data they've got on a character, Liam Kilburn.'

'Any particular officer, sir?' the orderly asked, turning to go.

'No, just Royal Ulster Constabulary HQ,' said Thane. 'The officer in charge of their end of this case retired a couple of years ago, so it'll have to be a general inquiry.'

As the orderly vanished, Phil Moss got up and also moved towards the door. 'I'll get this query put through now,' he told Thane. 'Though it's nearly eleven now. We'll probably need to wait till morning for the reply.'

Thane paused in the middle of turning a page. 'That time already? Well, there's not much more we can do tonight anyway. I'll pack it now myself—you do the same, Phil, after you pass that request on to the prisons.' He lifted the phone, and asked, 'Give me my home, please.'

The ringing tone beat twice, then a voice answered.

'Mary?' Thane's voice was suddenly softer. 'Me—how are the kids?' He listened, chuckled. 'Little devils. Well, I'm just leaving for home—put the kettle on in fifteen minutes, will you?' He listened again for a moment, an almost boyish grin lopsided across his face. 'At that rate, make it ten minutes,' he said, hung up and swung round, facing Phil Moss again.

'How long since you were married now, Colin?' asked Moss.

'Twelve years. Why?'

Moss shrugged, wooden-faced. 'Almost indecent, the pair of you still behaving like that.' The wood crackled and his eyes glinted mischievously at Thane's surprise.

'You lay off, you—you walking chemist's shop,' spluttered Thane. 'Mary was simply telling me she'd laid in some of my favourite brand of pickle.'

'A likely story, as the duchess said to the—'

Moss jumped through the door a second ahead of a well-aimed phone directory propelled by thirteen stone of outraged brawn.

For the second night running, Thane's sleep was broken by a telephone call. The bell rang at three-twenty-two. It took ten seconds to wake him, another twelve before he could come to life sufficiently to answer.

It was the Millside duty officer. 'Message from Perth, sir. Asked that it get passed on to you immediately. Patrick Kilburn escaped at 0154 hours this morning, and is still at large.'

Thane gave a deep groan. 'Well, he's not hiding in my house,' he grumbled. 'Thanks anyway—phone me if you get any further word from Perth.' He replaced the phone, yawned, and burrowed down again.

'What was it, Colin?' asked his wife sleepily.

'Kilburn's jumped... jail,' he yawned again. 'Tell you in the morning. Night.' And he was asleep again almost before he had finished.

CHAPTER FIVE

THANE WAS BACK on duty at 8 a.m. First, he ran a quick eye over the CID occurrence book at the Millside main office, then, satisfying himself that it had been a fairly quiet night in the divisional area, he detailed two detective constables to follow up a stolen property inquiry newly arrived from Coventry.

Upstairs, in his private office, he settled in his chair and took a quick glance at the morning papers. Two of them had managed to squeeze Kilburn's escape into their final edition. Neither had managed to gather details of the break-out in the short time before the edition. There were roadblocks on the main highways, a lookout was being kept at rail stations in the area—all the usual routine of a fine-mesh dragnet was in operation.

Thane picked up his phone. 'Morning, Jean,' he greeted the station operator. 'Get me Warrander House—the "open" near Perth. I want through to Governor Maxwell.'

The girl got through in record time.

'Maxwell here,' came a tired voice over seventy miles of phone wire.

'Morning, Governor. Thane. Any luck so far?' asked the detective. 'I got word last night, of course, but it seemed a bit early for us to panic at this distance.'

'I didn't expect you to,' agreed Maxwell. 'There's little news so far. Kilburn fooled us neatly. We put him in a cell for the night—we've got two of them in the building, just in case any of the prisoners get troublesome. My idea in doing it was more for his own protection than anything else. An officer took a peep inside every hour.'

'Sounds sensible,' Thane commented. 'What went wrong?'

The governor sighed audibly. 'Everything. The warder came around on his usual check just after one o'clock. Kilburn was on the floor of his cell, rolling in agony and groaning—or so it seemed. My man opened the cell and went in.

'The moment he bent over Kilburn, the devil stopped acting, and punched him in the stomach. The warder is no light-weight, but he just didn't have a chance. Kilburn gave him a right to the jaw, kicked him in the guts, then bashed his head on the floor. My man was knocked unconscious. He came to after about five minutes, and the bird had flown. He had broken a corridor window and jumped from the first floor to the ground.'

'But there was a special patrol on the grounds,' said Thane. 'Didn't they see him?'

He waved a greeting to Phil Moss, who had appeared in the doorway, and gestured towards the extension earpiece hanging beside the receiver.

Moss nodded, and listened in as the governor continued.

'The patrols were all engaged in making sure no one got in. You know the type of establishment we have here—we need minimum security as far as the prisoners are concerned. Being able to serve a sentence here is too important a privilege for them to ever try anything stupid. Kilburn had just a few minutes to get away, and knew it.

'From what we gather, he made straight for the fence. When

the warder came to and raised the alarm, the patrols searched the whole compound area. They found where he had got through the wire—it had torn a couple of strips of cloth from his battledress. Then the police returned, the alarm went out, and that's how it stands at the moment.'

'Not particularly happy, is it?' Thane gave a grimace to Phil Moss. 'We'll keep in touch with the search, and place a watch on any of Kilburn's old haunts around Glasgow.'

As Thane hung up the phone, Phil Moss scrabbled in one pocket of the loose tweed suit he was wearing.

'Looks as if Kilburn broke out because he was scared the next try on his life would be third time lucky,' he declared. The notebook was opened now. 'I got the gen we wanted from the prisons people last night. First, the father, John Kilburn. While awaiting trial, he had visits from his wife and eldest daughter on several occasions. His other son, Liam, made two visits. They applied for further visits after the sentence, but the father refused to see anyone.

'The son, Patrick Kilburn, had visits from the family too—right up till sentence—then he turned down any callers. There were some other applications when he was transferred to Perth Prison, but when he continued to refuse to see anyone, and refused to answer letters, they seemed to give up trying.'

'Did anyone outside the family attempt to see the Kilburns?'

Moss gave a polite burp, fished in an inside pocket for a bicarb tablet, and popped it in his mouth.

'Yes, quite a few. I recognize some of the names—reporters using their home addresses, I'd say, trying to get a story interview. Kilburn senior saw only two outsiders, a Jon Barlby and a Peter Angello. His son...' He shook his head. 'No outsiders.'

'Barlby and Angello,' mused Thane. 'Barlby sounds familiar. Wasn't he involved in a betting fraud case? Something about sending telegrams with faked time stamps?'

'That's him,' said Moss. 'He and a sub-postmaster down in

the Borders. The case didn't stick—the judge threw it out for lack of evidence. Records checked his file for me. He's got previous for fraud, jewel theft, and black-market currency deals. There's nothing on file for Angello, but Records are contacting Scotland Yard to see if he is listed there.'

A buzzer sounded mildly, almost apologetically.

Thane stretched out a hand and pressed one of two buttons set in a small switch plate screwed to the side of his desk. Outside in the corridor, a light flashed behind a "come in" notice. The other button controlled the "engaged" sign.

The door opened, and a familiar head of curly red hair appeared round the gap. Jock Mills, the Evening Bugle crime reporter, was making his usual morning round of police calls, checking at each division for the copy necessary to feed his insatiable news editor.

'Come on in,' invited Thane. 'Frankly, I'm disappointed. I thought it was someone bringing the tea. What can we do for you, Jock?'

'W...ell.' Mills hesitated a moment, rummaging in the pocket of his dirty white raincoat.

Dirty white raincoats were fashionable that year among reporters. The previous season it had been plastic coats, before that, government surplus duffels. He pulled out a crumpled newspaper clipping.

'You'd see this story in the morning about Kilburn escaping from that open prison—'

'We know about it,' agreed Thane, expressionless.

'Is he heading for Glasgow, in your opinion?' asked the reporter.

'Maybe,' shrugged Thane. 'Phil, how about chasing up that tea? And tell whoever's making it I want my three teaspoonfuls. You'd think the stuff was still rationed, the way they dole it out.'

'Maybe they're thinking of your weight problem,' cracked Moss acidly, winking at the reporter as he strolled to the door.

'Frankly, Jock, I don't know where he's heading. Obviously, we're on the lookout for him, just in case,' said Thane.

'When we got that flash about the van he stole—' began Mills.

'Van? What van?'

'The news editor radioed it to my car a few minutes ago. Our correspondent had just phoned in a brief story. Seems Kilburn—well, we suppose it was Kilburn—thumbed a butcher's van on a side road about six miles from the prison. The driver stopped to give him a lift, and Kilburn threw him out of the van and drove off. The butcher got to a farm and phoned the police.'

'You know more than I do,' admitted Thane. 'I'm still waiting on word from the local police. They've got their hands full at the moment.'

'Well, I'll get on my way—' The reporter turned to leave.

'Not so fast, Jock. Maybe you can help me now.'

Mills swung round. 'Do I get a story?'

'No—let's say this is in the nature of helping good relations. Were you on the Kilburn case?'

'Aye.' The newspaperman ran a hand over his red hair. 'I was mainly on the background stuff—you know, trying to poke into the things that weren't said in court.'

'Were you one of the men who tried to see Kilburn? Phil's got the list, but I haven't a copy here.'

'*Tried* is the operative word,' sighed Mills. 'I thought I stood a pretty good chance too. We'd have paid big money for the story. I lined up a pal of Kilburn who said he'd ask him to send me out a visit chit so that I could talk to him at the prison. But Kilburn wouldn't hear of it—the father, that is—when I followed up Barlby's visit with a letter.'

'You used Barlby?' Thane was interested. 'Were they close friends?'

'Not close. Barlby reckoned that John Kilburn had only one really close friend. And he was a man who wouldn't stand any monkey business. Nobody ever got near him, that I know of... The friend was an Italian, though I can't remember his name right now.'

'Was it Angello?' prodded Thane.

The reporter gave Thane a look of peeved inquiry. 'What are you asking me for, when you already know? What's it all about?'

'Can't tell you yet, Jock. But don't worry, you'll get a lead on it when it comes out. What do you know about this Italian?'

'Only what Barlby told me. Angello, it seems, is an honest man, more or less. He came up to Glasgow when Kilburn was arrested, but went away again soon after the trial. Barlby had only met him once or twice. He didn't know much about him—except that he'd met Kilburn during the war.'

'What was Barlby's interest in visiting Kilburn?' asked Thane.

'Him? He was just out for what he could get, I gathered. He wanted to take over Kilburn's watch-smuggling business,' said Mills. 'That's all I know, I'm afraid. Here's your bodyguard with the tea—I'll need to go.'

He left, nodding cheerfully to Phil Moss as the latter came in, balancing two filled mugs on the station's biscuit-lid tray.

The inspector set the tray down, picked up his own milk-white tea, and apologized.

'Sorry I was so long. I stopped to pick this up from the teleprinter room. It's the reply we were waiting on from Belfast.' He handed over a sheet of red-edged paper.

'I've found out a little about Barlby and Angello,' said Thane, rapidly sketching his conversation with the reporter. 'I think it will be worthwhile locating them both. Barlby should be easy enough, and if Angello is a native Italian, then the Aliens Department should have some note of his whereabouts, even if he has no record.'

He turned to the teleprinter message, read it quickly, slowed, and read the last portion again.

'You've read it?' he asked Moss. The smaller man nodded, and perched himself on the edge of the desk, whistling thinly between his teeth. Phil Moss had a pretty good idea of what was coming next, and was mentally resigning himself to fate.

'The family are still living at the farm,' mused Thane. 'As far as Ulster police are concerned, they rate the remaining Kilburns as a reasonable bunch—tough as nails, except for the mother, who has been in poor health. The son, Liam, was arrested once, just after his father was hanged—for assaulting a man called Barlby.

'"But the charge was dropped due to circumstances,"' he quoted. 'That's a nice Irish way of putting it, I imagine. Looks as if Barlby went over to see if the family would hand over some of father's contacts, and got more than he bargained for.' He took out his cigarettes, passed one to Moss, and offered him a light. Then he blew a thoughtful column of smoke skywards.

'Put me out of my misery,' begged Moss. 'Yes, I'll go to Ireland and see the family. Yes, I know the time of the next plane from Renfrew airport—I looked it up before I brought the message to you. But I warn you, when I'm on the operating table at the Royal Infirmary getting my ulcer amputated, I'll tell them all whose fault it was.' He stared gloomily out of the somewhat grimy window, seeking comfort in the desolate tenement landscape.

'If you get the morning plane over, you might get back tonight,' encouraged Thane. 'Then you can come over to our place for supper, and watch cowboys on the telly.'

While Detective Inspector Phil Moss yielded himself to the efficient shepherding of British European Airways, Colin Thane went in the station duty car to Police Headquarters.

"Aliens" was a quiet, peaceful-looking room, with a long wooden counter running its full length. Thane told the duty officer what he wanted, promised to look back in a few minutes, and strolled across the way to the police laboratory.

Two white-overalled technicians looked up from their apparatus as he entered.

'The man we're looking for,' bellowed a voice from the other corner of the room. 'Colin, would you like to see what we got out of these rifle bullets?'

His frayed "working" jacket unbuttoned, pockets bulging with everything from acid-stained handkerchiefs to a dog-eared black notebook, Dan Laurence, superintendent in charge of the scientific bureau, gestured Thane towards the comparison microscope mounted on his bench.

Thane peered obediently through the twin eye-pieces, while Laurence commentated, 'These are the bullets we had sent down from that open prison you took a joyride to yesterday. The one on the left came from a wall, the other from the grounds. Both from the same gun, of course—a .300 Lee-Enfield. We can tell you this—it's been used a lot, judging by the state of the rifling marks on the bullet.

'And the other point—all right, you can stop looking, the show's over—the other point is that the rifle's firing pin is hitting the cartridges well off centre, judging by the sample case that came down wi' the bullets. Routine stuff, I know, but it may help later.'

'It usually does,' said Thane. He'd lost count of the number of times Dan Laurence and his squad had used their test tubes and microscopes to clinch the case against hoodlums with seemingly watertight stories, or to point to a completely new possible solution to a crime. He gestured towards the two white-coats. 'What are they on?'

'Nailing a particularly nasty poacher,' growled Laurence. 'These ruddy savages who poison a stream and scoop up salmon by the barrowful should be fed a dose of their own medicine. The stuff keeps going down-river, and wipes out anything in its way. They'll spoil half the rivers in Scotland if they keep on. We've got this fellow's gear, his clothes, and water samples. The poison in the water matches powder traces on the rest of the stuff—we've put him right up the creek.'

Thane spent a few more minutes prowling through the laboratory. He found it a fascinating place at any time, and some of the wrinkles he had gathered in his talks with Dan Laurence had been of major help in subsequent fieldwork, when time was precious, and the bureau men were miles away. Then it was time to go back to Aliens. The duty officer was ready waiting.

'Found your Angello all right, sir. We had only a few details, regulation stuff, but I checked with London by phone to tie it up. He came here five years ago, stayed two months, then returned south. Then he went back to Italy. We've no note of any return visit since.

'Here's his entry: "Peter Angello, born Rome 1910, home Via Aosta, Rome, profession, dental surgeon. No record advises."'

'That's one I can strike out,' sighed Thane. 'Still...'

He noted the details, thanked the Aliens officer, and headed back to Millside, intent on getting the latest report on Kilburn. It was waiting on his desk.

Kilburn had crashed a police roadblock with the butcher van five miles from where it had been stolen. Then he had abandoned the van another mile down the road, one wheel in a ditch, and had disappeared into the thick woodland that fringed the area, taking with him the butcher's raincoat and cap, the van's starting-handle, and a pocketful of meat pies from the vehicle's stock. The starting-handle meant only one thing.

A further warning had gone out to all police in the hunt: 'Consider this man dangerous, and likely to attack. Warn all local inhabitants to be on their guard.'

Inspector Roy had added a footnote to the report. One of his plain-clothes men, continuing the quest around Warrander House, had found a young farm boy who had seen a light-coloured saloon car parked two miles from the prison the day before the first attempt on Kilburn's life. The place was only a short distance from the moorland where the prison party that Kilburn had been assigned to was engaged on reclaiming work.

And the boy had seen two people, a man and a woman, return to the car and drive off about an hour after the work party arrived. The man had been carrying a long, cloth-wrapped object. But the boy hadn't been close enough to get the car's registration number, or to be able to give anything but a hazy description of the couple.

Thane gave a thin whistle. The inference in Roy's message was obvious. The couple had gone hunting Kilburn, had found him gone, and had stalked him down the next day.

But if they had been responsible for the notes which had panicked Kilburn, for the shots that tried to kill him, what was their motive? And who was their contact at Warrander House—for a contact they must have, to get the note into Kilburn's bed, to know where he should have been on the moorland project, and, most important of all, to be able to get information quickly enough to replan their hunt and strike within twenty-four hours.

Why, who, where were they? And, strangest of all, why had Patrick Kilburn been so stubbornly determined not to reveal their identity?

He took out his cigarettes, and began searching his pockets for matches.

CHAPTER SIX

LIKE AN UNTOLD NUMBER of frequent plane travellers, Phil Moss hated flying. He climbed aboard the BEA Viscount, fastened the safety belt with practised precision, then, as the engines began their screaming whine, stared fixedly at the back of the seat in front of him, thinking that at least he wasn't married.

As the plane turned into the runway he swallowed, licked his lips, and tensed in his seat, hands tightly clenched round the paperback Western he had bought at the terminal bookstall.

The plane charged down the runway, Moss repeating over and over to himself, 'Get up... up...' and then, before he realized it, they were in the air, climbing smoothly and rapidly.

That was that... but he had just settled down, swallowed, yawned, and blown his nose in approved fashion to clear the popping in his ears, and seemed to have just begun reading his book, when on came the "fasten your safety belts" light again, and the plane began sinking.

He groaned inwardly, gazed enviously at the six-year-old staring excitedly out of one of the plane's windows across the gangway, then settled down to his own personal landing drill.

That meant don't, whatever you do, look out the window at the approaching ground below. Keep thinking as hard as possible on the work that lies ahead once the plane lands. Without making it too obvious, shrink as far down in your seat as you can—then wait for it.

And, like every other air passenger, the moment the plane's wheels touched ground, and it began running in without blowing up or overturning, he thought just how wonderful a form of travel it was.

An RUC officer, revolver strapped round his waist, was waiting in the Belfast Airport lounge. He welcomed the Glasgow detective, then ushered him out to the car park.

'There's a car and a plain-clothes driver waiting for you,' he said. 'I gather you want to get straight about your business, so I'll just say good luck to you—but give us a look in on the way back, if you've got time. And if you hit trouble, don't hesitate to radio in.'

The sixty-mile journey took the best part of two hours, during which the talkative plain-clothes driver kept up a colourful torrent of comment on the misbegotten character of every other Irishman on the road.

They passed Fordnacloy shortly after noon, and a few miles up the road the driver drew in, stopped, and checked his map.

'The farm is off a little road on the left, sir,' he confirmed. 'About half a mile on. Do you want to go right up?'

'Might as well,' agreed Moss. 'I don't suppose there would be much sense in quizzing any of the neighbours, anyway.'

'Around here, sir?' The driver sniffed. 'Sure, and you're right there. Five minutes after you'd started, and half the country would know you were here. Gossip... you've never come across the like of it. There's only one thing they like better than gossip around here, and the other stuff's too damned dear by half now. I should know—I was born not fifteen miles from here.'

He slid the car into gear, and as they moved on again, added,

'I met the Kilburns a few times, years ago. Och, the old man and Patrick were a tough pair of rascals, though I never thought John Kilburn would be a killer.

'At home here, you know, he was a decent enough family man, though stubborn, mind you, terribly stubborn. One rule he had—he'd never mess his own doorstep. Then I joined the Force myself, and that was the end of it. You can't drink a man's whiskey and try to nail him to the wall at the same time.'

The car bumped off the main road, and onto a narrow, cart-rutted track, high-hedged and muddy. The driver swore as they splashed through a deep puddle. '—muck. Hours it'll take, cleaning her up again. There now, that's the farm on ahead.'

It was a low, grey-stone building, shaped like the letter L, small, many-paned windows studding its thick walls. A group of chickens ran screaming from the car's path, and a brindle calf, only a month or two old, stared at the vehicle for a moment, then loafed off across the cobbled courtyard.

The Irishman switched off the engine, pulled on the hand-brake, and wound down his window, sniffing the farmyard air. 'That's the stuff to put real life into a man, now— Will I come with you, Inspector?'

Moss shook his head. 'You'd better stay with the car,' he advised. 'I'll give you a shout if I need an interpreter. I want to try and have a friendly talk with them, and one man can often get away with that where two would simply land in trouble.'

He got out, closed the car door, and looked around. Smoke was drifting lazily from one of the four broad chimneystacks. In usual farm style, the big front door was shut and locked, and looked as though it hadn't been open for years.

Moss walked the length of the building, and gave a grunt of satisfaction as he saw washing hanging on a line, and, as he turned the corner, a kitchen door lying open.

Sidestepping a scrawny cat, he thumped the door knocker, and waited, noting the pans bubbling on the big black range, the kitchen table covered in gay plastic, set with cutlery for two. After a few moments, he knocked again.

'What do you want?'

Phil Moss spun round at the unexpected voice from behind him. She was a girl of about twenty-three, he guessed, small, dark-Irish, with just that touch of features that suggested some far-distant Spanish ancestry. Perhaps, like so many other Irish families, dating back to some shipwrecked Armada sailor who had married into the race with whom he found refuge.

'Who are you looking for?' the girl asked, a mixture of impatience and suspicion in her voice. In one hand, she carried a white enamel bucket, half full of milk. Obviously she had been in the farm byre when he had arrived.

Moss touched the brim of his trilby. 'Miss Kilburn? I'm a police officer. I've come over from Scotland to see if your family can help us. It's a matter involving your brother, Patrick.'

'Oh.' The girl's face hardened. 'All right, come in.' She swept past him into the kitchen, placed the bucket in the spotless white sink, then turned towards him.

Standing just inside the doorway, Moss took out his warrant card, and offered it for her inspection.

She glanced at it without touching, nodded, and asked, 'Why are you here?'

Moss moved over towards the dresser. 'Did you know your brother had escaped from prison?'

A flicker of interest crossed the girl's face. 'No—but he's not here. He's not likely to come here either,' she said coldly, turning her back to the detective again, and stirring the contents of one of the pots on the range.

'You're Katrina, the youngest daughter, aren't you?' mused Moss. 'Are the rest of the family home?'

'My brother and Margot are out,' she said, without turning.

'Will they be long?'

'Perhaps. I don't know.'

'Where's your mother, then, Katrina?' persisted Moss. 'Maybe she'd like to know—or might be more friendly.'

'Friendly.' The girl turned, pot-lid still in her hand, dark eyes bright with anger. 'Do you expect her to be friendly? You police who hanged our father. Do you expect us to welcome you, to ask you to our table, perhaps?' Her voice rose. 'If Patrick has escaped, do you expect me to help you? Do you expect my mother to help you... now?'

Moss shifted his weight from one foot to the other. 'Your brother's on the run because someone is trying to kill him,' he snapped. 'You're not helping him, or yourself, like this. If you won't help, perhaps your other brother Liam will. When will he be back—because I don't intend leaving this neighbourhood till I've seen him?'

'I—' The girl broke off, suddenly anxious. The inner door of the kitchen had opened as they spoke, and another woman, older, plump and pleasant-faced, stood there smiling. 'I thought I heard a visitor,' she said. 'Who is your friend, Katrina?' She came forward, the smile never leaving her face. There was something wrong with that smile, something lost and meaningless, as childlike as the half-querulous note of her voice.

Moss hated himself as he ignored the silent appeal in Katrina's whole manner and said, 'I'm a policeman, Mrs Kilburn. I want to see your son, Liam. Where is he?'

'Liam's away,' she replied in the same child-like tones. 'He's gone away with Margot to see London.'

'Mother...' The girl's manner was verging on sudden hysteria. 'You remember Liam told you the holiday was something you weren't to talk about? He said you weren't to say anything about it?'

'Oh...' The woman blinked. 'Oh, yes...' Her lips quivered. 'Now I've spoiled the secret, haven't I? What will your daddy think when I tell him? It was to be such a surprise, too, and now I've spoiled it.' She saw the table set for lunch. 'Is your friend staying for lunch, Katrina? Katrina's a very good cook, you know, Mr... I don't know your name, or do I? I forget things so easily.'

'Moss, Mrs Kilburn,' said the detective gently. 'No, I won't be staying for lunch, though I'm sure it will be nice. I just want to speak to your daughter a little longer, and then I'll need to go. There's a man in a car waiting for me.'

'Yes, Mother, we won't be long,' said the girl desperately. 'You go and do some more knitting, and I'll call you when it's time.'

'All right.' The woman beamed her innocent, empty smile again, and left the room.

Katrina Kilburn closed the door behind her, then stood with her back against the varnished wood. Suddenly, she seemed exhausted, anxious, her anger almost dissipated, grief and worry written large on her attractive young face.

'I'm sorry, lass,' said Moss. 'We didn't know—but even if we had, we've a job to do. How long has she... how long has your mother been ill?'

The girl went over to the table, pulled out a chair, and sat down before she replied.

'The day my father was hanged. She collapsed then... she couldn't take any more. It had been bottled up inside her all these weeks before, and then her mind couldn't take any more. She was in bed for a fortnight, under drugs most of the time. When she came to, she was completely out of her mind. She's got it into her head Dad's still alive. She... she writes him once a week and gives us the letters to post.' She buried her dark head in her hands, not crying, just giving a long shudder of suppressed emotion.

Moss hesitated, fumbled for his cigarettes, then touched her gently on the shoulder.

'Thanks.' The girl took one with a trembling hand, accepted a match, and took a quick, womanish draw of smoke. 'I don't want to see her hurt any more, that's all.'

Moss watched her, silent. He felt his ulcer give a sudden twinge, and bit his lip at the quick, grumbling pain.

'Mind if I take some of that milk?' he asked.

The girl shook her head.

He went over to the sink, took a clean cup standing beside it, and plunged it into the milk pail. Slowly sipping the liquid, giving his stomach something to work on, he was conscious of the girl watching, waiting. He felt suddenly inadequate to the whole situation. His imagination had suddenly conjured up an almost ridiculous possibility, one without reason apparently, but one that...

'Does your mother write to Patrick?' he asked. The girl nodded. 'Then why doesn't he get those letters?'

Katrina moistened her lips. 'We... we don't send them.'

'Why not?'

'Liam decided we shouldn't. My mother thinks that he's somewhere abroad, just like she thinks Dad is. Time means nothing to her.'

'And you agree?'

She took another puff at the cigarette, and nodded.

Moss finished the last of the milk, put down the cup, and continued his quiet questioning. 'When did Liam and Margot leave on their holiday?'

'About three weeks ago,' said the girl.

'Do you have a London address where we can contact them —or will they be back soon?'

'No... I don't know.' The girl flushed red as she tried to explain. 'They didn't book a hotel. All I know is they'll be back at the end of a month.'

Moss sighed. 'Look, Katrina, as a liar, you're pretty hopeless. Try again. What was the surprise your mother mentioned—the one you were so anxious she shouldn't talk about?'

She gave a nervous laugh. 'Nothing... She... she had just got it into her head that—'

'That they might meet your brother Patrick?' Moss sent each word hammering home. 'Isn't that the secret, Miss Kilburn?'

The girl sat silent, a red flush sweeping over her face. Then she moistened her lips.

'You're wrong, very wrong indeed, if you think we had anything to do with Patrick escaping. You have my word that we wouldn't help him...' She gave a harsh, brittle little laugh. 'Help him—'

'I didn't say help him,' corrected Moss. 'You've got it in for your brother, haven't you? I told you someone was trying to kill him. Someone who took a couple of shots at him with a rifle. Does Liam have a rifle, Katrina? And do you know why someone—maybe someone close—might want to see your brother get a bullet through the head?'

Katrina got up, and walked over to the still-open kitchen door. 'You're the policeman—you find out,' she snapped. 'There's nothing more for you to be told here. Go and catch Patrick, and ask him if he wants to tell you more.' Her voice held an underlying note of hysteria again as she finished: 'And remember this, Inspector. You police have made one mistake already. Pray—pray hard that you don't make another.'

All the way back to the car, Phil Moss was conscious of the girl still standing there, watching, waiting. Twenty minutes had passed, and now he knew what his report must be. Never had he had such a strange mixture of fact and conjecture to present. Never had the possible conclusion boded so grim a task ahead.

CHAPTER SEVEN

PATRICK KILBURN SCANNED the scene below with infinite care. Slowly, tenderly, every muscle aching, he lowered himself to a kneeling position behind the rocks and tried to work out his next move.

After fourteen hours on the run, he had reached a stage of quivering exhaustion, his original desperate energy given place to plodding fear of pursuit. When the stolen van had slid a ditch, he had scrambled up the wooded slope and had headed into the rough terrain at a stumbling run, doubling back roughly parallel with the road for a time, then heading west, away from the farm-scattered lowland, straight for the broken country that was the foothills of the Grampian mountains.

He had no plan, other than to get clear of the searching police and to find some way of getting to Glasgow, where, at any rate, he had the means to help a fast disappearance. He had had no plan, other than to get out, when he had faked his illness and attacked the warder in the prison those long hours before. For if he had stayed, they would have got him, he knew.

He shivered, and drew the butcher's coat tighter round his body to keep out the cold, penetrating drizzle of rain. They wouldn't give up, these two figures from his branded past, with their cold determination, their deadly purpose. Even if he had told those detectives, and they had acted, it would have given only a temporary period of safety, then those stalking hunters—or perhaps others, following in their path—would have resumed again.

And he couldn't, daren't, tell—and live.

Kilburn felt in the raincoat pocket. He had eaten the last of the pies two hours ago, washed down with water from a hillside stream. All that was left now was a handful of small change, and a half-empty box of matches. He peered over the rock again at the place below. It might be his last chance, the crazy sort of chance that was desperate enough to come off.

Five houses, a filling station, and a hotel made up the hamlet, strung along the roadside. The rock-scattered slope levelled out about two hundred yards from where Kilburn knelt, and the hotelier had roughed out a car park in the short length of waste ground behind the white-washed building.

Three big touring buses, two of them a sober cream, one a vivid red, were drawn up on it, filling most of its width. While the drivers sat together, gossiping, in one of the coaches, the majority of the passengers from all three vehicles were milling around the hotel door, or drinking in the long bar that protruded its single-story length from the bulk of the main building. Football supporters' parties often stopped there, giving the bar a hectic, money-clinking half-hour before they headed off again, throats serviced for the game ahead.

'Nothing to lose,' muttered Kilburn. He pulled a grubby handkerchief from his prison battledress, soaked it in a rain-pool in the rock beside him, and wiped as much of the mud and grime as he could from his face and hands.

Combing his wet, wind-tangled hair into rough order with his fingers, he rubbed the worst of the clinging soil from his boots with the rag, and rose to his feet.

He made no effort to hide his progress down the slope and into the park. None of the groups of laughing, talking supporters paid any attention as, keeping as far away as possible from the coach where the drivers were still gossiping, he headed for the hotel.

The two cream-coloured buses were from Perth, he noticed. The red coach bore the name of an Arbroath firm —and in its rear window was a large, hand-painted placard proclaiming that it was on hire to the brake club.

Kilburn grasped the handful of coppers in his coat pocket, and marched boldly into the crowded, smoke-filled bar. The warm, stuffy atmosphere seemed a caressing comfort after the bleak cold of the hills, the buzz of voices music after the monotonous whimper of wind on the moors. Almost grateful to the packed mass of bodies through whom he had to bore, he made his way to the bar and ordered a beer. Then, glass in hand, he edged away again, towards the quieter outskirts of the rosetted throng.

Over the edge of the beer-glass, he saw the man. Middle-aged, with a straggling mousy-brown moustache, a red-white-and-blue rosette in his coat lapel, he was drinking by himself against the wall. As Kilburn watched, the solitary drinker fished out a packet of cigarettes and, with the skill of a practised elbow-bender, flicked them open and thumbed one into the corner of his mouth.

'Light?' Kilburn took his opportunity, offering the matchbox, which was his only possession.

'Thanks,' grunted the moustache, and Kilburn struck a flame, then returned the box to the raincoat pocket.

'Where are you blokes bound for?' he asked, sipping his beer. Moustache drew a hand across his lips. 'You with the Dundee lot? I'm with the works bus from Arbroath.'

'No... no, I work at the farm over the way there,' said Kilburn, waving vaguely with his free hand. 'How long are you stopping here?'

'Another pint or so, probably,' grinned the other. 'We knocked off at four, and this is the first stop. We usually manage a quick one at Stirling too. Grand things, these floodlit games, eh, man?' He drained his glass, contemplated it owlishly for a moment, then invited, 'Like another?'

He didn't wait for an answer, but wriggled through the crowd and returned with two more foam-topped pints.

'*Slainch.*' Kilburn took a deep swallow, then plunged. 'Where are the rest of your pals?'

'Me? Och, I'm more or less on my own,' his companion said, sinking a good half of the beer. 'My son got the seats— I'm no' with the works. I'm with the Gas Board. Then Willie was told he couldn't get away. They needed him for a bit of maintenance work. Nice overtime, but he cursed fit to burst, missing the game and all. So, he passed his ticket over to me, and here I am.'

His head went back, and the rest of the pint disappeared in a series of gulping swallows. Again, he inspected the empty glass, then turned a speculative eye at Kilburn.

Thinking quickly, Kilburn took another drink, and volunteered, 'My turn.' Then he timed a moment's hesitation, and declared: 'Look, how about coming round to the other bar? It's just a small one—only the locals around here use it. But the beer's better, and it's a darned sight quieter.'

Moustache gave the matter serious consideration. 'No' a bad idea. Where is it?'

'Round the back, outside,' said Kilburn, hastily. 'Come on, you've got that bus to catch—and you'll never get near this bar in time for another pint.'

He turned, placed the beer glass on a handy window-ledge, and headed for the door without glancing back. He sensed the little man following him, and breathed a silent prayer of thanks. The bus park—it was to the left. He turned right at the door, walking past the group of men still congregated there, and struck along the front of the hotel.

'Here, it's a hell of a long way,' complained the little man, catching him up.

'Round here,' said Kilburn. 'Just at the back.' He turned the corner, headed up the far side of the hotel, and gestured, 'Just behind that outhouse.'

The little man grunted, and came on. They turned the corner together. Kilburn took a quick look round. No one near. He put a hand in his pocket and offered, 'Cigarette?'

Moustache came close—and Kilburn used every last dreg of energy in a chopping, edge-of-the-hand blow which began with his right hand starting from waist level and ended in a hollow, flesh-smashing blow which hit his unsuspecting victim along the throat three inches below his right jaw. Moustache gave a vomiting grunt, and collapsed.

Kilburn grabbed the man as he fell, and dragged him close under the outhouse wall. Working quickly, every second counting, he took off his coat, then his prison blouse, and then began stripping the little football fan's coat and jacket, keeping a constant lookout, still able to hear the occasional sound of laughter or a raised voice from the front of the hotel.

Three long minutes, and Kilburn was wearing his victim's jacket, had refastened his stolen coat, and had gagged and bound the other man, using his tie, coat-belt and braces. A hiding place now...

He grabbed the unconscious figure by the shoulders and, with a grunt, dragged him, heels scraping the ash surface, towards a mound of empty beer cases. There was a small space between them and the hotel wall.

He slid Moustache in, then, as a sudden afterthought, plucked the coloured rosette from his coat and put it over his own buttonhole. The hotel staff were obviously still struggling to cope with the tide of customers... with only the slightest clink of bottles he shifted four of the cases, to blank off the narrow space between wall and mound, screening Moustache from sight.

A suspicion of a smile twisted one corner of his mouth. He turned away, the comforting feel of the little man's wallet against his chest, and walked boldly and confidently back to the front of the hotel.

He stopped at the pavement's edge, took out the cigarettes from his newly acquired jacket—it was just a little tight across the shoulders—lit up, pulled in the sheer luxury of the smoke, then walked on, across the road, and into the telephone box which stood beside the filling station.

Lifting the phone and placing it against his ear, just listening to the dialling tone, he kept his back to the crowd outside the hotel, and watched them through the phone-box mirror.

He hadn't long to wait. A bus horn blared three times in the parking lot, and the football fans began heading in its direction. The last few stragglers came running out of the bar as the first bus began to leave the waste ground, and it slowed to allow them aboard. Then it accelerated away, followed by the Arbroath coachload.

The third bus began to draw out and Kilburn threw open the door of the telephone-box, and sprinted across the road towards it, shouting. The driver saw the rosette on his lapel, and stopped, and a burly man in a maroon scarf threw open the door. Kilburn jumped aboard.

'Thanks,' he gasped. 'Thought I'd be left behind.'

'You're no' with our lot, are you?' queried the door-opener.

'No... I'm with the Arbroath bus. They've gone off without me.'

The man chuckled. 'Och well, we're full up, but we'll squeeze you in somewhere, Mac. What were you doin' in that phone box?'

For a moment Kilburn was caught off guard. Then, 'Trying to get through to the shop where my kid sister works—a message I forgot to give her. Then I saw the buses leaving, and had to run.'

His questioner nodded sympathetically. 'You're Irish, by your tongue,' he declared, and as Kilburn agreed, the last barrier crumbled. 'Thought so—my old woman's from County Tyrone. Come and join the party, Paddy, we're just going to get a sing-song going.'

The bus rolled on its jolting, singing way. Kilburn squeezed himself onto the edge of one of the front seats as the big man with the muffler led the choruses. They had gone about three miles down the road to Stirling when the red hull of the Arbroath bus appeared ahead, stopped by the grass verge.

They must have discovered they were a man short, he realised. He should have thought of it—it was bound to happen. They had him now— unless...

Kilburn caught the arm of the big man between choruses. 'There's my bus ahead,' he said. 'They must have missed me at last.'

'Oh!' The chorus leader looked along the road. Two figures were standing beside the other bus, waving. 'Want to switch over, chum?'

Their guest shook his head. 'I'm happy here—enjoying the singing. Still, they'll be wondering what's up. I'd better let them know I'm aboard.' He waited, hoping.

'I'll do it,' volunteered the other. He turned to the driver's dividing window, rapped on the glass, and slid open the hatch. 'Slow down at the bus up there, mate—I just want to give them a shout that their pal's all right.'

The driver nodded cheerfully. He liked driving football parties. There was usually a nice tip waiting at the end of the day.

They slowed to a crawl as they drew abreast of the other

bus. Muffler leaned out of the doorway, and shouted, 'We've got one of your boys aboard—he's staying for the sing-song. Okay?'

The two Arbroath men on the roadway gave a wave of agreement. 'See you at the game,' shouted one.

And, suddenly light-hearted, Kilburn sat back with a grin and pulled out his victim's cigarettes while the big cream coach accelerated away.

They were stopped two miles down the road at a police checkpoint. But the uniform men barely glanced at the busload of rosetted fans from the entrance doorway, asked them to keep an eye open for anyone trying to thumb a lift, then sent them on their way with the request, 'Give the team a cheer for us, boys.'

'Wonder what that was all about,' said Kilburn's newfound friend.

He laughed. 'Just as well we know where you're from, mate, or they might have grabbed you by mistake.'

Just as well, agreed Kilburn mentally, forcing an answering smile. A few minutes later, he was joining in a rousing rendering of "The Star o' Rabbie Burns."

CHAPTER EIGHT

THE EVENING PLANE from Belfast brought Detective Inspector Phil Moss back to Renfrew Airport just after eight that evening.

One of the Millside divisional drivers was waiting. 'Mr Thane wants you right away, sir,' he explained. 'Big flap on—that escaped con Kilburn has made it to Glasgow.'

Moss hurried after him to the police Jaguar, settled into the passenger seat, and, as the driver pressed the starter, asked, 'Where are we heading for?'

'Hampden,' said the driver. 'Mr Thane's there now with Sergeant MacLeod and a squad. That's about all I know, sir.'

'When did it break?'

The driver concentrated on overtaking two lorries, which in turn were busy trying to overtake a bus. ''Bout forty minutes ago, sir,' he replied, sliding the gear lever back into top as they cleared the heavier vehicles. 'Have a nice trip?'

'There's no such thing as a nice trip,' grunted Moss. 'There's only the kind of trip where you're miserable and the kind of trip where you wish you were back home. Anything on the blower recently?' He gestured towards the two-way radio's speaker.

'A one-three-eight out Blackhill way,' answered the driver. 'Look at that idiot—' he sawed at the steering wheel to avoid a drunk who had lurched off the pavement.

'Welcome to Glasgow,' muttered Moss. 'Fu' as a puggy. How half of them get home alive I'll never know—drunks seem to have more lives than a cat when it comes to crossing roads. A one-three-eight —rowdy crowd fighting, cop requires assistance, right? I've never been able to memorise that new code, since they brought it in to stop radio fans snooping on our wavelength.'

'It would hit the newspapers too,' suggested the driver. 'Sometimes I've seen them working so fast, they've arrived at a job before us.'

'Not a hope,' said Moss. 'Get a newspaperman to admit they "milk" the police radio, and you'll get an extra pension. But they had a full code list in every office within four days.'

As they talked, the car ate the distance between the airport and the giant football stadium. The driver struck off the main road and headed for the crowded bus park, where scores of coaches were waiting. A roar of cheering hit their ears.

'Another goal for us,' said the driver. 'There's Mr Thane, sir. I'll take the car over.'

Colin Thane left a little group of men and came over as Moss got out of the Jaguar.

'Any luck?' he asked.

Phil quickly sketched the results of his journey. 'I've got the RUC checking whether Liam Kilburn ever was known to have a rifle, and going round any of his pals to see if they have any idea where he is at the moment,' he concluded. 'Though I've got a pretty good guess that wherever his brother is, Liam isn't far behind.'

Thane shook his head. 'If you're right, then he isn't far away now. We got a phone call from up north less than an hour ago. Someone attacked a football fan when a busload of them were stopped at a pub. He tied up the fan, took his jacket and money, and then hid him behind a pile of beer crates. The poor devil lay there for nearly two hours before they found him. The description he gives of the man who jumped him tallies with Kilburn. I've traced the bus drivers, and we made a loudspeaker appeal for the organiser of one of the parties to come out of the game—otherwise, we'd have to wait until the match is over. We'd never find him in a forty thousand attendance.'

They walked over to the waiting group. One of the men, in a dark green busman's uniform, looked far from happy.

'This is Strothers, the driver of one of the Dundee buses,' explained Thane. 'They picked up an extra passenger after the pub stop.'

'But I didn't know the cops were after him,' protested Strothers, anxiously fingering one of his tunic buttons. 'He just seemed like a bloke who'd missed the Arbroath bus—he even got us to tell them he was on board.'

'That's right, Mac,' boomed a voice behind them. 'What the devil's goin' on anyway, dragging me away from the game like that?'

Thane turned to the new arrival. 'Mr Fergus? Thanks for answering our call. You're the organiser of the Dundee party?'

'Deputy organiser—I am in charge o' the second bus,' said Fergus, tightening his muffler. 'I came as soon as I could—though I had to wait to see that goal. Puts our boys well in the lead, eh?'

'We're trying to find out something about a man who joined your bus near Perth,' said Thane. 'Remember him at all? He said he had been left behind by his friends.'

'Och—the Irish bloke. What about him? I told his pals he was all right. Don't tell me he got lost again at Stirling?'

'Stirling?' Thane pounced on the town. 'Didn't he travel all the way down with you?'

'No.' The football fan sniffed, then drew his coat-sleeve

across his nose. 'We stopped at Stirling for a quick break—near a pub on the Glasgow side. The Arbroath bus had pulled in too, and he said he'd better get back to his own mob. That's the last we saw of him. Why?'

'Radio in to headquarters, Phil,' snapped Thane. 'We're probably too late, but ask them to pass the word to Stirling police in case Kilburn's still hanging around the town. Why?' he addressed Fergus again. 'I'll ask you a question instead. Why didn't you tell the police when your bus was stopped that you had a stranger aboard? Was this the man?'

He handed the Dundee man a full-face photograph of Patrick Kilburn, taken from the police files.

'Lemme see.' Fergus squinted at the picture in the glare of a policeman's torch. 'Aye, that's him. But he was with the Arbroath boys—they stopped to look for him. He even had a favour on his coat, like me,' he declared, gesturing to his red-white-and-blue rosette. 'What do you want him for anyway?'

'He's an escaped prisoner,' said Thane. 'He's serving life for murder. Satisfied?'

Fergus's confidence evaporated, and he swore. 'Look, Mac, he was just a bloke who'd missed his bus as far as we knew, honest. A nice, quiet Irish-speaking bloke. He joined in the sing-song on the way down.' His dismay was almost comical.

'The harm's done,' said Thane. 'We'll want a statement from you, and from some of the others who were on your bus.'

'Right now?' Fergus looked wistfully back at the football stadium.

Thane relented. 'After the game. Bring a couple of the men who sat near him on the bus. A constable will get you back into the ground if you want to go now.'

Fergus cheered up, but only a little. 'On the run... the club committee will roast me,' he moaned, as he went off in the direction of the turnstiles again.

Thane detailed Sergeant MacLeod, one of the Millside

detectives present, to collect the Dundee spectators after the match and get their detailed accounts of the surprise passenger they had had in their midst.

He shivered. The temperature dropped quickly these autumn evenings. Tens of thousands of other men in civilised jobs would be having a "night at the fireside," reading the evening paper, complaining about the dull television programme, wondering what was for supper. The big detective shrugged. He must be getting old.

'Come on back to the car,' he suggested to Moss. 'I want to hear more about the Kilburn family. They seem a pretty interesting collection.'

Phil Moss was thankful to obey. They got into the CID duty Humber and lit cigarettes. Then Phil produced his notebook, in which he had scrawled a rough account of the strange conversation he had had with Patrick Kilburn's mother and sister at the farmhouse.

His companion waited until he had finished, flicked a half-inch length of grey ash off the top of his cigarette, and commented, 'Take it as read that wherever Liam Kilburn and the girl—what's her name, Margot?—are, they are very interested in their brother Patrick. From what the girl told you, and the general atmosphere, they aren't particularly concerned with seeing that he gets tucked up nice and warm in bed at night.

'I'm on your side in this, Phil, but at the same time have we reason enough to believe they're out there in the dark somewhere, gasping for a chance to gut-shoot Kilburn? It seems to me we have got three different jobs to do here. Find Kilburn, find his brother and sister—and find sufficient evidence to link his relatives with these attempts on his life.'

Moss took out a handkerchief and blew hard on it. One of his ears still seemed dull after the plane journey. He folded the handkerchief away again and pointed out, 'If they weren't involved in this, why all the mystery? And why did his sister seem not in the least concerned that somebody was trying to bump off Patrick? If you're looking for a motive, couldn't it be the fact that their mother has literally gone out of her mind with worry about the whole affair?'

'Not enough, Phil. Maybe that's enough to make them hate their brother Patrick, but it isn't enough to make them want to commit murder. I wonder—just exactly what did that girl mean when she said, "Pray you don't make another mistake"?' He stared moodily out of the car window, then leaned forward, and stubbed his cigarette on the facia ashtray. 'We won't find any answers here—let's get back to Millside and see how things are shaping outside the city.'

At 9 p.m. a plainclothesman brought the teleprinter message up to Thane's office, along with two cups of tea and a couple of unhappy-looking chocolate biscuits. The CID chief finished his telephone call, hung up the receiver, and took the cup Phil Moss shoved across the desk.

'No luck at Stirling,' he said. 'They've watched the trains, checked buses and other traffic, and toured the town. Not a sign of him.'

He picked up the teleprinter message. 'Here's Belfast's contribution. "No details of Liam Kilburn having access to firearms. But must be borne in mind that due to activity of illegal terrorist organisations, etc., and quantity of wartime small arms known to be still held without licence, possibility cannot be ruled out. No air or sea passages booked by Liam or Margot Kilburn, but as no passport control they could have used assumed names. Liam Kilburn has four minor convictions for breach of the peace and assaults, all of village brawl variety. Served three years as private in Irish Guards during last war. Nothing known officially re: Margot Kilburn, though understand from local inquiries was at one time suspected of assisting in cross-border smuggling of jewellery, etc." And that's that... At least we know that they didn't want anyone knowing where they were heading.'

He took a sip of tea, then asked, 'Isn't it about time we heard from the team we put on checking the Glasgow bus and train ends? They've been at it over half an hour.'

'Give them time, Colin,' soothed Moss. 'They may be finding it pretty difficult to trace some of the bus crews—the buses may be out on another run by now.'

'You're right,' admitted Thane. 'But I find it damnable sitting on my backside like this, chewing the cud.'

He picked up the pencilled list before him. 'We'll give them another hour, then run the rule over these characters.' The list gave eighteen addresses—the homes of men and women Patrick Kilburn was known to have associated with before his trial for murder.

Thane picked up his pencil and underlined one name on the list—Jon Barlby, who lived in a flat just off Cathcart Road. Barlby, the man who had wanted to take over the role of crime courier, and who had been repulsed by Patrick Kilburn's father. Mr Barlby was due a visit, it was obvious. Mentally, he made one of these hop-skip-jump reactions, which occasionally drove Phil Moss up the wall.

'Remember that Italian, Peter Angello, the dentist who lives in Rome? See if he's got a home phone number—you'll get it through Continental Trunks. Quicker than going through Interpol. I'd like to have a word with him. Oh, and Phil, while you're waiting, see if you can get hold of Jock Mills of the Bugle. Tell him our deal still stands at the end of the day, but that right now I want him to see if the Bugle picture files have a photograph of either Liam Kilburn or his sister Margot. Remember what it was like during the trial? Anyone who had an auntie connected with the murder was photographed. If we get a print showing them, then at least we'll know who we're looking for.'

'I'm hungry,' complained the long-suffering inspector. 'When do I get to eat?'

'As soon as I've spoken to Peter Angello, I'll stand you sausage and chips in the canteen,' grinned Thane. 'Goodbye.'

As Phil left, two uniform constables came in.

They had been breaking up a simple bottle fight in a nearby tenement– and had found a nice cache of stolen property under a bed that had been overturned during one of the struggle's wilder moments.

Both cops were youngsters, keen as mustard, eager to learn, and Thane willingly brushed his worries aside for a quarter-hour to guide them on the way to trace the origin of the stuff—three cartons of shoes and a case of woollen underwear—and to give the man encouraging freedom to carry on with the job instead of turning it over to the CID.

'I'll square it with your Super,' he promised.

Once—it seemed a long time ago—he'd been like these two young cops. Except that a senior CID man had given him a monumental chewing for getting in the road. Thane hadn't forgotten how he had felt that night. And with a desperate shortage of good recruits, it would be madness for any force to do other than nurse along keen lads like the pair before him.

He lit another cigarette and got down to some of the routine paperwork piled on his tray. The pile of letters were signed, and he was checking a batch of expense sheets when Phil reappeared. There was a grim look of satisfaction on the smaller man's face.

'You can take it Kilburn's in town,' he said, picking the twenty packet from the desk and helping himself. 'Got a match?'

Thane tossed over the box. 'Where'd they trace him?'

'One of the plainclothes detail located the conductress of a Stirling-Glasgow bus that got in about seven-thirty. She's convinced Kilburn was aboard. He took a single ticket to the terminus, and borrowed an evening paper she had. Then he got off on the outskirts of the city—she remembered telling him there was a bit to go before the bus reached town, but he just grunted at her.'

Thane ran a thumb along his chin, feeling the beginnings of a rough stubble. 'Have you passed the word?'

Phil Moss nodded silently.

By radio message to police cars, not only in Glasgow, but in half-a-dozen surrounding counties; by teleprinter flimsy to divisional stations; by word of mouth from duty inspectors to beat men as they took over shifts, a small army of blue-uniformed men would soon know that Kilburn was lurking somewhere in their area.

The information lent a new urgency to every report of a stolen car, every 999 call of a break-in, every complaint of an unknown prowler. For a man on the run could be anywhere, doing anything—and when the escapee was of Kilburn's desperate nature, there could be no "all clear" until he was back behind bars.

'I got through to Jock Mills at the Bugle office. He's looking through their files right away—and bursting with curiosity,' he told Thane. 'But your Italian call will have to wait. Angello's on the phone all right, but he won't be in for a couple of hours, according to Continental Trunks. They got through to his home, and spoke to a housekeeper. I booked the call. Okay?'

'Fine,' agreed Thane. 'That gives us time to take a run round some of Kilburn's former pals. You've had that meal, Phil—we'll grab some sandwiches on the way out.'

CHAPTER NINE

SOMEHOW, when a man breaks jail and the heat's on, an immediate metamorphosis overtakes his friends. They tell his hunters they must have made a mistake—they've only met the man a couple of times. Their home would be the last place he'd think of coming—they quarrelled, hadn't the cops heard? Or, if he did show up, the first thing they'd do, they say, would be to scream for the police.

Thane and Moss had heard it all before. They'd also caught men on the run before, hiding under the bed of their "worst enemy."

They had fourteen names and addresses, fourteen people to be questioned, to be warned—and then to be watched from cover by a hidden plainclothesman.

They visited two billiard halls where the clientele immediately thinned. A fashionable "bridge club" where they knew watchers had given the tick tack even before they reached the foot of three long stairs, causing two faro tables and a roulette wheel to be hurriedly dismantled. A back-streets dance hall where the M.C. switched the radiogram back on and patrons hid their bottles and straightened their clothing.

And then they came to the block of flats. A solitary Morris stood out like a sore thumb among the array of opulent radiators in the white-roped parking space.

The black plastic register of tenants showed Jon Barlby lived on the top floor. They walked across the sea-green mosaic floor, and took the walnut-lined, crystal-buttoned lift up the six floors. The door opened with a polite sigh, and Thane stepped out into a brightly lit hallway, covered in soft grey carpeting.

'This I like,' whistled Moss. 'The day my eight draws come up, you'll find me in a layout like this.'

Barlby's apartment was second on the left. Thane rammed the bell with a gust of indignation at the optimist who first coined the opinion that crime didn't pay.

After a minute, the door opened. Barlby was a plump, middle-aged man, with brushed grey hair, a neat goatee beard and a smile.

'Police?' The smile remained as Thane showed his warrant card. 'Come in.'

They followed him into the flat through a short hall to a large lounge. The decor was subdued, modern, and expensive. Central heating made the focal point of the room a large twenty-one-inch television set, switched on and showing a screen littered with dancing girls.

Barlby flicked off the picture and waved them to seats. 'Now?'

'You know Patrick Kilburn has broken out of prison?' asked Thane.

Barlby perched on the arm of a settee, carefully adjusting the crease of his dark-brown suit. 'It's been in the papers,' he agreed. 'I thought someone might call sooner or later to see me, Chief Inspector. But you're wasting your time. I know nothing about it.'

'Kilburn got to Glasgow tonight,' said Thane quietly. 'We thought he might pay you a visit, Barlby.'

The smile faded a little. Barlby got up and crossed to the tiny cocktail bar in the far corner of the room.

'Care for a drink, Chief Inspector? And your friend?' He shrugged at their refusal, and poured himself a dry sherry. Glass in hand, Barlby looked at them for a moment. 'It's no secret I've got a record. And that I knew,' he emphasised slightly, 'knew the Kilburns. In point of fact, I endeavoured to make a business deal with Patrick's father. But it fell through. And, you'll probably see from your files, I have been behaving myself for quite some time.'

He tapped his glass delicately. 'This is my business now, quite legitimate, I assure you. I'm a wine broker—a handy form of middle-man between producer and wholesaler.'

Phil glanced round the room. 'Business must be pretty good,' he commented drily. 'You wouldn't have some side-lines?'

Barlby's little goatee beard quivered with amusement. 'Do you know of any that I have?' he fenced. 'Seriously, gentlemen, you see before you a man whose only current criminal activities consist of seeming to always leave my car parked in a "no waiting" zone. As for Patrick Kilburn, I have no wish to see him, no wish at all.

'I presume, Chief Inspector, you will be placing the regulation watch on my flat. In fact, as a citizen, I feel tempted to demand it. I meet my old acquaintances from time to time, admittedly, but the neighbours around here wouldn't quite understand, I'm afraid, if the wrong type of person began using this building. Now, if you'll excuse me.' He gave them no option but to follow him to the door again.

And the door was shut firmly behind them almost before the two detectives realised it.

They glanced at each other, and Moss gave a sudden, indignant protest. 'How the devil did that happen?' he asked.

'Barlby just happens to be one of the most prim-mouthed smoothies we've ever come across,' said Thane ruefully. 'He didn't give me time to get a word in edgeways. God help anyone he does business with–he could "con" them into buying Buckingham Palace. But somehow, I think he would be rather unhappy to see Kilburn. Slap a couple of men on the job, Phil, one back, one front. Seems to me Kilburn's more likely to visit here than Barlby would wish. Who's next on the list?'

'A girlfriend called Ivy,' said Moss.

'The clinging type?' asked Thane, poker-faced.

As Phil Moss put it, somewhat crudely, it was bad enough dealing with neds without having to cope with comic cops in the bargain.

They worked through the rest of the list, and finally, a few minutes before midnight, returned to the welcoming warmth of Millside Police Station.

A large envelope was waiting on Thane's desk, marked "Urgent." He ripped it open, and pulled out two photographs–Jock Mills' contribution from the Bugle picture files.

The first showed Liam Kilburn, and had obviously been taken on the steps of the High Court during his father's trial. It was a "snatch" picture as the man strode into the building, but the photographer had captured a good three-quarter face of his subject.

Liam was dark-haired, with the same high-boned cast of features as his brother Patrick, but he was taller, and his powerful frame, like that of so many men who live by the land, seemed trapped and uncomfortable within the city suit he was wearing.

Obviously, Liam had spotted the cameraman at the very moment the shutter had clicked. His expression was one of forming anger, his eyes, even in the black-and-white reproduction, seemed bitter, and there was something more–something the ten-by-eight print Thane held in his hands could only hint at, in the tight line of the mouth, in the tired lines on that face, pleasant and weather-beaten, so like and yet so different from that of Patrick Kilburn.

Thane laid it down, and was picking up the second photograph when the phone at his side gave a long ring.

He lifted the receiver, and the station switchboard girl said, 'Continental Trunks on the line, Mr Thane—will you stand by for your call to Rome?'

'Right...' He tensed eagerly as a humming undertone with the faint sound of barely audible background voices reached him along the line.

He picked up the second photograph with his free hand, and frowned in surprise. A happy, laughing girl of about nineteen, dressed in a swirling froth of a dance frock, smiled at him from the glossy print.

He turned the photograph over. On the reverse side the reporter had scrawled, 'Sorry—this "collect" picture, taken at a party about a year before the Kilburn trial, is the only one we have—we never had a chance to get one of Margot Kilburn during the case.'

He turned the picture over again. Margot had the Kilburn high cheekbones, but they only served to accentuate the sparkle in her eyes, the milk-smooth perfection of her face. Her black-Irish hair was cut bubble-short, and—

'Rome on the line,' warned Continental Trunks, cutting into his reverie. 'Go ahead, Glasgow.'

''Allo? Peter Angello speaking. Who is this?' Despite the distance, the voice, with only a faint foreign intonation, almost lost by the metallic reproduction, was clear, and puzzled.

'Good evening, Mr Angello—sorry to call you so late in the evening,' apologised the detective. 'My name is Thane, of Glasgow police.'

'Is not so late, sir,' reassured the Italian. 'We have none of your special summer time. Is only jus' after eleven here—the night is still beginning.'

Thane stifled an almost overpowering, up at seven in the morning, yawn. 'That's not so bad. I'm calling concerning old friends of yours, the Kilburn family.'

'Go on, signor,' caution had slid into the still friendly voice. 'It is true, I knew John, whom you hanged, and that I am still happy of that friendship. His family, I also know. What do you wish—for I have not seen them for years, though sometimes I still write?'

'John Kilburn's son Patrick has escaped from prison,' said Thane, wriggling in his chair and heaving himself into a position that was as peculiar to see as it was, to him, comfortable, feet planted flat on the seat until he was nearly but not quite sitting back on calves of his legs, his knees resting on the ledge of his desk. Phil Moss had returned from an excursion to Edinburgh Zoo, declaring he'd seen an orangutang in the same pose, but nothing else.

'Does this concern me?' asked the Italian, tone more withdrawn than ever.

Thane sighed. 'Frankly, Mr Angello, I don't know. It may, and it may not. But you are spoken of here as one of John Kilburn's few friends. I'm phoning you directly to save time. Because right now someone is trying to kill Patrick Kilburn, and we need any help we can get. I'll put it bluntly. The man is terrified of someone, but won't say who. He's more than terrified, he's becoming desperate. He broke out of prison after two attempts to shoot him down. So far, he has assaulted three people in the course of this getaway.'

The buzzing background noises were unbroken for a moment. Then, very slowly, the Italian asked, 'And who do you think is making this fear that makes him run so hard?'

'That's why I'm on this call to you,' said Thane patiently. 'Because, apart from a man called Barlby, you are the only person outside John Kilburn's family who visited either of these men in prison. Because right now we cannot trace either Liam

Kilburn or his sister Margot, and because two people, one a man, one a woman, were involved in the attempts to kill their brother. We're trying to do more than catch an escaped convict, Angello—and you may be the only one who can give us a hint of the reasons behind it all.'

'Mother of God,' groaned the other man. Then, quickly, determinedly, he told Thane, 'By telephone, I cannot help. There is only one way—I will come to you. There is a plane early tomorrow. I will be on it. Do not ask me more, signor.

'This I tell you. I loved John Kilburn as no other man. To you, he was many wrong things. To me, he was a man who risked all to help a stranger, not once, but three times. And you are right, I can help. It is not the police I come to help, but my friend's family. Tomorrow, when I see you, I will say more. Now, I must go—I must make arrangements.' And the line carried the click as he hung up.

CHAPTER TEN

THE DRIZZLE of rain that had begun at midnight had given place to a more steady downpour by 1 a.m. The wind was just strong enough to swirl the occasional fallen autumn leaf along the pavement until it came to a damp, sponging halt at some puddle's verge.

In a shadowed doorway, the man on the run shrank far back as a solitary car, headlights blazing, passed along the road, tyres whispering on the wet tarmac.

Across the road, and about three hundred yards away on the slight downhill slope, the squat bulk of luxury flats was now in darkness apart from the lighted entrance hall with its wide glass doors. There was no one in sight. But Kilburn knew he was not alone.

Ten minutes before, another passing car had swept down the same road, and its lights had given him a quick glimpse of a waiting figure standing in the doorway of the first of a small row of shops only a few yards from his goal. He'd guessed someone would be there—his other attempt, to find a way round the back of the building, had been ended by the sudden glow as another watcher lit a cigarette in the otherwise perfect concealment of an outhouse.

Kilburn gazed up at the top storey of the towering block. Barlby would be in bed now. He might have known Thane would have slapped a watch on the place. But he'd got so far now, two plainclothes snoopers weren't going to balk him.

And once he got through to Barlby, Thane could search as long as he wanted. He could handle the police—there were far more deadly foes to worry about, foes who would know some of the things he must do once the Barlby matter was over. Still, he'd be ready then. Let them come.

He contemplated the block again. From where they were posted, the two cops could between them see all four sides of the block. But Thane had forgotten something.

Kilburn looked up, sixty feet above street level. Almost invisible in the darkness, a fire escape stairway ran down the side of the flats. It halted opposite at roof-level of the office building just across from him. And between the two, a safety-conscious builder had slung a narrow metal bridge.

Fifteen minutes later, Kilburn was at the back of the office block—he had had to make a considerable detour to keep out of range of the watchers. Without tools, the next move was a crude, basic affair.

He took off his raincoat, folded it into a square pad, held it against the low-set window by his side, and lunged. The glass spangled inwards. He cursed the noise, but the worst of it had been absorbed by the muffling cloth.

Eagerly, he thrust an arm through the jagged hole, grunting with pain as a knife-sharp edge sliced at the flesh of his wrist and a trickle of warm blood flowed. But his fingertips could just reach the retaining window-snib. It was stiff to move, and his muscles bulged with the effort. Then, at last, it slid.

Three forced doors took him to the office-block roof and the edge of the 'tween building catwalk. Lacing his prison boots together and slinging them round his neck, he moved on stocking soles across the metal and onto the opposite fire escape. Glancing down only once at the barely discernible street scene below, and blessing the rainclouds masking the moon, he began to climb towards the flat roof of the luxury apartments.

Barlby woke to the repeated chiming of his doorbell. With an effort, he rolled out of bed, pulled on his shot-silk dressing gown and, yawning, rubbing his eyes, went through. The bell rang again as he approached the door.

'A'right, all right,' he said loudly. 'Coming... Who is it?'

'Police,' the voice answered harshly.

'Huh...' He shot back the bolt, turned the lock, and opened the door a fraction. A shoulder forced it wider—and Kilburn was in, slamming the door behind him.

'Surprised?' he asked.

Jon Barlby swallowed. 'At this hour, yes—look, Kilburn, this place is "hot" for you—there are cops outside, and Thane, the Millside dick, has been here already.'

Kilburn sneered. 'No one saw me, Jon. And I had to have a little chat, a private chat, with you. Right now, I need a drink.'

'Sure, sure, Paddy.' Barlby licked his lips. 'Through here—you gave me a scare. I've been sleeping.' He couldn't take his eyes from the stubble-framed, vicious-mouthed figure.

'Through here,' he repeated, leading the way into the lounge, where a few hours before he had talked to Thane and Moss. Kilburn knocked his hand away from the light switch, and, by the glow from the hall, strode across the room, opened the curtains and peered out. The window looked over the back of the building.

'I'll put on the table lamp,' offered Barlby. 'With the curtains drawn, it won't be seen.'

Kilburn pulled the curtains to again, carefully, and agreed. 'But don't try to fool about,' he warned.

Barlby switched on the lamp. As its soft glow lit the room,

he crossed to the cocktail bar, pulled out a bottle, and poured two stiff drinks.

Kilburn snatched one, swallowed it, then took the bottle himself and refilled the glass.

'Cigarette,' he demanded. The older man hurried to obey, then stood waiting, obviously frightened. His guest slumped down on an armchair with a loud grunt, and took another long drink.

'You still have good whiskey, Barlby,' he said, smacking his lips. 'I needed that.'

'I—I'll get you some food,' offered the other.

'That can wait. You know why I'm here.'

'You need help—' began Barlby.

'Help be damned,' interrupted Kilburn. 'I want the stuff you've been keeping these five years. Remember? You're my private, personal bank, and right now I need to collect, quickly. Where's that box I left with you?'

'It—it's not here,' stammered Barlby. 'Now take it easy, Paddy, take it easy. I've kept it well guarded for you. But I didn't want to keep it here, where it might be found. It's in my safe deposit box at the bank.'

'You useless...' cursed Kilburn. 'You were supposed to keep it here. That was the whole... reason I gave you it. I've got bank accounts of my own, in plenty of different names. But you were meant to be the emergency fund.'

He tossed the still-lit cigarette onto the carpet and ground it out under his boot, oblivious of Barlby's anguished expression.

'I've got to get that box. There's money, a passport, and a gun in it, and a few other things I need if I'm to get clear and take up the business again.' His eyes narrowed. 'That box had better be where you say it is, friend. If I thought... if you even took a snoop through that box, I'll have your guts.'

'The box is untouched, I tell you.' Barlby fingered the cord of his dressing gown. 'What are you going to do once you get it?'

'Clear out, fast,' said Kilburn. 'Get over to the Continent. I'll contact one or two people I know over there, and get back to business again. There's plenty of money to be made over there by anyone who knows his way round the frontiers and can take what one man's got to another man who needs it.'

Barlby smiled slyly. 'That's what I thought too. But your father seemed to think differently when I tried to do a business deal with him. We couldn't talk very easily, with those warders beside us. But he just refused to even answer my hints.'

'The old man was getting soft,' said Kilburn. 'He had been moaning about some of the stuff we were running even before we got picked up. But I had bigger ideas, and I've got them still.'

'Is that why you got out, Paddy?' asked Barlby, with unctuous interest. 'Any of the lads who saw you "inside" said you seemed to have lost interest in everything. They thought you'd cracked up.'

'Keep your damned nose out of my life, Barlby,' snarled the Irishman. 'All I want is my box. After we've got that settled, maybe we can do some business—I'll need a man here once I get organised. Right now, I'm hungry, and I need a clean-up.'

'Sure, Paddy, sure,' soothed his unwilling host. 'I'll get you some food and heat some coffee. You'll find anything you need in the bathroom. Don't worry about lights there—they both look onto a central courtyard.'

Kilburn stripped off his coat and jacket, and followed him through. He gave a grunt of satisfaction as he saw the pastel blue tiled room, with its gleaming, matching porcelain and the waiting towels.

'I'm next door,' said Barlby with a toothy smile. 'Help yourself.'

Opening a mirror-fronted cabinet, Kilburn laid out shaving cream, lotion, and injected a new blade into the chrome-handled safety-razor. Then he filled the basin with steaming hot water, and gave himself over to the luxury of a wash. From the kitchen, he could hear the sound of cupboards opening, a pan rattle, and Barlby moving about. He was busy creaming his stubble beard when the latter looked in.

'Eggs and bacon suit you, Paddy?'

'Sounds fine,' agreed Kilburn, feeling almost well-disposed towards the world for the moment.

Barlby disappeared again, and the kitchen tap began running.

Whistling softly, Kilburn swept the razor down the line of his jaw, wincing a little as the blade rasped at a rough patch. Up-strokes now, from his throat... then he stopped, puzzled.

That tap was still running.

Some inbred instinct made him suddenly suspicious. He raised the razor again, stopped with it at chin level, then softly laid it down on the edge of the basin. On tip-toe, he moved to the door, out into the hall, and up to the half-open kitchen door. He peeped through the narrow space at the doorjamb.

The room was empty, the tap running at the sink, a pan warming on the electric cooker. His face hardened, and he moved quietly across to the opposite door, which was open only a fraction.

Kilburn heard the faint whirr of a telephone dial and threw the door open. Barlby was back in his bedroom. The bedside table's small drawer was wide open. A small black automatic lay on the peach silk quilt, only inches away from the man. And as Barlby swung around, the telephone in his hand, the shocked, terrified look on his face needed no analysis.

As Barlby's free hand shot towards the gun, Kilburn sprang across the room like an enraged tiger. His whole weight hit Barlby's chest, and the little man went over like a skittle-pin, the gun he had just succeeded in touching flying from his grasp, the phone receiver hitting the floor. With a soft, subhuman snarl, Kilburn took seconds to seize the phone cord and rip it bodily from the junction box on the wall.

Barlby began to lever himself from where he had been thrown, huddled against the bed. A half-formed scream dissolved into a short falsetto of agony as Kilburn's foot took him square on the mouth. He sprawled on the floor again, making faint panting whines. One hand went out in a pleading gesture, pawing Kilburn's trouser leg, fear-filled eyes entreating, blood pouring from his shattered lips.

Kilburn picked up the automatic from the bed. Blind, bitter anger poured through him as he recognised the gun, the gun that was supposed to be in the "bank safe deposit" with the rest of the contents of his all-important box.

Barlby's hand dropped away from his leg. The man tried to pull himself further into the angle formed by the bed and the wall. In the dim light of the bed lamp, Kilburn's figure threw a tall, menacing shadow.

His foot swung back once more, and the heavy boot smashed home again and again—and again and then, as control boiled completely over, his whole body seemed to quiver while the figure before him crumpled beneath the torrent of kicks.

Suddenly he found himself gasping for breath, swaying. He sat on the bed, looking for a moment at the broken, hideous thing lying at his feet. Then, carefully averting his eyes, he loosened his laces, and, careful not to let his hands touch their now sticky toecaps, took the boots off.

Thrusting the automatic into his trouser pocket, he padded through to the kitchen. The frying pan was hot and ready. He opened a cupboard, found some eggs, broke two into the pan, and, as the fat sputtered, felt the shaving cream that still covered the right side of his face. He glanced at the eggs once more, switched on the coffee percolator, and went back into the bathroom.

While, almost within earshot yet unknown to the two watching police, Barlby slid from merciful coma into death, Colin Thane ground on at his task.

CHAPTER ELEVEN

PHIL TOOK the two press photographs to Headquarters, to have the photographic staff take copy negs and run off a batch of proofs for distribution to the men engaged in the strange double-hunt.

Thane put an orderly on the job of checking BEA's flight schedule to locate the plane that would most likely bring the Italian to the city, then phoned "Buddha" Ilford, chief superintendent of the city's detective force. Ilford growled and grunted at being wakened at his home, but listened intently.

'You're right,' he agreed. 'Technically, we can't pull in the other two Kilburns. We've only supposition and theory to go on. But we've still got to find them, and quickly. When should this Italian arrive?'

'Early tomorrow afternoon, if we're lucky,' said Thane. 'In the meantime, I'll keep up the search for Patrick Kilburn as hard as it can be pressed. And I'm hoping that the prison authorities may come up with a lead on how that warning note came to be found in the man's bed. We might just manage to tie something in on that.'

'And the motive?' asked Ilford.

'Their mother went clean out of her mind when the father was hanged,' said Thane. 'The brother remains, as a symbol. Maybe they want to wipe out that symbol. Maybe... let's wait until we see Angello, sir.'

The BBC's 8 a.m. news reported Patrick Kilburn having reached Glasgow. In a small hotel twenty miles from Perth, a young couple sitting at breakfast heard the bulletin, finished their tea and toast, and asked for their bill. There was still a faint nip in the air as they got into their car and headed south towards the city.

The girl took out her lipstick, fixed her mouth, using her handbag mirror, and gave a faint smile of encouragement to her companion. He nodded grimly, then concentrated on keeping the little saloon at a fast but unobtrusive fifty miles an hour.

At eight-fifteen, Jon Barlby's "daily" used her latchkey to enter his flat and prepare breakfast. The apartment was quiet, and the curtains were still drawn. But there was nothing unusual about that, as her employer seldom wakened before nine.

She gave a "tut" of annoyance as she surveyed the untidy kitchen, with its unwashed dishes and crumbs of unfinished food. She cleaned up the place, set a tray with orange juice, toast, and coffee, and knocked on the bedroom door. She knocked a second time on the half-open door, then, smiling, went in. The bed light was still glowing.

Then she saw what was lying beside the bed. She didn't scream—being in the ARP during the war knocked that sort of nonsense out of a woman. She laid the tray on the bed, saw the phone ripped from the wall, left the room, and was sick in the kitchen sink. Then, locking the outside door carefully behind her, she went out to find a telephone.

Thane's car, the first of three, reached the flats within twenty minutes. His arrival was the first the two look-out men knew of the murder.

They had taken over from the night shift at 6 a.m., getting an "all quiet" report—and now they waited for a blistering comment from their chief.

It did not come.

Thane knew his men. Whatever had happened, he'd find out first, then, if necessary, hold his own private inquest. He took the lift to the top floor, where the "daily" and the building's caretaker were waiting outside Barlby's apartment.

Inside, the murder squad got to work with smooth efficiency. The curtains remained drawn, every light was switched on, and, though nothing was moved or touched until the Identification Bureau van, with photographer, fingerprint and scientific specialists arrived, each room was closely examined.

Barlby's body lay in its crouched position, head battered almost beyond recognition, a dark-red, congealed pool of blood soaking the wallpaper, carpet, and bedcover. Fragments of bone and several teeth had been knocked from the ugly, twisted gash that had once been his mouth.

'Putting it mildly, not a pretty sight,' said Phil Moss, wrinkling his nose in distaste.

'Anything but,' agreed Thane grimly. 'A battering half that degree would have killed him. Whoever did it must have gone crazy once he started. Wait a bit—take a look.' He dropped on his knees on the carpet close by the body, peering at the thick pile.

Phil knelt beside him, and whistled softly as he saw the faint outlined stains.

'Kicked to death,' he murmured.

'Looks like it,' said Thane. 'The shape of the shoes—or boots, more likely—is pretty clear. The lab boys should tell us quite a bit from these.'

A chime of the doorbell heralded the I.B. squad. Superintendent Dan Laurence heaved his untidy bulk into the flat at their head, his men deploying behind him and unpacking their gear. An inch-long ash fell from his cigarette and dribbled unheeded down his waistcoat front as he took in the scene.

'Nobody ever does a nice clean murder anymore,' he complained. 'Blood, blood all the time. What's it this time, Colin, a housebreaker with a jemmy?'

'More likely an escaped con with a pair of heavy boots,' replied Thane, indicating the telltale staining.

'Kilburn, eh?' Laurence perked up, and squatted down beside the body. 'Man, if he could kick a ball like that I know a couple of teams that could use him. I take it this character won't exactly be sadly missed by society?'

'I won't send flowers, if that's what you mean,' said Thane wryly. 'I had two men watching the place all night. How Kilburn got in is a large blank at the moment.'

'Hey, Willie,' called Laurence.

The police photographer, Speed Graphic and electronic flash assembled, poked his head round the door.

'Start in here,' instructed the Bureau chief. 'Get these stains, half-a-dozen angles on the body, some general views. Then get Mick to start in here with his powder and brushes. We're dealing with a wild man, and wild men are awfully careless, lad.'

As the man got to work, the three officers got out of his way into the hall. One of the plainclothes watchers came forward, still more than a little unsure of his reception.

'The lounge and dining room have been pretty well taken apart by whoever was here, sir,' he declared. 'And it looks as though someone had a nap on the couch.' They followed him through, and he gestured, 'These rugs have been thrown back and you can still see the faint outline of a body on the cushions.'

'Aye, you're right,' agreed Laurence. 'We'll take a picture of it first, then run a chalk line round the outline, Colin, and drop another plate on it. Okay?'

Thane turned to the "daily." 'Did you come into this room at any time before you found Barlby?' he asked.

The woman was emphatic. She had gone straight to the kitchen, cleaned up there, and then taken in the tray. 'Once I've done that, I usually start to tidy the rest of the house,' she declared. 'I've never seen the place in a mess like this, ever... Mr Barlby was a tidy soul, almost too neat at times.'

'Pity you washed these things up,' said Laurence. 'We might have got the odd fingerprint off them. Oh... by the way, you won't mind us taking a sample of your "dabs," will you? Don't worry, it's just so that we can rule out any of your prints we find around. We'll be doing the same on Mr Barlby.'

'You won't find many things like that around here,' said the woman indignantly. 'I dust this place from top to bottom every day, mister.'

'I know, I know, but we don't need to find dust to find prints,' explained Laurence patiently. 'There's hundreds of little sweat pores in your fingers. Touch almost anything, and you leave a mark. Probably you can't see it, but if it's there, we can find it.'

The woman agreed. While a detective constable led her away to have the job done, the second plainclothes watcher came into the flat again. He seemed happier than before.

'I've found out how he got in, sir,' he exclaimed. 'There's an unlocked door leading onto the roof... you get to it by a short stair at the end of the corridor. From the roof, there's a fire escape that leads to the next building. I've followed it down.' He told of the trail of forced doors, and the smashed ground floor window. 'There's a smear of blood on the glass, sir—whoever it was has a nasty little gash.'

'I didn't think he'd get past you too easily,' murmured Thane.

The man brightened still more.

Some chief inspectors would have your brains for breakfast, he thought. But it was nice to have a boss that gave you an even break.

'Get back down to that window,' instructed Thane. 'Make sure no one messes about with it until Mr Laurence's men get down. We'll want to test the area for fingerprints, and a blood sample too. And—'

He caught sight for the first time of two small articles lying just under the couch. Without moving them, he got down on his knees once more and inspected them closely. One was a small bedside alarm clock. The alarm hand was set for 4 a.m. The second was a stubbed-out cigarette end, which had burned a small hole in the pile of the carpet.

'Prayer sometimes helps,' cut in a voice from behind.

Thane scrambled to his feet again as Doc Williams, the police surgeon, came into the room.

'Morning, Colin,' said the medical man. 'What have you got there?'

'The killer took a nap on this couch,' explained Thane. 'According to the clock, he probably got away from here sometime after 4 a.m. And he stubbed out a cigarette beside it.'

'Obviously a single man,' commented the doctor. 'Any married man has been terrorised into using ashtrays within a week of going to the altar. You thinking of that English case, Colin?'

Thane nodded. 'And we've got a blood sample from a window he smashed in getting here,' he added.

The case the two men had in mind had happened not so long ago. It had taken scientific detection another long stride forward in the relentless struggle against crime, a struggle in which under-strength forces, faced with more and more violence and trickery, needed every card they could play to trump their anything-but-unskilled opponents.

Two cigarette ends had been found at the scene of a major robbery. Under the laboratory microscopes, they had been examined for saliva, which had been finally grouped.

Chemists had proved that it was completely practical to group saliva in exact correspondence to the blood group of the man who had smoked those cigarettes. And samples of the suspects' blood and saliva had matched the group characteristics of the saliva traces on the stub.

It wasn't sufficient evidence in itself to convict, but it was a very important link in a chain that had meant ten years' preventive detention to a very surprised robber.

Since then, the technique had been used successfully on the gummed flaps of envelopes containing blackmail letters. Now, for the first time in Thane's experience, it might trap a killer.

Superintendent Laurence lifted the stub with tweezers, and placed the squashed tobacco in a small transparent envelope.

'It's a strange thing, Colin,' he grumbled. 'With so much blood splashed around that bedroom, I'd have thought there would be traces of it elsewhere around the flat. The fellow had to tidy up somewhere. We'll take the swan-neck from the waste pipes in the kitchen and bathroom. We may get something from them.'

Phil Moss wandered over. 'This is interesting,' he said. 'Don't worry–it's been checked for prints. But the lads tell me the entire place seems to have been wiped clean.' He had the safety razor in his hand. 'Take a close look at it. It's been washed under the tap all right, but there's still quite a few stubble hairs clinging round the edges. Whoever used it last didn't bother to take out the blade.'

'Can you do anything with it, Dan?' asked Doc Williams.

The superintendent gave a shrug of his shoulders. 'We'll try. Face hairs are of different diameters and colourations. The microscope's the answer.'

In another hour's search of the flat, they found little else.

Kilburn had been careful, very careful. Everything he might possibly have touched had been wiped. When the dead man's prints and those of his "daily" had been eliminated, the police were left with only two faint smudges, neither of them sufficiently clear to classify.

Some articles were missing—underwear, a shirt, other small clothing, a coat. Barlby's suits were intact—none of them would come near to fitting the taller, more heavily built Irishman, realised Thane. But the dead man's shoes did, apparently.

A pair of brown hand-sewn brogues were absent, according to the "daily." His wallet had gone, and nowhere among the scattered papers was there a trace of the money they were told he habitually kept around.

An empty whiskey bottle, carefully wiped, lay on the cocktail bar. But apart from the forgotten cigarette stub and the few millimetre-long hairs on the razor, Kilburn, a man who could settle down for a nap with his victim lying dead and two police on watch outside, had left no other apparent evidence behind.

'Phil and I will get on our way, Dan. We've plenty to do,' said Thane. 'Keep in touch, will you? And I'll ask Records to dig out Kilburn's blood group if you want.'

Dan Laurence growled his thanks. He was busy with the kitchen trash bin, into which the "daily" had swept the odd crumbs of food left lying on the table. One item was a crust, with a clearly defined bite mark left on a tiny portion of adhering butter.

The two Millside men were glad to leave the flat and get into daylight again.

Ignoring the elevator, they walked down the stairway, glad of the exercise, silent. Somewhere outside, in the big, sprawling, smoky city, a mad-dog killer was loose. Patrick Kilburn had crossed the line where any remaining sympathy for his fears ended, and let loose on himself the full cold efficiency of a murder manhunt.

The CID duty car was waiting outside the building. One or two passers-by gave curious glances, and a large tweedy gentleman, occupier of another of the flats, took time off starting his Daimler as Thane had a quick word with the uniform constable standing discreetly by the door.

Then, Phil at his heels, he climbed into the duty car and told the driver, 'Back home to the station now.'

Moss took out an off-white handkerchief, blew his nose loudly, and asked, 'What next?'

'A phone call to Warrander House first,' said Thane. 'Maybe Governor Maxwell has made some progress on the note Kilburn received. Someone inside handled it. Then I want to get a teletype off to the Yard bringing them up to date. Kilburn may move quickly now, and the Channel ports are as likely an escape corridor as anywhere. Will you check the Irish boat-train watch is maintained, and pass the word to the airport security teams?'

Moss nodded. The round-the-clock watch was already in being. But now still more men must be put on duty, customs and immigration officials quietly alerted, hire-car firms discreetly warned.

The car slowed at traffic lights, picked up again as the red changed to amber, and swept through on the first flicker of green. The radio came to life with a crackling request for a traffic patrol to sort out a bus and lorry smash out along Alexandra Parade.

'Ambulance summoned,' added the police officer, then a moment later acknowledged a reply from the mobile unit.

There would be more calls like that before noon, guessed Thane. The misting rain would turn most of the older stretches of road surface, and especially the granite-sett paved streets, into slippery skid-pans ready to ruin any driver's no-claim bonus.

He was rather pleased about the rain, though. He'd taken a big chance transplanting a plum tree from a relative's garden a good month before the accepted time. Its roots were cosseted with bonemeal and a liberal helping of beautifully matured compost, and a nice steady damping, not too little, not too much, might save the day.

Back to work. 'Where can we find Snouty Leith at this hour?' he asked his companion.

Moss glanced at his wristwatch. 'Pubs don't open for more than an hour. He'll still be asleep,' he replied, from long knowledge of the little ex-con of whom Thane spoke.

"Snouty" earned his name from his acknowledged skill at smuggling tobacco, any prison's unofficial currency, into smoke-starved inmates. His other, less-known function was to act as an occasional ear for the law in places where a policeman would have stood out like a temperance worker at a meth-drinking competition.

'Putting him to work, Colin?'

'I'd put Charlie Chan to work on this one if I could,' said Thane softly. 'Kilburn must have gone berserk when he booted Barlby's head in that fashion. What's to stop him doing it again? And until this fellow Angello arrives, we can't compete with the relatives who're looking for him.

'Let's face it. From all the cards we've seen, Liam and Margot Kilburn will quite cheerfully gun down their brother on sight. We can't just wait to step in and pick up the pieces, Phil. Even if we wanted the family to settle up its little quarrel, there's every chance that some innocent outsider might get caught in the middle of a shooting session.'

He patted his pockets, frowned. 'I'm out of fags again—how about it?'

With a mumbled, half-meant, wholly unprintable comment, Phil Moss dug into his jacket. He caught the driver's eye in the windscreen mirror. 'All right,' he assured him. 'You'll get one too. I'm a one-man police charities fund.'

Thane's third phone call was his most successful. From

Governor Maxwell, he learned that an intensive grilling of the open prison's occupants, with much threatening of possible withdrawal of privileges, had produced some definite results.

A trusted star-class prisoner, who worked on his own at a "civvy" job outside the prison, returning every evening, had owned up to bringing in the sealed note addressed to Patrick Kilburn and laying it on the bed in his cubicle.

'He says he was paid £10 for the job—the money was sent home to his wife. One evening, when he went to get a bus back to prison, a woman stopped him and asked him to deliver the note. She said she was a friend of Kilburn's, and the message was a highly personal one, not the sort of thing she wanted any screws reading, so she couldn't post it in.

'Our man fell for the story, not being the brightest of characters, and besides, he knew his family could use the money. The woman met him again the next evening, handed over the note, and disappeared.'

'Could he identify her again?' asked Thane.

'Probably,' said the governor. 'But I can't see the people you're after taking as big a chance as that. They could have used a third party for the job, or the woman could have been made up out of all recognition. He says she wore glasses, a headscarf, and looked about forty. The only thing that may help is that she spoke with a faint Irish accent.

'I'll have to deal with the man, of course, stop some of his privileges and take him off the outside job for a start. The damn fool's due for release in three months, too.'

They grabbed a quick cup of tea in the station canteen, listened sympathetically to the uniform superintendent's opinion of Glasgow magistrates, whose idea of sorting out juvenile hoodlums was to give them a five-minute lecture, then set off for Snouty Leith's abode.

The drill was simple, and established. Even before the duty car had drawn to a halt outside the gloomy tenement, dirty-faced kids had abandoned their games on the chalk-scrawled, glass- and rubbish-strewn street and were running over with the cheerful interest that came from regularly seeing relatives and neighbours lifted by the slops.

One tousled-haired brat, secure in the knowledge that he had four months to go before his eighth birthday brought him of age to come before a juvenile court on any charge, began a short, monotonous, and pungent three-word chant suggesting what citizens at large should do to "the polis."

Several tenement windows slid open, and housewives brought cushions to make more comfortable their "lean oot." The prospect of an arrest was much more interesting than attempting to clean the stinking homes to which they were condemned. And, with luck, they could pass the time until the television programmes began at one o'clock.

'Keep an eye on these kids—or they'll pinch the wheels off the car,' warned Moss as he swung open his door.

The driver was already aware of the multitude of mischief-seeking hands around his precious, polished Jaguar, and was remembering another police driver who had returned from a similar job to find rude messages scratched with a nail on the police car's boot. As Thane and Moss disappeared into the tenement close mouth, he sent up a little prayer that they wouldn't be long.

Snouty Leith lived two up right, in a room-and-kitchen he shared with a couple of stray cats and a screwsman currently doing six months at Barlinnie Prison because of a slight oversight.

It was fifteen minutes to opening time, so Snouty was up and dressed and was, in fact, brewing himself a cup of tea when Thane pounded on his door.

An interested audience of neighbours were gathered round the stairhead when he emerged.

'Want to see you, Snouty,' said Thane, as the stocky little

man's mouth dropped open. 'How about coming down to the station and telling us what you were up to last night? Someone knocked off a nice parcel of jewellery in a break-in near Argyle Street, and it was such a nice professional job we thought of you.'

'Not me,' protested the little man. 'I've got an alibi—honest, Mr Thane.'

'We'll take a turn down anyway,' said Thane. 'Hurry up, Snouty, I've got a busy day ahead.'

'A'right,' sighed the ex-con. 'Wait till I get my jacket.'

The spectators stood back, with loud promises that 'I'll feed your cats' and 'We'll come and visit you' as Snouty re-emerged and joined the two detectives.

They walked down the stairs again, through the children still clustered round the car, and squeezed into the rear seat. The driver scattered the youngsters with a blast of the Jaguar's horn, gave a last glare at the seven-year-old who had begun his chant again, and moved off, one tyre crunching over a tin can in the process.

The little man relaxed as soon as the car had turned the street corner. 'You might have waited till I'd had me breakfast, guv'nor.' He grinned. 'What's it this time?'

Thane told the uniform driver to head in the general direction of Millside, but to take it slowly. He pulled out the cigarettes he had bought at the police canteen, stripped off the wrappings, and offered one to Snouty, who accepted eagerly, digging Phil Moss in the ribs with his elbow in the process.

'We want Patrick Kilburn, Snouty.'

'Gawd.' The little man let the grin slide from his face. 'I knew he'd blown. But I don't like it, guv'nor. Paddy Kilburn's big trouble, and he knows most of the rough boys. I'd rather do a handful inside than have him know I grassed on him.'

'He killed someone this morning, Snouty,' said Moss. 'The courts will top him this time.'

A flicker of interest crossed Snouty's unshaven face. 'Chiv or shooter?' he asked. 'Paddy Kilburn used to carry them both.'

'The boot,' replied Thane grimly. 'Sorry, Snouty, but this time we can't take no for an answer.'

Resignedly the informer sat back for a moment, while the car purred on. Then, 'Drop me at the next corner, guv'nor. I've got an idea which might pay. Pal of mine who's a burglar, doubled as a bodyguard to a forger a few years back. Paddy Kilburn and his old man used to move some stuff for his boss. But, guv'nor, if he catches on I'll get more than a bashed face. I'll end up in the river.'

It fitted, Thane knew. If, as Snouty said, the Kilburns had taken phoney banknotes abroad for the forger, then the escaped prisoner might well go there for refuge. And Snouty's pal would be as well placed as anyone to know what was happening.

'Pull in,' he told the driver.

Snouty made sure the street was clear, then hopped out. He suddenly stopped on the pavement's edge, and asked hopefully, 'Expenses?'

'Here's two quid,' said Thane, stuffing the notes into the grubby, outstretched palm. 'And don't booze it.'

Snouty gave a quick mock salute, and faded.

CHAPTER TWELVE

THE FIRST REPORTERS arrived at the block of luxury flats almost an hour after Thane departed.

They were just in time to see Barlby's body being carried out in a mortuary shell, and in the near-panic rush that followed as they tried to get a story scraped together for the mid-day edition, which had an 11 a.m. press time for both papers, they could only agree on one thing—thank the Lord no one had a lead on the other.

That they had arrived almost simultaneously was due to a quiet tip-off given to their papers' court reporters by a friendly official, who had just been informed that the police surgeon wouldn't be able to attend as a witness in an assault trial.

The caretaker of the flats was reticent, knowing that his employers were going to be unhappy enough about the publicity to come. But the "daily" had no such qualms, and delighted the waiting notebooks with a technicolour description of her discovery. She posed for pictures, spoke at length of Barlby's tidy ways and nebulous background, and finally, rather reluctantly, wandered off. She just missed, by seconds, the late arrival of a television sound-and-vision film unit, and thus missed her greatest chance of winning immortal fame among her neighbours.

Jock Mills of the Bugle had finished clearing his copy by phone. As usual, his office car's two-way radio had broken down at a time of crisis and could receive, but not send. This situation sometimes made the desk-bound news editor behave like a raving lunatic, and Jock had long since decided that telephone boxes were much to be preferred. He hung up, put his notebook back in his raincoat pocket, and walked back along the road to the flats.

In deference to what he knew would be Thane's wishes, and because, for the moment, the news editor knew nothing about it, he had kept out of his story the connection between Barlby and the Kilburns. 'But' he promised himself, 'when I break this story, I'll be all set to put the screw on for a rise in pay.'

Fifty or so people were now gathered outside, with that mute, detached, expectant air adopted by any crowd who aren't sure what's going on, don't want to admit it, and aren't going to miss anything.

'Excuse me.' The stranger touched his arm, and Jock, his story cleared, raised a friendly eyebrow. 'What's happening over there, chum? There's some talk of a murder—and I saw you with these other newsmen earlier.'

'Man called Barlby got killed,' said Jock. 'Someone broke into his flat.'

I know you, he puzzled, know you from somewhere. The stranger—only he wasn't really a stranger, Jock was sure now—involuntarily tightened his grip on Jock's arm.

'Barlby? Are you sure?'

'Yes. Why, did you know him?' asked the reporter, then, suddenly, he realised who this was beside him. 'Wait a bit,' he exclaimed.

But the tall man had already turned, and was moving quickly through the crowd, away from him.

'Hey,' Jock Mills called after the man whose face, younger, without the moustache now on his upper lip, had stared at him from a photograph the previous night.

He started after Liam Kilburn, and as he cleared the crowd broke into a jog-trot. But the other man was hurrying too. He jumped into a waiting car, and the small saloon ripped away from the kerb, going through the gears at almost peak revs. Jock Mills was left standing open-mouthed.

Then he shoved his hat to the back of his head and cursed aloud. A woman had been driving, he was sure of that. But why the hell hadn't he had the sense to spot the registration number of the car? A small green saloon... For a moment he struggled with temptation. Then he headed back to the phone box and dialled 999.

CHAPTER THIRTEEN

THE VISCOUNT AIRLINER swept in to land along the runway with a turboprop whine, there was a momentary scream of rubber as tyres met tarmac, and then it was rolling to a gradual halt. The engines whined louder again, and the nosewheel turned as the pilot brought it towards the disembarking bay at the airport terminal building.

White-overalled mechanics whisked a wheeled gangway up to the passenger doorway, it swung open, and, clutching an odd assortment of hand luggage, its occupants came out into the sunshine.

It wasn't difficult to spot Peter Angello. Swarthy, medium height, clean-shaven, the Continental cut of his brown gabardine suit, and the flash of colour from his near-yellow pigskin shoes set him apart from the other travellers from London, where he had joined the Scots-bound aircraft.

Thane met him at the doorway leading into the airport passenger lounge, and the Italian dentist pumped him by the hand.

'Good trip?' asked the detective.

'Ver' nice,' said Angello. 'But what is the news?'

Thane led him through the crowded lounge over towards the luggage bay.

'Bad, I'm afraid. Kilburn is still on the loose, and has killed a man, an old acquaintance. Our guess is he had double-crossed Kilburn over some crooked deal. And Kilburn's brother and sister are in town. A friend of mine spotted them hanging around the flat where the man was murdered. But they got away before he could warn us.'

The Italian groaned aloud. 'Then I am not here a moment too soon. You see, it is to me you must blame all this, signor. Me and no one else,' he finished, shaking his head.

They rescued his luggage, a large green travel bag, from the porter's trolley, and went out into the parking lot, where Thane's car was waiting.

Angello looked around him and sighed again. 'Signor Thane, this I must tell you now. Now, while we are here alone. Later, I can tell others, if need be, but please—'

'Go ahead.' The detective stopped and half-turned towards the obviously anxious man.

Angello began his story with an open-palmed gesture of his hands, and kept moving them as he spoke, as if voice and gestures were interdependent.

'To understand, you must realise that I am the friend of John Kilburn, and not his son. And you must understand the debt I owed to the man, a debt that by foolishness I have repaid by bringing his family tragedy—and now this.'

It had been towards the end of the war in Europe, when Italy, resistance to the Allies collapsed like a burst paper bag, its leaders swinging to join the fight against Germany, had become a jungle in which bands of alleged "guerrillas" operating under the banner of resistance were settling old scores indiscriminately. Fascist units were indulging in a last orgy of looting and killing, and former British POWs walking out of their prison camps, were wondering who would arrive first—the Germans from the north, or the Alfie's from the south.

'I had been a Fascist!—but only, like so many others, because it was, to a professional man, a matter of convenience. I had served in the Italian Army, but was wounded at Bardia, and was very happily sent back to my work as a dentist in my hometown.'

And then the terror came. The guerrillas worked from house to house, dragging out men, women, and children, beating the fortunate ones, hanging, vilifying the others. Sometimes they had reason for their savagery, in terms of tortured, slaughtered comrades. But often they had not. In Peter Angello's case, he was dragged out of bed with his wife and child, bundled down to the street corner and, still in his night-clothes, thrown to the ground beside the local police chief, a Socialist union leader, and a young Black-shirt corporal, home on leave with a bullet-smashed leg. His wife and child were dragged away, screaming.

Angello took out a flowered silk handkerchief and openly wiped his eyes.

Thane scuffed the ash surface of the car park, frankly moved by the Italian's barely suppressed emotion.

'They hanged the police chief and the corporal from a lamp-post. But they had no more rope. The union man struggled, and one man clubbed him with a rifle butt. I asked for a priest, and they laughed.'

Then John Kilburn had appeared, neat in his battledress, a Schmeisser submachine gun held at waist level. Angello recognised him as one of the POWs he sometimes treated at the nearby camp. And Kilburn fired one short burst along the ground, shouted in camp-learned Italian that he was lead man of an Army patrol, and gave the "resistance" men two minutes to get clear. Two more khaki figures were running up, shouting. The others disappeared and the two unarmed POWs helped Angello to his feet.

'I told him of my wife and son,' said Angello. 'He just walked away, telling me to wait. He came back twenty minutes later, bringing them both. My wife's arm was gashed, her dress torn. Kilburn had no bullets left. And the next morning, your soldiers arrived.'

That had been the beginning. Angello's wife died months later from the things that happened to her that night. Kilburn went home to Ireland, but the two men wrote to one another. Kilburn returned to Italy not once but several times, and Angello, a widower now, twice came to his friend's farm for long holidays from his prospering new practice in Rome.

'We got on well—and I owed him everything,' said Angello. He took out a slim gold cigarette case, paused until they had both lit up, then, the tobacco burning unheeding in his fingers, went on. 'John never hid from me that what he was doing was wrong. Sometimes I argued with him, sometimes I pleaded. But I knew that he told me the things he did because there was no one else. His wife knew he had become a smuggler. But she did not know the other things.

'Patrick, his son, gloried in it all. He brought some of the worst things, the dirty things best unseen, into the business. Sometimes his father was angry. But always, eventually, he gave in. For John Kilburn loved his boy, loved him because he was strong and cunning, because all the time they worked together. His family, too, he loved. But they knew only little things, and they had the farm.'

Thane threw down his cigarette and rubbed out the glowing stub with his heel. 'Did you help him in the courier work he did for the gangs?' he asked bluntly. 'Even if he was a friend, shouldn't you have gone to the police?'

Angello raised his hands in a gesture of despair. 'True, signor, I should have gone to the authorities. But he was my friend, he saved our lives. Would you do it?

'I kept my hands clean. Never, even if he had asked, would I have helped. But he did not ask me. And, because he could trust me, he told me all his plans and schemes, the people he worked with, the goods he carried, the criminals he smuggled to safety. You have a storybook hero, the Scarlet Pimpernel, I know. John Kilburn would joke of himself as the Black Pimpernel. He said the only difference was that he was smuggling the mobs to safety from the aristos.'

The airport clock showed it was nearly three-thirty. Thane tried to hurry the Italian. 'So how do you blame yourself for what happened?'

'I am slow in the telling,' apologised the swarthy dentist. 'You are in a hurry?'

'We've to meet my colleague, Inspector Moss, in the city in twenty minutes,' said Thane. 'Can't you continue in the car?'

The Italian agreed. The part of his story that most affected him emotionally was over. He got into the rear seat of the Jaguar, Thane sitting in front beside the uniformed driver, and the car started off.

As they travelled, Angello came to the vital part of his tale. When Kilburn and his son were charged with murder, he had flown over to see how he could help. But John Kilburn did not want to talk, except about his family outside, and to inquire how his son, in similar isolation in the same prison block, was bearing up.

'When they were sentenced I wept,' said Angello. 'For whatever happened, John Kilburn was still my friend. I went back to Italy, for I could not stay and see him and his family suffer so.'

And then came the letter. It arrived four days after John Kilburn was hanged. Written the evening before he died, it seemed a simple message of thanks for Angello's attempts to aid and comfort the doomed man.

'But, Signor Thane, it was more, much more. John often showed me a very simple code he used when writing to his contacts abroad. You take the first and last words in each line, and there is your true message. And the message he sent me was that he did not shoot the policeman, that his son Patrick had done this—but he could not see the boy hang. He had lived his life, and now he must help Patrick the only way he could. But someone had to know the truth. He wanted it to be me. And I was to keep it secret from all.'

Angello wiped his forehead.

In the silence, the police driver, mouth half open, suddenly realised he had gone past the road junction where they should have turned off, so intent had he been to hear their passenger's story.

But Thane hadn't noticed either. Slewed round in his seat, he demanded, 'But the family found out?'

'*Si*.'

'You told them?'

Angello nodded. 'I went to Ireland three months after I got that letter. I found my old friend's wife had gone out of her mind. I found his son Liam brooding and bitter. And his lovely dark-haired girls— Signor, I feared for their sanity. Then I thought, "If I tell them of their father's sacrifice, they will have a new, proud memory to keep in their inner heart, one that will make the bad things seem less real." And I—I did.'

'What happened?' pressed Thane, knowing what was to come, realising that the thing he had feared was shaping into final reality.

'Liam cursed his brother and wept. The two girls were so quiet, I was almost afraid. They asked me to show them the letter. I did. Then it was Liam who sat silent, and the girls who wept. The next day, they seemed brighter, as if a darkness had been raised. The word I brought made no difference to their mother—she can no longer understand, except that her husband is somewhere distant.

'They thanked me, and I left. I came back only once, three

years ago. But my friend was dead, his family were not close to me—and I did not come back, nor want to, until you telephoned.'

Angello drew himself forward, both hands clutching the leather of the seat in front. Softly, slowly, he said, 'I have come here to help, Signor Thane. To repay a debt. I will do that with you—not to help your police, but to help my friend's son and daughter. I will repay the debt—by stopping them from killing their brother. He deserves to die. I would not raise one finger to prevent that. But if Liam and Margot kill him, what is justice to them will be murder in the eyes of the world. Do you accept me, signor?'

Thane took a deep breath. Then, 'I do,' he agreed. 'If you are ready, we will start as soon as Inspector Moss has joined us and has reported. You remember the hiding places John Kilburn told you about?'

Angello nodded. 'I remember—and I have notes. Sometimes I would say I should tell the police and would make notes after he had gone. But secretly, I knew I could never do it.'

Phil Moss flagged them down in Eglinton Street, not far from the city centre. He brought a mixture of good and bad news.

'The Scientific Bureau phoned over a preliminary report, Colin. Your hunch about the saliva test has worked. Blood samples from the office window Kilburn smashed match up with the saliva grouping on the cigarette. And Barlby was in a different blood group. Now they're trying to group the blood forming that shoe-shape stain on the carpet.

'But most important, they found a clear set of prints on the window-snib at the office... Records say there is no doubt they match up to Kilburn's "dabs." Oh—and Doc Williams reckons Barlby had been dead about seven hours when he was found. He says it can only be a pretty rough estimate, but he would probably place the murder at about one-thirty in the morning.'

Moss had just come from a quick meeting with Snouty Leith in a quiet South Side pub where the little informer was unknown. 'Snouty says there is any amount of excitement about Kilburn being on the run, but, so far, no one seems to know anything about where he is. Strange thing is, Snouty says, the word is being spread that one of Kilburn's old customers is very anxious to contact him. Before you ask, Snouty doesn't think this is his brother and sister. All he knows is that one or two of the strong-arm men from the dock-side mobs are letting it be known there's money waiting for any "ned" who puts Kilburn their way. And all Snouty can gather is that he's wanted for some pretty strange and crooked job that's coming off.'

'When is he contacting us again?' asked Thane.

'Tonight—after the pubs shut,' said Moss, carefully unwrapping a digestion tablet, and popping the pill into his mouth. 'Know anything about stomach ulcers, Doctor Angello?'

'Sorry, I am a dentist,' smiled the Italian apologetically.

'Hm...m, I forgot,' grunted Moss. 'Well, take it from me, a rampant ulcer is four or five times worse than the most hellish toothache ever known.' He sucked away while Thane sketched in the skeleton details of Angello's story, raising an expressive eyebrow, but refraining from comment, as the Italian told of the letter in which John Kilburn had laid the murder of the detective at his son's door.

'That's it, Phil,' concluded Thane. 'And now, we're going to start looking up some of John Kilburn's old bases. The first is about five minutes' run from here.'

CHAPTER FOURTEEN

THE ROOM HAD A DAMP, stale smell about it. The faded Victorian wallpaper bulged loose in one corner, and the small washbasin's porcelain surface was criss-crossed by a network of black-veined cracks and chip marks.

Patrick Kilburn poured the last of the beer can's contents into the coarse glass tumbler and drained the liquid down. Then he lay back on the bed again, the springs creaking as he curled himself into a more comfortable position. The Beretta dug sharply into his side, and with a muttered curse he took the gun out of his jacket pocket and laid it close to hand on the rickety bedside table.

'What a dump,' he grumbled. 'What a stinking dump.'

The faded board outside proclaimed this was the Pleasance Hotel. Inside, from the faded, stone-floored alcove that was the reception desk to the plastic-covered tables in the "dining-room," the whole place looked exactly what it was, a third-rate rooming-house in an East End back street.

The handful of residents were mainly broken-down casuals who came in at night to sleep and left again first thing in the morning. But it was safe—that was why he and his father had chosen it all those years ago as one of their scattering of hideouts.

The owner was a fat, dirty woman of indeterminable age and dyed blonde hair, showing dark at the roots. The twin factors that Kilburn had money and that more than once in the past she had, for cash, helped store some of the goods and men the two Irishmen smuggled through had been sufficient persuasion to let him have the room.

It would do till nightfall, anyway. And then— He chuckled and felt the reassuring bulk in his jacket pocket. That rat Barlby— But at least he'd managed to find two of the bankbooks, still untouched, when he took the flat to pieces. There had also been two spare clips of ammo for the butt-loading automatic, and, most important of all, that little red-covered notebook with its entries covering half a dozen countries.

Barlby hadn't been able to "break" the book and its precious information, thanks to that simple code the old man had worked out. Kilburn pushed the thought of his father quickly into the background—think instead of the money, a hundred and fifty quid between Barlby's wallet and cash-box, another three hundred he'd drawn that morning from one of the bank accounts. "Victor Sewell" was the name it had lain under all these years, and the manager had been pleased to welcome him back from abroad.

The old prison kit was in the river now, safely sunk. He'd paid three quid for a grey pin-stripe from a second-hand store where they didn't worry too much about customers' appearances. The stuff from Barlby's wardrobe had done till then. Now it was all in the river, for the second-hand store stocked every need.

He had to wait till evening, now, for the next stage. With a little bit of luck, it would be smooth enough.

'Pick up a few of the old strings,' he muttered. 'Slide down by the docks, make a couple of phone calls, and I'll be set up sweetly.'

Suicide to try to board a ship in port. But he knew one or two characters who'd run a small boat out from farther down the coast, one or two foreign coaster skippers who would happily pull him aboard there and put him ashore after dark off their home coastline—provided the pay was right.

God, life had been a foul mixed-up mess. The craven terror of waiting for the rope, the dumb misery of prison that sapped him dry of everything but a cringing urge to do whatever the prison screws wanted, for that meant good conduct marks, and maybe weeks, months, perhaps years off his time. Time—five years rotting, another five years at least ahead, and only mugs try to escape, because you lose all remission.

Damn his brother and sister—but at least they had forced him to take the gamble. Damn them, however they had found out...

When he woke, it was with a sudden start. He glanced at his watch... three hours since he had dozed off to sleep. Five o'clock now—almost time. Kilburn scooped up the automatic from the table and slid it back in his pocket.

Rolling off the bed, he inspected his reflection in the mirror above the wash-basin and ran a hand speculatively over the dark stubble that had formed on his chin. It had been 1 a.m. that morning, in Barlby's, when he last stood close to a blade. The quest he was about to set out on demanded a tidy, assured appearance.

Adjusting his tie, smoothing his hair back with his hands, Kilburn left the room and went quietly down the hotel stairs. He could pick up the necessary shaving gear from the chemist shop at the corner.

The razor, soap, blades, and a toothbrush were in a neat brown-paper package as he left the shop minutes later. He took three steps forward, then stopped and slipped back into the doorway again, a wave of stomach-tightening, heart-pumping panic sweeping through him.

There was no mistaking the two figures who were mounting the five steps up to the Pleasance Hotel, swift-footed, shoulder to shoulder. Liam and Margot had arrived.

Behind him, the shop door opened, a bell clanging. The elderly woman coming out had to ask him twice to let her pass before he realised she was there. He kept in the doorway, shrinking to one side, and she squeezed her fat form past with a mutter and a glare.

Kilburn shoved the paper package in his jacket pocket, rested his right hand round the Beretta's butt, and edged out a little. They had gone inside the Pleasance.

Half-expectedly, he scanned the street. But there was no one else in sight, except the stout woman, puffing her way along the pavement. The Irishman licked his suddenly dry lips, squared his shoulders, and headed after her, directly away from the hotel. For the moment, he feared neither crook nor cop, but the devils out of hell would be welcome company compared with his own kin.

CHAPTER FIFTEEN

MARGOT DID the talking in the hotel. She usually did—Liam preferred it that way, for, though when the mood moved him and only friends were around he could show sudden, unexpected eloquence, normally he was slow of tongue. He knew his job—while his sister talked to the dyed-blonde landlady, he kept both hands deep in the pockets of his loosely cut tweed overcoat, ready for the slightest movement on the stairway.

The woman was frigid from the start. Wiping her hands on the dirty apron hanging round her middle, she denied from the word go that Kilburn was, had been, or ever would be in the Pleasance.

'I've never heard of him,' she declared.

'You can't read papers, then,' Margot threw back at her. 'Hasn't his name and his photograph been in them all today, telling how he escaped from prison?'

'Suggest just once more, just once more, that I would have a convict in this hotel, and I'll fetch the police,' cried the woman. 'I run a decent place here.'

Margot rested one hand on a slim waist. 'Decent be damned,' she told her overweight opponent. 'I've told you, we're family! Look, does this satisfy you?' She delved into her tooled leather handbag and pulled out a snap-shot. 'There...' she thrust it into the blonde's unwilling hands. 'It was taken years ago, but there's my father, with my brother here beside him, Patrick, myself, and the others. Now do you believe me?'

The woman fingered the photograph. 'Anything else?' she demanded.

'Driving licence, some old bills—and here, another picture of my father,' said Margot, producing the articles.

The blonde was still undecided. 'You say your father used to come here. Where would he keep his baggage?'

Liam's eyes never left the stairway. 'In your kitchen, woman, where else? In the space behind the false back of your kitchen cupboard. Now, will you tell us—or do we have to be taking the place apart ourselves?'

She relaxed, at any rate. 'Upstairs—room eight. But you can tell him again I don't want him here. The sooner he goes, the happier I'll be. I'm scared stiff, I tell you—that's why I was so cautious.'

'We'll tell him,' promised Margot. 'But don't worry. We've come for just that purpose, to take him off your hands.' She took a step nearer to the woman. 'Go back to your kitchen. In fifteen minutes you can come out again, and we'll be gone. All that's left is for you to forget you've ever seen any of us. Do that, and you'll be well looked after, as you were before.'

'But, missus,' said Liam softly, purposefully, 'your memory had better be bad if anyone comes asking questions—or we'll be back to settle in another way.'

They waited until the woman, gladly accepting their orders if it meant getting rid of her unwanted guest, had gone back into the dim, sour-smelling passageway leading to the kitchen.

Then, Liam leading, the girl on the opposite side of the treads, a mere three steps behind, they climbed the stairs. The big man moved quietly, a trifle stiffly, left hand unbuttoning his coat as he advanced. As the last button slipped, the edge of the coat swung and blued metal glinted for a moment before the cloth fell back into place. They halted on the landing, then Margot gestured to the left, down the corridor.

But room eight was empty when they threw open its door. The crumpled bedcover, the stub-filled ashtray, told part of the story. Margot took off one fawn leather glove and felt the grey-white top mat. The disarranged centre still seemed faintly warmer to the touch than the surrounding material.

'Only minutes away,' she murmured.

Liam swung the sawn-short muzzles of the shot-gun he was no longer troubling to conceal. 'Want I should check the other rooms, Margot?'

The girl nodded. 'But softly,' she cautioned. 'There's not likely to be anyone in them, but we don't want to scare some innocent roomer—if this flea hive has such a thing.'

They searched—and found nothing. Liam tucked the gun back under his coat and, an iron-bitter look on his face, followed his sister back down the stairway. Together they went into the kitchen.

Even as the blonde, breaking off peeling potatoes at the grimy sink, began to protest that she had no idea where her missing roomer might be, they heard the creaking groan of the street door. Margot chanced a quick glance into the hallway and her breath came out in a hiss of surprise.

'Peter Angello—and what look like police,' she whipcracked. 'You two get rid of that gun, then join me. We can't do anything but meet them.' Without further hesitation, she stepped smartly out of the kitchen. Her Cuban-heeled shoes sounded loud on the stone flags.

'Hello, Uncle Peter,' she said boldly. 'I might have realised you would show up sooner or later.'

CHAPTER SIXTEEN

THE SUDDEN HEAD-ON encounter with Margot Kilburn came as a complete surprise to the trio before her.

With the little Italian dentist as their guide, Thane and Moss had covered plenty of ground since they accepted his offer to guide them round the Kilburn network. Only two of the places he took them to were known to the police. The others, as quiet, out-of-the-way spots as the Pleasance Hotel, had brought frightened reactions from the occupants... though not all had been inhabited.

Two were gone, demolished with the rest of the surrounding buildings to make way for new development. One was a ramshackle hut in the middle of a score of allotment gardens. Another, the most cunningly hidden of all, was in an underground petrol storage tank lying to the rear of a quiet Giffnock garage. The garage owner had taken over the tank, with its two fitted bunks and tiny heater, for his own purposes.

Thane, wriggling through the inspection hatch that led to the big steel cylinder, had emerged with the satisfaction of knowing where some of the motor accessories stolen in a recent wave of garage break-ins had found a resting place and Sergeant MacLean of Millside was there now with two Renfrewshire CID men and a resigned garageman.

The Pleasance was number seven on their fist.

'Don't you recognize me, Uncle Peter?' asked the girl again.

Angello's face lit up. 'Margotta, my child, I had been praying to find you,' he exclaimed, moving towards her.

'Me? I thought it would be Patrick you and your friends would be after,' she said drily. But there was no doubting the affectionate hug she gave the Italian. 'Liam's here... Liam, come on out.'

The Irishman's bulk appeared in the kitchen doorway. Slowly, he, too, came forward, the blowsy owner of the Pleasance trailing behind in her flapping carpet-slippers. Liam gravely shook hands with Angello, then stared determinedly at Thane and Moss, a few steps away.

Hurriedly, the little Italian began introductions.

'That can wait,' said Thane. 'Miss Kilburn, do you know where your brother is?'

'I can tell you he isn't here,' she replied, meeting his gaze and holding it steadily. 'And I can tell you if we knew where he had gone to from here, we wouldn't be hanging about exchanging the time of day with you.'

'He's been here?' Phil Moss moved to the foot of the stairway as he spoke.

'Been and gone, unless he comes wandering back in while we're waiting,' said the girl, silencing the fat blonde woman's protest with a curt gesture.

'Look away if you like, Mr Detective. He was in room number eight, according to this one here, but Patrick always was the lucky one at getting out of places just before trouble arrived.'

Phil caught Thane's faint nod and went up the stairway to make a routine check. Liam Kilburn watched him go, face expressionless, then pulled out a battered cherrywood pipe, slipped off the metal storm cap, and began fumbling for matches. Angello beat him to it, and the Irishman mumbled a thanks.

They waited silently, until Phil Moss came back down the stairway. He carried the beer can carefully in his handkerchief, and in his other hand was a small transparent envelope in which he had emptied the contents of the ashtray in room number eight. He was remembering the stub found at the Barlby murder flat—these would be good for comparison tests.

Quietly he squeezed past the blonde woman into the kitchen, looked around, and reappeared again.

'Satisfied?' asked Margot Kilburn, two small spots of red appearing on her cheeks.

'Routine,' said Thane, with no hint of apology in his tone. 'I didn't expect your brother to be waiting around. You aren't the best of friends, are you?'

Peter Angello stopped the girl before she could answer. 'Be careful, Margot, these men are not fools. They know what has happened. I have told them.'

'Told them? Why?' She was obviously puzzled.

'For your own sake,' said Thane. 'Angello's a pretty good friend to have, Miss Kilburn. He scorched over here by plane from Italy today after I had telephoned him.'

'And has he told you that you hanged the wrong man?' asked the girl bitterly. 'How do you feel about that, knowing the blood of an innocent man is on your hands? Oh, I know you were not on my father's case. I'll remember the faces of the men who were as long as I live.'

'He's told us,' said Thane, tipping his soft hat back on his head with a sigh. 'It isn't a pretty tale, I admit.'

The girl shrugged her shoulders. 'Oh, I'm not blaming the police. At first I hated everyone I saw. But you get over that feeling in time.' She changed tack suddenly. 'Did Patrick kill Barlby?'

'Maybe.'

'No great loss, that one,' growled Liam Kilburn. Then, conscious of attention having switched to him, he faced away, puffing furious clouds of smoke from his pipe.

'Mr Thane...' Peter Angello hesitated. 'May I speak... speak to them freely?'

Colin Thane pursed his lips. In terms of hard, practical fact there wasn't a thing he could pin on the escaped man's brother and sister, even if he had every reason to be sure they were the snipers who had twice tried to kill Kilburn.

'Go ahead,' he agreed. 'But with this warning to all of you—be careful.'

The Italian nodded vehemently. 'That is what I want to say... be careful, Margot, be careful, Liam. What you plan is wrong, foolish. Do not stop me now. I know, and what the police do not know, they guess. Go home, go back to your mother. Let these men find your brother. This man he has killed—when they find Patrick, he will have to stand trial. You will see, he will not escape a second time. Vengeance is not for you; it will only bring more black sorrow to your home.' He stretched his arms out towards them, appealing.

Margot carefully traced a neat design on the stone-flagged floor with one neat shoe.

'We haven't said anything about our plans for Patrick,' she at last answered. Then challengingly, she demanded, 'Do you want to arrest us, policeman?'

'Maybe I do,' said Thane. 'Maybe I want to, for everybody's safety, including your own. But right now, I'll admit I can't.' Despite himself, he couldn't help liking the dark-haired, soft-voiced girl and her big, slow-moving brother.

'Right. You can't. Then we can go?'

'Margotta.' Angello was almost in tears. 'You must understand what may happen to you. Stop this mad foolishness while you can.' He gripped her by the arm.

The girl gently shook herself free. 'Liam and I know what you are trying to do, Uncle Peter. But there's nothing you can say that will change things.'

The little Italian stepped back and turned appealingly to the stolid figure by her side. But Liam Kilburn gave no answering sign of emotion.

'Can we go now?' Margot repeated her question to Thane.

'In a moment.' He slipped forward suddenly and ran his hands quickly over her brother's clothes. Liam's eyes flickered, but he made no protest. Thane was a tall man, but Liam Kilburn topped him by a good inch. If the Irishman had made trouble, thought Thane wryly, they would have had a lively time.

'What did you expect to find, a gun?' asked Margot mockingly, as the detective stood back.

'Perhaps. Can I see your handbag?' The girl flushed, but obeyed. Thane gave the contents a perfunctory glance, then returned it. He ran a deliberate eye over her slim figure and with intentional irony declared, 'I don't propose to search you—it would be pretty difficult to conceal anything under your rig-out. But listen to me. You'll be watched, you'll be waited for. We're giving you some rope—for God's sake, don't use it to hang yourself.'

The girl flushed. Her brother gave a low growl of anger, which died away at her silent command. Together they left the hotel, unbowed, with a grim purpose that gathered round them like an impenetrable cloak. And yet, as they went, Thane felt something akin to pity for these two, caught up in tragedy, attempting to bludgeon the present to achieve their conception of justice for the past.

As the outer door swung shut, Phil Moss headed after them. Two plainclothesmen were waiting a little way along the street, left there in case the hotel had proved to be "hot." Now their job would be to tail the Kilburns. The familiar wiry frame of their inspector appearing on the hotel steps, and his slow nod in the direction of the couple, walking rapidly along the pavement, was all the signal they needed.

One plainclothesman stopped studying the display in the corner chemist's window and began strolling after them on the opposite side of the street. Behind him, just keeping the shadower in sight, the second officer was at the wheel of an unpretentious buff-coloured observation van. It moved slowly, engine little more than ticking over, while he radioed in for another team to assist them. For a good shadowing job needs ample numbers so that the giveaway factor of one man constantly "tailing" can be eliminated.

Back in the Pleasance, more police arrived, another comb was made of the building, and finally they left, leaving one man on guard against the unlikely return of Patrick Kilburn. And only the frightened blonde, once more busy preparing the evening meal for her returned lodgers, knew of the sawn-short shotgun lying concealed in the kitchen hiding place that had sheltered many strange bundles before, but none more deadly.

Standing outside the Pleasance Hotel, the duty car waiting by the pavement, Thane knew he had on his hands one of the trickiest situations he had ever known. And worse, for once he was completely robbed of the initiative.

There were three more addresses in the Kilburn network still to be visited, according to the Italian. But if Patrick Kilburn now knew his brother and sister also had details of the network, he would be certain to avoid it like the plague. The runaway would have to contact some of his friends sooner or later—but in the waiting time, he remained armed, desperate, and ripe for trouble.

Colin Thane had to pin his hopes on Snouty, the patient

little informer—and there were four hours to go before Snouty could be hoped to show results.

The grim-faced chief inspector turned to Angello. 'We'll visit these other hideaways on your list,' he said. 'Then get you into a hotel for the night. You've tried, man… What happens, or who it happens to, at least you've tried.'

They got into the car, and it purred away.

CHAPTER SEVENTEEN

IF THERE DID HAPPEN to be any compensations to the task of being a policeman's wife, mused Mary Thane, it was high time someone told her about them.

She eyed the brown coffee spouting regularly into the glass top of the percolator, decided the liquid was now sufficiently dark, and disconnected the base plug. At eight o'clock she was usually just summoning courage to engage in the nightly battle to get the kids to bed and the eruption into the house of two hungry cops didn't help. Still—she smiled and shrugged as the conversation drifted through the open serving hatch from the living room.

'Dad said he'd repair it, Uncle Phil—but he still hasn't,' complained young Tom Thane, holding the current pride of his life, a small battery-operated model sports car finished in authentic British racing green.

Phil Moss forked the last segment of scrambled egg from his plate and examined the model. 'What's up with it anyway, youngster?'

'The reversing lever...' The schoolboy gave his father a withering look. 'It stopped working nearly a week ago.'

'It just needs a spot of cleaning out,' explained Colin Thane. 'What else can you expect when you get it covered in dirt in the garden? When I was your age...' He gave up. 'Look, I'll fix it. But not tonight.'

He was saved by his wife's arrival with the coffee.

'Bed,' she declared firmly. 'Now, Tom. You too, Kate.'

The girl glanced up from the corner of the room, where she was sprawled beside a storybook, gauged her mother's possible patience, and decided it was best to obey.

Thane waited until the two children had thumped their noisy way upstairs, Mary close behind.

'We'd better get moving soon,' he declared. 'I've to check in at Headquarters about nine. Really shouldn't have come out at all, come to that.'

Moss snorted. 'Couldn't do much good hanging about Millside at the moment. Ah...' he settled back, lighting a cigarette. 'Nothing like home cooking.'

'You can hardly call scrambled eggs a complete sample,' apologized Thane. 'But—'

'At this hour, Mary would have been justified turfing us both right out again,' grinned his friend. 'No, just coming home like this to the kids, a fireside, and knowing there's a welcome, I mean. You're a lucky man, Colin.'

'Then why guard your bachelor status so fervently?' asked Thane slyly, pouring another cup of coffee. 'Don't tell me your landlady has stopped making eyes at you?'

'Since she found that her new bank manager's a widower, she's lost interest in humble coppers,' said Moss. 'And a good thing too—it was getting beyond a joke.' He changed the subject. 'Think Snouty will have turned up anything?'

'He'd better, for everyone's sake.' Thane's tone was serious. 'The chief constable's climbing the walls, the papers are having a Roman holiday, and the information room are getting about three phone calls every five minutes from well-meaning old ladies who think they've got an escaped con under their beds.' He tossed his cigarette end savagely into the glowing fire. 'And I'd hate like hell to end up pulling in the Kilburn girl and her brother on a murder rap.'

'Only luck has stopped them so far,' agreed Phil. 'Can't we lock them up quietly until we get their brother Patrick again? Barlby's murder is a capital charge—you'd think they'd be satisfied as long as he swung for that.'

Thane shrugged. 'It's a fixation, Phil. A deadly, bloody-minded fixation. Call it a mixture of their Irish temperament and what they've gone through, knowing their father ended on a rope, seeing their mother go crazy, then finding out dear Patrick was to blame. Probably the whole show drove them pretty close to crazy themselves at the time. And now they're wound up, they'll keep on. Give me one good reason for locking them in a cell and I'll do it for their own good as much as anything else. But they've been careful, and just as cunning as their old man used to be. We know they're behind a lot, but just tell me any charge we could stick on them, with the flimsy evidence we've scraped together so far.'

He was right, Phil knew. 'Damn Paddy Kilburn,' he muttered. 'Let me see young Tom's toy car, Colin, maybe we can fix it—we're not due to be collected for another five minutes.'

They reached Headquarters dead on time. A series of reports were waiting from the police lab. The cigarette stub in the Pleasance matched on saliva with the one found in the murder flat. Paddy Kilburn's prints were all over the beer can. The others were technically valuable for any later court hearing, but took Thane no further.

Leaving Phil in the inspectors' room of the Headquarters canteen, he crossed the road to the Central CID office.

"Buddha" Ilford, chief superintendent and head of the entire city CID force, listened quietly. He didn't like the idea

Colin Thane put forward. But, after sitting for a moment, hands folded across his ample stomach, he finally agreed.

'It's been done before, Colin. A phoney charge to help a case along by keeping someone out of circulation. It could cause a stink—still, you're right. Breach of the peace, theft, assault—take your pick, and pull them in. And may the Lord have mercy on us if we don't find Patrick Kilburn before we've got to let them go.'

Fate didn't mean it to be so easy. Thane was on his way out of the Central building, back to Headquarters, when his name was shouted.

A young uniform man hurried down the corridor towards him, a message form in his hand. Phoned over from Millside station, it was short and simple. 'Officers shadowing Liam and Margot Kilburn report lost contact.'

CHAPTER EIGHTEEN

SIMPLE TRICKS ARE ALWAYS the best.

Liam and Margot Kilburn walked down the road, turned off at the first corner, and climbed into the hired saloon they had parked there. The car purred away, the CID shadow van "tailing" in the distance. But the Kilburns seemed unaware of them. They made no effort to increase their pace. Liam steered quietly through the city, then pulled off the road at a garage on the outskirts, stopped at the petrol pumps, and got out.

The CID van stopped well short of the garage. One detective slid from the van and strolled along towards the pumps. A garage attendant was filling the tank of Kilburn's saloon—then the bonnet went up for an oil check.

As the "shadow" stooped, pretending to fix his shoelace, Margot left the car and went over to the cigarette dispenser. She drew a packet.

Crash—the mechanic slammed the bonnet back in position, finished his oil check. He turned round puzzled. And the watching tech suddenly realised: neither Margot nor Liam were in sight!

Wiping his hands on a piece of rag, the mechanic headed

into the garage. Outside, the "shadow" waited in an agony of suspense. He might jump too soon—the Kilburns could return any second. Yet if he waited...

Long moments went by. Then another car drew up outside the pumps. The attendant reappeared, shouted back into the garage, shook his head in bewilderment, and began to push the Kilburns' car out of the way. The "shadow" sprang to life. But he was too late. Brother and sister had simply walked through the garage, gone out of the rear door, and vanished.

So, Thane and Moss discovered when they arrived. The abandoned car was "clean"—not a trace remained of its occupants.

'They probably checked in at an hotel somewhere before starting out to find their brother, Patrick,' suggested Phil Moss.

'Not this family,' growled Thane, angered at the ease with which the couple had slipped him. 'My bet is there's another car waiting somewhere with their bags aboard. An hotel would be too obvious a way of tracing them. Get a call out on the radio for another prod round the hire-and-drive companies—though somebody else probably rented this car for them and would do the same for any other transport they wanted.'

'You in charge?' a surly faced figure in a crumpled lounge suit confronted him. 'This car's in my way. What am I supposed to do with it?'

Thane struggled to refrain from telling him. 'Better give it a home inside for the time being,' he advised.

'Who'll foot the bill?' demanded the garage manager. 'We put five gallons of petrol in it, and a quart of oil.'

'Your attendant says three gallons and a pint,' retorted Phil. 'We'll worry about that later.' He fell into step with Thane as the burly policeman walked back towards the black radio car. 'Robbing shower, some garages,' he muttered. 'Where to now? It's almost time to meet Snouty.'

'That's as good an idea as any,' nodded Thane. 'Where have

we to contact him?' 'Back row of the Florinda cinema,' grinned Moss. 'Snouty says that since the telly got going that's as quiet a meeting place as you can find.'

The programme at the Florinda wasn't particularly calculated to wean anyone away from the small screen. A second-rate gangster film was in process of killing off some spare characters as Thane and Moss joined Snouty in the back balcony, slipping into seats one on either side of the little informer.

Snouty turned his attention from the screen and got down to business. 'Kilburn's been found, guv'nor,' he muttered. 'The word's gone out to the boys who were after him.'

'D'you know where he is, Snouty?' asked Thane in equally cautious tones.

The little man shook his head. 'Sorry, guv. All I know is the heat is off. I was in this pub, see, knowing that big Eddy Argot was prowling around for whoever wants to get your pal. Well, when Eddy does come in, he looks sour. So, I chinned him over a few drinks, casual like, and he says he's just lost a nice easy twenty quid—that another character did him out of it by less than five minutes.'

'Who found him, then?' asked Thane.

'I'm just coming to that, guv'nor,' chided Snouty. 'Big Eddy doesn't blab too much, and he's got a thirst—I had to use some of my own money, keeping the drinks going, like.' He paused suggestively, sighed when Thane failed to budge, and continued, 'The man you want is Norry Lebrook. 'Least he's the bloke Eddy says done him out of the cash.'

Snouty could add nothing more. The two detectives left the cinema, and ordered their waiting driver to head back to Millside Police Station.

As the car moved off, engine purring through the gears, Thane flipped the transmitter switch on the radio panel, and lifted the hand-mike.

'Fourteen calling...' he waited until the distant radio-room, set high on Cathkin Braes overlooking the city, gave him the go-ahead. 'Chief Inspector Thane. I want a man, Norry Lebrook, brought in—his CRO number is on file. He should be somewhere around the city centre—have a check made there first. He lives in a lodging house, city centre, address on file. I want him brought to Millside. Over.'

'Roger,' the radio room operator's voice crackled back over the loudspeaker. A few minutes later, they could hear the control dispatching patrol cars, the message giving a detailed description of the wanted man.

Thane knew the drill so well he could picture the scene. The patrol crews knew where to look. City centre corners were where the male and female dregs of the city, the thugs and their women gathered. Then there were the half-dozen back-street meeting places, where touts offered bottles of cheap wine at an exorbitant profit, Scots early-closing licensing laws and their customers' craving, guaranteeing ready sale.

A car at each end of the alleyway, and the animal-like shapes their headlights disclosed, would submit peacefully to a quick scrutiny. "Neds" didn't like roughing it with cops, unless the odds were in the nature of twenty of them to one uniform. They much preferred beating up drunken sailors or solitary youngsters.

Norry Lebrook had no reason to think the police wanted him. A Central Division car found him arguing with some cronies under the big, shop-lined bridge that generations have called the Highlanders' Umbrella. And a radio call advised Thane that a protesting Lebrook was on his way at the same time as the chief inspector's car was entering the Millside yard.

Lebrook didn't look the vicious type as he was marched into Thane's office. His fingernails were black—but his shirt collar was starched and white. His black homburg hat perched cockily on a dark, well-oiled mop of hair. His tie was perhaps a trifle out of place—Norry certainly hadn't been in the Brigade of Guards.

A dark grey suit, quiet and conservative in cut, was spoiled in its effect by his heavy crepe-soled shoes.

But when Norry was seventeen, he had fractured a rent-collector's skull with an iron bar, the start to a long career of brutal assaults, many of them under fee-paying direction. Small, smart, and savage, like a hundred others from the same jungle, Lebrook was no stranger to the "wanted for questioning" process. His face held in a gold-toothed smile, he let his eyes flicker round the room while a uniform man held one sleeve with a firm twist-grip.

Thane leaned back on his chair, arms folded. 'I want Patrick Kilburn, and I think you can help me, Lebrook,' he said slowly, softly. 'We know you acted as contact man tonight, so you might as well make it easier for all concerned and start talking.'

Lebrook allowed a look of hurt surprise to filter across his smile. 'Me, Mr Thane? No—not me. Someone's made a mistake, gents. Must have been someone who looks like me—happens all the time, me bein' mistaken for some other fellow.' With his free hand he pulled a packet of chewing gum from a pocket and began to raise it to his mouth.

'Knock it off, Lebrook,' Phil Moss took a step forward, and with a backward flip of his hand, sent the gum spinning out of Lebrook's grip. 'We're not here to play games with you.'

'You can't—' Lebrook blurted but got no further.

'Shut up.' Thane reared from his desk and took a giant, threatening stride towards him, towering over the crook. 'I've no time to waste on your kind, Lebrook. This is a murder investigation. We want Kilburn. You got twenty quid tonight for putting a contact through to him. Still got the money?'

The uniform man pulled Lebrook's other wrist back, and Thane, standing a little to one side out of range of a possible knee-lunge, swept swiftly through his pockets. The money—fourteen pounds of it, anyway—was in the man's right-hand jacket pocket.

'Spent the rest?'

'I won that at the dogs last night,' protested Lebrook, beads of sweat glistening on his forehead, one snaking down to his upper lip. 'You know you can't mess me about like this.'

'No? Oh... sorry, my mistake.' Thane turned away, and his feet crunched down heavily on the man's suede-covered toes.

Lebrook gave a howl of agony.

'You did that on purpose, you swine,' he wept.

'That's naughty,' said Phil. 'When all we're looking for are a few nice, simple answers. Where's Kilburn?'

Still held fast by the impassive uniform man, Lebrook licked his lips. 'If you're going to arrest me, what will the charge be?'

'Helping an escaped prisoner, accessory, a few other things —if we charge you,' said Thane. 'Maybe, instead, we just keep you in overnight and let the word get out that you're the fellow who's been putting the finger on one or two of your friends recently. Of course, that wouldn't make you very popular, especially among their friends. Let's see, Black Harry got nine years for razoring, and then there was that little tip that sent the Cliff brothers away for that mail-van job...'

'They'd never believe you. I've never grassed in my life,' gasped the man, white-faced.

'But if they did,' pointed out Thane, 'it could be awkward. Of course, we'd give you what protection we can, but there just aren't enough recruits coming forward these days.' He sighed.

'You're bluffing.' Lebrook was trembling.

'Perhaps. You're a gambling man—what odds do you offer?'

The two detectives gazed impassively at Lebrook. The ticking of the wall clock seemed loud in the long silence.

At last, he spoke. 'You win. I did contact Kilburn. He was in a cafe down by the docks—one of the places he used to meet some of his sailor pals.'

'What happened?'

'I passed on the message and took him in a taxi to the fellow who needed him.' Lebrook was reluctant, but there was no sign of mercy in the men before him. 'All I had to do was tell him this bloke would strike a bargain with him—help him out of the country if he did a job in return.'

'And the name?' pressed Thane.

'Giore Paxidena—he's a Greek or some-thin' like that. Runs a couple of restaurants. That's all I know. I ran Kilburn over to his house, got paid off, and was going to forget all about it. Who tipped you off anyway?'

'Just a friend,' said Thane. 'Lock him up,' he instructed the waiting constable. 'And here'—he handed over the banknotes—'once you've got a receipt for his property, get me a list of these notes. There isn't much chance of their being traced back to Paxidena, but we'll make the attempt anyway. Oh, and have a try at getting a couple of cups of tea for us—try the switchboard girls. They've always got a kettle on the boil.'

Phil Moss waited until the door had closed behind the prisoner. Then, sucking thoughtfully on a digestion tablet, he asked, 'Ever heard of this character Paxidena? He's a new one on me.'

Thane walked over to the window and gazed out into the black night. 'The name rings a very faint bell. Nothing more. But I think Lebrook's telling the truth—let's see if there's a way of finding out.' He turned and picked up the telephone. 'Get me the Special Branch at Headquarters,' he asked the operator. 'And while I'm on, there's a cop on his way down in search of tea. Any left in the pot?'

He chuckled at the girl's reply and waited.

'Special Branch? Thane of Millside Division here. Can you help us on the Kilburn case—yes, the escaped con. Got anything on a man Giore Paxidena? I don't think Records will have him—he's probably a borderline character.'

There was a long pause while the Special Branch man left the phone to search the gallery of metal filing cabinets that housed a host of strange dossiers, some of which would have caused public explosions if their very existence became known beyond inner police circles.

Thane picked up a pencil and began writing busily on his desk pad while the Special Branch detective reported. There was a file on Mr Paxidena all right—not as fat a dossier as the people who gathered it would like, but more than sufficient for Thane's needs. He asked a couple of questions, thanked the man at the other end, and hung up, a grin of satisfaction crinkling the corners of his mouth.

'Stop looking like a cat with a saucer of milk,' begged Moss. 'I presume our Greek friend isn't on the side of the angels?'

'Greek, or whatever else he is,' said Thane. 'Paxidena is in the restaurant business all right, but Special Branch had a look at him when he appeared out of nowhere two or three years back. His papers seem in order, but his past, and where he got the money to get started, is just a big blank. They've a feeling he has his fingers dipped in one or two troublesome little activities —and he's got some unusual friends.'

Phil raised an expressive eyebrow. 'He must be behaving himself pretty well, now at any rate, or we'd have heard something about him.'

'Or else he never does his own dirty work,' pointed out Thane. 'He may have come to Britain to lead the quiet life, or, for all we know, he perhaps decided things were getting too involved around his former stamping grounds. There have been one or two strange "jobs" done lately, remember, "jobs" that didn't fit any of our local patterns.'

'Headquarters seems to think a London gang did at least a couple of these,' protested Phil. 'And even if Paxidena has been the real culprit, why come out into the open at this time when he knows we've got nothing on him to date? Why take a chance by having a character like Lebrook drive a bundle of red-hot trouble like Kilburn to his own home?'

'It's out of pattern,' agreed Thane. 'Unless, of course, there is really urgent reason for it, so urgent that Paxidena couldn't waste time working through middle-men.'

'He wants Kilburn to do a job and will help him out of the country.' Moss frowned in concentration and fumbled for another tablet. A faint gnawing pain was giving him sullen warning of his body's refusal to tolerate much more work that night. Well, he reckoned, he had a few hours to go before the pain reached the mincing machine stage. 'The Irishman had dealings with terrorists before. Remember the file, Colin? Hints of arms smuggling, money, explosives, getting "hot" characters over the Channel—the ruddy lot.'

'There's no suggestion that Paxidena comes under the "terrorist" heading,' warned Thane. 'Security has plugged most of the holes in that particular dyke. Mind you, Kilburn's network has been lying dormant for five years while that young thug has been in prison. If it came to life suddenly, MI5—and all the other numbers too, whatever they do for a living—would be left sitting on their cloaks and daggers.' He frowned. 'I prefer to keep this as a nice, respectable criminal matter until someone shows me I'm wrong.'

'Can't we shout for help?' asked his friend half-seriously. 'I'd love to see some of these secret service boys, and meet their expense accounts.'

Thane grinned a little. 'Maybe later. Right now, I'm going to put out a special search request for Paxidena's car—Special Branch had it on file. Then we pick up a search warrant and head out to interview the gentleman.'

'Bull in a china shop stuff?' queried Moss.

The big man shrugged. 'Maybe. But we haven't got time to waste.'

A description of Paxidena's car, a six-month-old Sapphire, was on the air with a "special search" priority request as the two detectives drove away from Millside. The broadcast gave the firm instruction: "Do not attempt to stop this car. Report position and follow at distance with extreme caution."

The Greek's home was in the West End, a flat in one of the large, now converted mansion houses that dominated most of the area. A Flying Squad car was already parked, lights out, down the road a little from the driveway entrance. Thane's Jaguar drew in behind it. The Millside chief knew its crew and wasted no time.

'We've recced the grounds and the lock-ups at the rear,' the squad sergeant told him quietly. 'No sign of Paxidena's car, sir.'

'Leave your driver here, put your other two men on the rear of the building, and come along with us,' instructed Thane.

They crunched up the gravel surface of the driveway, half-hidden in the tree-lined shadows, and stood for a moment before the dull oak-framed glass door. Gently, Thane tried the handle. It turned, and the sergeant and Phil Moss followed him in. A dim light burned in the entrance hall.

'First floor left,' said Thane.

They went up the wide, thick-carpeted stairway, and halted outside Paxidena's door. Thane knocked on the wood, waited, and knocked again. Faint noises came to their ears, and then, after a fumbling of locks, the door opened a few inches.

'What you want?' demanded the pretty olive-skinned girl who peeped round its edge. A security chain still held the door secure at its inches-wide position.

'Police,' said Moss. 'Giore Paxidena at home?'

'No.' A glint of fear in her eye, the girl started to shut the door again.

Moss's shoe toed into the gap, stopped it short.

'Better open the drawbridge,' he advised. 'We want to talk.'

She hesitated, then, biting her lip, released the chain with a chatter of links and stood back to let them enter.

Thane walked through the short hallway, and into a room where an expensive-looking Hi-Fi radio was moaning softly.

The girl—she looked even better in the brighter light, with her jet-black hair swept back and up in a top-knot style, decorated with a large silver clasp—moved gracefully across the carpet, neat in black velvet slacks and a plain white-wool sweater.

'Mrs Paxidena?' queried Thane.

She shook her head. 'Just a close friend. Why do you want to see Giore? Has there been trouble at the restaurant?' Confidence returning, she went on, 'He has gone out to visit friends. I do not know when he will be back. But I will give you the address of the restaurant manager. He can take care of the matter.'

'How long since he left?'

'An hour, maybe more. The manager's name—'

'We're not interested in the manager, I'm afraid,' said Thane bluntly. 'Is there anyone else in the flat?'

She took a step forward, took a cigarette from an open box on the sideboard, held it suggestively, then, flushing a little, lit it herself using a silver table-lighter. 'There's no one else. The housekeeper has gone away for a couple of days. Why are you asking me this?'

Thane nodded to Phil Moss.

The latter produced a large envelope from his inside pocket and told the girl, 'We have a warrant to search this flat for a man, Patrick Kilburn.' Then, offering the paper for the girl's inspection, 'Haven't seen him under one of the beds, have you?'

She was more frightened than angry as she snatched the paper. 'There's no one here—I told you. When Giore comes back, he will take care of this nonsense.'

'It can't wait till then,' Thane told her. 'What's your name, miss?'

'Does that matter?'

'We're not here to play games,' he snapped. 'Who are you, what are you doing here—and where's your boyfriend?'

'Maria Colante.' She rubbed her free hand nervously on one

hip. 'I... I am on a visit from London. I am a dancer in cabaret there.'

'Right, love—what's the name and address you give the Employment Exchange?' asked Moss, notebook out.

'That's my real name,' she protested, though the attractive accent had faded. 'I come from Stepney. Nothing wrong in that, is there? And Giore is out. I haven't a clue where he's got to.'

'Did he take the car?' asked Thane.

The girl nodded.

'Kilburn with him?'

She was really angry now. 'I don't know this man Kilburn,' she shouted, throwing the half-smoked cigarette at the fireplace. 'Go ahead and search the house if you want. Search all you can, copper. Force your way through. But this time, you'll make real trouble for yourself. Giore has friends—important friends. They will hear how you treated me.'

'Never mind the political speeches,' sighed Thane. 'Phil, get the driver in from the car to keep an eye on the lady. Better call up for a policewoman to be sent out too, in case Miss Colante thinks up a fairy story about sex-starved detectives. I'll start in here.'

Half an hour passed. While a neat-uniformed woman officer kept a quiet eye on the fuming dancer, the police team continued a minute search of the restaurant owner's seven-roomed flat.

'Irish, Italians, Greeks,' muttered Moss, ploughing his way through the dressing-table drawers in the absent owner's luxurious bedroom. 'It's time we turned this lot over to UNO, Colin.'

He pulled out another drawer, up-ended its contents on the floor, and began again. It left a nasty mess behind, this kind of search. But every cop knew it was the only way you could be sure nothing was missed. A nice polite, careful not to crumple examination was as unreliable as the average town hall clock.

'Nice taste, this fellow.' He held up a cream silk man-tailored shirt for inspection, then dropped it as his eye caught a small yellow folder lying next on the pile. He picked up the folder and pulled out a small bundle of photographs. 'Huh—holiday snaps. How do you like this one of the girlfriend?' He passed it over to Thane, who grinned at the bikini-clad form posing by a caravan door. Then the big man suddenly froze.

'Take another look,' he asked. 'Where would you say that was taken?'

Moss peered at the background of hills and water. 'Looks familiar. Couple of big ships lying off there, too. Warships, maybe.'

'The Gareloch?' suggested Thane quietly. 'There are one or two small caravan sites around there.'

Moss sucked a hiss of air through his teeth. 'And a nice quiet caravan in the middle of nowhere—'

'Would be a perfect place to keep someone like Kilburn snugly out of the road,' finished Thane. 'Especially late on in the season, when most holidaymakers have gone home. Let's ask the girl.'

Maria wouldn't talk. She didn't have to. The startled expression that flashed across her face the moment the picture was produced was enough on its own.

'If you won't tell me, I'll just have to go down and find out for myself,' Thane told her.

'I'll get my hat,' volunteered Moss.

'You'd better stay here, Phil, and keep the search going,' said his friend. 'There may be some very interesting stuff around, if we look long enough. And if this is a phoney lead, it'll be better for one of us to still be in the city. Better hold the girl for questioning till I get back. I'll take our car, leave the driver with you, and handle it myself. Will you get on the blower and ask for a couple of the local cops to meet me at Garelochhead?'

Reluctantly, Phil agreed.

CHAPTER NINETEEN

THE RUN from Glasgow out of the main Boulevard, running high above the straggling shipyards and lower docks of the Clyde, is a fast, smooth one late at night.

Thane slid the Jaguar quickly and quietly through Dunbarton and along the narrow coast road, enjoying the feel of driving. No matter how good the police crews were—and there were few better on the road—like every other man who holds a licence, Colin Thane always felt happier behind the wheel himself.

He kept the speedometer needle at a comfortable 55-60 on the narrower road beyond Helensburgh and felt almost disappointed as the lights of the mammoth ship-breaking yard at Faslane loomed ahead, marking the near-end of his journey. They were working nightshift in the breakers, oxy-acetylene burners busy disembowelling what looked like an old aircraft carrier.

The local car was waiting just a few yards before the village of Garelochhead. Two Dunbartonshire uniform men came over and saluted in the dim glow of sidelights as Thane crawled the Jaguar to a halt behind their Riley.

'Sergeant Mackeson and Constable Machrie, sir,' reported the older man. 'Your Inspector Moss has spoken to us, and the superintendent says just let him know if you need any other assistance.'

'We'll do for the moment,' Thane thanked them. 'You know about the photograph?'

'Aye. Could we see it, sir?'

The uniform men took the picture handed them and studied it at torch point. The sergeant grunted a reprimand as his companion gave a faint whistle.

'Never mind the wumman, man. Away and get the map.'

Thane joined them as they spread a large-scale map over the Jaguar's bonnet.

Under the torch-beam again, Sergeant Mackeson explained, 'There's a wheen of wee places about here where folk have a caravan or two lying parked. It's obviously no' one of the big, organised sites, eh, Machrie?'

'Wrong background,' agreed the constable. 'See here, sir,' he placed the photograph on the map. 'These two peaks you see on the left here, almost in line, are The Strone and Beinn Mhanaich—not what you'd call real mountains, but big enough. And the water here, with the ships, gives us a further line to come back along.' His finger traced over the map from the hills, across the Gareloch. 'It would be about here, I would reckon, Sergeant.'

'He's right for once, sir,' agreed the sergeant. 'Aye, I think I know the exact spot. Up off one of the side roads on the way to Clynder. Not more than twenty minutes away.'

'Lead on then, Sergeant,' nodded Thane. 'We'll stop a fair distance short and finish it on foot.'

He tailed the Dunbartonshire Riley through Garelochhead, followed it as it struck left at the road fork, and stayed a hundred yards or so behind as they swept down the main road. He slowed as the Riley's trafficator began winking, and then followed it as it swung off the road to the left, onto a bumpy, narrow route that was little more than a glorified track. Like the Riley's driver, he switched on to sidelights after a short distance, then braked thankfully to a standstill when the car ahead finally stopped, lights winking out.

The two uniform men waited for Thane to join them at the bonnet of their car.

'The road's too narrow for anyone to get past coming this way by car,' said the sergeant softly. 'But at this hour, there shouldn't be traffic up here—unless the men you're after try to make a run for it. The place we have in mind is about six hundred yards on, sir. I thought we'd better walk from here.'

He waited respectfully. Chief inspectors were occasionally an unknown quantity, and all he knew about the man from Glasgow was that he was reckoned to be a man sergeants didn't play around with.

Unhappily conscious of the fact that his heavy shoes had been put in for mending that day by his wife, and that the pair he had on had a distinct tendency to leak at the mere suggestion of water, Thane peered into long-grassed darkness around.

'Fair enough. But we'd better keep off the track,' he said. 'Do you know your way around?'

'Och, it's just a wee bit marshy here and there, sir,' consoled the sergeant. 'We're high here, but there are no holes to fall down. If we go up the hillside a little, then turn left again, we'll be just a stone's throw off the caravan site.'

They scrambled into the deeper darkness, stumbling on the rough ground. Young Machrie swore long and softly as he tripped, sprawling, over a gorse root, and lost his hat. He began fumbling for it in the darkness.

'Leave it be, man,' snarled his sergeant. 'We can't stand around here all night.'

For a brief moment the sallow half-moon peered through a break in the heavy cloud above and glinted on the metal cap badge. Thane scooped up the hat and handed it to the youngster. But the moonlight had done more.

'Just ahead, sir,' hissed the sergeant. 'There's a car lying on the grassland, a few yards off the track.'

'Any sign of life?' whispered Thane, while all three men stood motionless, ears straining for any sound other than the faint whistle of wind through the tangled gorseland.

'All clear,' replied the sergeant at last. 'We'll go softly now, I think. A few more yards, and we should be about on the vans.'

He moved on in a half-crouch, the others following up the slight slope and freezing again as he raised a hand in signal. Then, belly down, they inched forward to the top of the rise, and stared down the opposite slope.

There was only one caravan left on the level piece of ground, which was little more than the size of a tennis court. Light shone from its curtained windows, and an occasional spark coming from the small chimney stack at one side showed that the occupants lacked none of the comforts of home.

It was one of the biggest vans Thane had ever seen—getting it up to that lonely site must have been a man-sized job.

He turned and wriggled his bulk over the grass to the sergeant's side. The uniform man, breathing heavily after the exertion, gave him a faint, questioning lift of one eyebrow. Thane took another look at the heavy clouded sky, the moon once more completely hidden.

'I'm going down to have a look around,' he murmured. 'I want you two to stay here. I'll make it purely a recce trip—the slightest sign of trouble, and I'll be back up here like a rocket.'

'They're supposed to be dangerous, probably armed, aren't they, sir?'

Thane nodded. 'Don't worry. I'm no hero. But if I do land in trouble, one of you stay here and keep a long-distance eye on things, while the other gets back to that car radio as fast as his legs will carry him and gets a squad up here.'

The constable, too, had moved close by this time. Hoarsely, obviously excited, he blurted, 'Shouldn't we get them now, sir?'

The sergeant gave young Machrie a withering glare. How dare the youngster challenge a top brass decision? No discipline, none at all these days, that was the trouble.

Thane rolled over on his elbow, eyes fixed on the dull outline of the caravan. 'If we knew Patrick Kilburn was in the van, that would be the right thing to do. But until we're sure, we'll wait.

'Now this is what I'll do. I'll move along this ridge about twenty yards to the right, then slide down to the level. That way, I'll be facing the tail of the caravan. There's less chance of my being spotted from that end—the kitchen usually fills most of the end space in these big outfits.'

Two worried cops strained to follow him as he crawled away, cat-like despite his bulk. Then, making sure of each foothold before he moved, knowing the slightest slip on the mud and grass might send him thudding and rolling down the slope to the caravan's very door, he began the next stage. He gave a sigh of relief as he reached level ground again. Now, a dozen steps would take him to the caravan.

Thane blessed the damp-soft turf as he crossed the dividing distance and reached the tail of the van. He pressed low against the thin metal skin as the muffled sound of voices came from inside. Feet tramped, a bottle clinked, and then there was a roar of laughter.

Thane pursed his lips and moved round to the near-side. The caravan's curtained window was just head-high, he could look straight into the brightly lit interior.

Three bottle-gas lamps, delicately shaded, sent their glare directly down on the caravan's midsection. And, apparently staring straight at him, Patrick Kilburn and Giore Paxidena sat side by side on a gaily-patterned couch. To their left, a small coal stove burned warm, and each man held a half-filled glass, a bottle handy at their feet.

They spoke again. And this time their voices were distinct.

'That was a neat trick,' chuckled Kilburn. 'I've heard some of the stunts fellows like you pulled in Europe... but to sell a character a load of stolen cloth, then pinch the lot back again as soon as he had tailored it up into costumes, that's really something.'

Paxidena, fleshy, pallid-complexion, with plastered-down dark hair, smoothed a crease from his expensively cut suit and accepted the compliment.

'It saved us the trouble of paying someone to do the manufacturing, and of course it gave us an extra profit without risk. He couldn't very well tell the police, could he? It was a method we used on quite a few occasions—in widely different places, of course.'

Kilburn drained his glass and turned to the swarthy restaurateur. 'All right, so you're a pretty smart organiser. And you say you can get me out of the country. What's the pay-off?'

Paxidena shrugged. His voice became softer, and Thane had to strain to follow.

'As I said, we will help you, and in return you will act as our agent. Even before I came to Britain, I knew that the Kilburn network was still almost unknown to the police, and that it extends to many countries. The people you used are not the type likely to be questioned and have no link with any other smuggling rings. With you at their head, they could soon be operating again—for us.'

'You're on that "us" again,' complained Kilburn. 'Just what is your game?'

'I'm just a restaurant owner.' Paxidena smiled sleepily. 'Since the moment I landed in Britain, I've never allowed myself to be directly involved in any crime. But I have been responsible

—in a purely planning capacity, of course—for several incidents which have annoyed the police.

'I have most respectable friends, all very useful when I need information, though they would never dream that little Giore here could do anything wrong. When I am ready, I telephone people I know in London, sometimes other places—even abroad, occasionally—and they come over and do the rest.

'Normally, I take only commission for my trouble. But this time,' he emphasised, 'things must be different. This is the dream of a lifetime, my friend—a fortune begging to be taken. I lack only one thing, someone who will work for me and dispose of the goods abroad, in many different places. For this job will be so "hot" that not a fence in Britain would come near it.' His voice rose. 'A fortune, Patrick Kilburn, such as I had never thought possible.'

Kilburn rubbed his chin. 'That's okay for you—but I'm no charitable organisation. I stand a good chance of getting out on my own—so what's in it for me if I throw in with you? In cash—not promises. Money today's better than a big hooray tomorrow, according to my book.'

'Don't worry, you'll get the rate for the job,' sneered Paxidena. 'My offer is six thousand pounds for this, plus what you have to pay for expenses, and we'll fix a regular percentage for the future. Quite apart from any stuff that turns up here, or from my friends down south, I've still got connections in my old country who might need you.'

Kilburn whistled softly, then he warned, 'I can't move stuff around myself like I used to. I'm too hot now.'

'We would ask you to do that only occasionally, after this mission,' Paxidena reassured his companion, lighting a cigarette. 'But you have vital contacts. And remember, this is going to be one of the biggest jobs ever. We are not handling your little suitcases with watches. When this load is collected, every policeman in this country will be seeking us.'

Kilburn picked up the bottle from the caravan floor. Outside, Thane felt a cramp creeping up one leg, and eased it gently back and forward, waiting. Every second where he was made the chances of discovery more likely—for those other empty glasses on the caravan table meant that Paxidena either had come out with men or had met them here.

But the muffled, blurred conversation held him spellbound, and it went on, even as he took time off to look once more into the surrounding darkness, in which the ridge where the two uniform men were waiting was only a hinted outline.

It was Kilburn again, the whiskey in him obviously restoring his long-buried, swaggering confidence. 'So, you're big boys. That doesn't scare me. I'll take your money, Paxidena—and give you a sweet service. But what's your idea for getting me out of the country? A plane?'

Paxidena shook his head. 'You are a trifle rusty, my friend—but then, five years in prison would do that. It takes time, lots of time, to arrange a plane now, thanks to the way this country's radar system is always on duty, and the rules that have to be observed. There must be reasons, excuses—and our plan is that you start your journey tomorrow night. We just got to you in nice time.'

'That, I like,' grunted Kilburn.

'Good. And as you leave, you will be working for us—for this very important "package" must be taken out of England with you,' emphasised Paxidena.

Thane tensed, waiting for the next words from inside the caravan.

And at that same second, twin beams of light slammed out of the darkness, pinning his figure in their glare. From behind one of the lights a voice shouted hoarsely. A loud exclamation, a smash of glass came from within the caravan.

Even as a wave of heart-thumping dismay swept him, the

policeman hurled his burly form from the caravan's side, trying to get free of the twin beams. The result was immediate—the snapping crack of a gun mingled with the orange flare from its muzzle and a sudden, whirling kaleidoscope of pain as the bullet slammed into his shoulder, spinning him into a tripping sideways fall that set a second shockwave of pain through his body.

Even as he tried to rise, fighting against swooning agony, there was a pounding of feet, the sound of hard, angry voices—and he was pulled roughly upright and dragged forcibly towards the caravan.

Thane kicked out blindly, felt his shoe strike satisfyingly home. Paxidena's voice swore shrilly, and a pistol butt thudded against the side of his head.

The daze lasted until he was thrown roughly into a corner. He raised his head—to find a sneering Kilburn bending over him.

'Mr Clever Thane, in person,' said the Irishman with a leer. 'Couldn't stay away, could you?'

Paxidena pushed Kilburn aside. 'How many of you were there, policeman?' he demanded.

The answer came from one of the two newcomers. 'Just him, and two others wearing uniform,' said the tall thin man with the knife scar on one cheek and a tightly belted raincoat. 'Grigor took one, and I the other—we crept up behind them.'

'Where are they now, Johnny?' snapped Paxidena.

'Where we found them. We spotted them as we watched by the road, the way you ordered. The big man left, and they were so busy watching him we could move right up. A thump on the head each, and we shackled 'em with their own handcuffs.' Johnny smiled, showing a row of broken teeth. 'They are quite peaceful, eh, Grigor?'

The second man, smaller, with a toothbrush moustache and a dirtier version of his companion's raincoat, nodded.

'This is Thane, the cop who came out to prison to see me,' grunted Kilburn. 'There was another skinny guy with him then.'

Paxidena shot a questioning glance at his aides. Grigor shook his head and said thickly, 'No more—only two cars, three men.'

'So...' he turned to Thane again, taking in the big man's wounded shoulder, the coat torn in the brief struggle outside. 'Let us see how you found us here—and remember, our guns go off.'

He thrust his hand inside the torn coat, and fished out the policeman's wallet. A flip through, and it was tossed to the floor. Paxidena tried again, and this time brought out Thane's black-covered police notebook. He removed the elastic—and as the book loosened, a flutter of paper caught his eye. He snatched it from the floor, and for a moment his face paled.

'The holiday pictures with Maria,' he muttered. 'You have been to my home, policeman. I am not often careless. But you were clever.'

Thane gave a mock bow, and grunted with pain at the effort. 'Your girlfriend's holding hands with a policewoman,' he retorted.

'Then we'll need to blow, fast.' Kilburn lit a cigarette nervously. 'If this fellow was listening outside for long—'

'Four, maybe five minutes,' Grigor told them. 'We had to move softly. We could not rush the job.'

'And that means you are a very large embarrassment, I am afraid, Mr Thane,' said Paxidena. 'Obviously, I cannot return home without finding others of your kind waiting. But also obviously, I cannot leave you here. Give me your gun, Grigor...' The smaller man obeyed. 'Now, you three, go and bring me the other two men. Do not trouble to be gentle.'

'What's the setup?' queried Kilburn.

'A simple one. The caravan rests level here. But push it a few yards, and there is another little slope down. At the foot of that slope, there is a cliff, and below the cliff, the sea. Be quick now, please—I do not want to waste time, in case Mr Thane's many friends grow anxious.'

With a mouth-puckering grin, Grigor turned and eased the door handle open. Then his mouth dropped, a cigarette falling heedlessly from one corner—and he backed from the half-open door, which swung wider. The bottle-gas light glinted harshly on the oiled blue metal of Liam Kilburn's sawn-off shotgun, held stomach-high and swinging in a tight, menacing arc.

Johnny recovered first. His hand dived to a shoulder holster.

With a look akin to pity in his eyes, Liam Kilburn fired.

The *blaam* of the shotgun reverberated in the caravan shell, a sting of cordite flushed the air—and, with a scream half-strangled, Johnny went down like a broken doll.

Grigor moaned, and turned his head. A twenty-bore duck cartridge at five feet range, fanning from the stubby muzzle, had cut Johnny almost in half with flesh-tearing obscenity. The shotgun swung in a shorter arc, and Liam Kilburn stepped over the threshold, carefully avoiding the limp body.

'There's still the other barrel,' he warned in his blunt Irish voice.

Tenderly, Thane eased himself into a sitting position, hearing Liam go on.

'I've no particular quarrel with you fellows. But my brother here, now—Margot and I have been looking all over for you, boy.' He took another step forward, a quiver of tension rippling through his body, tightening knuckle-white the big hands that seemed to almost enfold the cut-down shotgun.

Grigor shrank further back, until his small body was pressing tight against the caravan wall. In the corner with Thane, Patrick Kilburn breathed harshly, nervously. Only Paxidena, the gun he had borrowed from Grigor still in his hand, could take his gaze off the still-smoking shotgun and find voice to answer.

'You are his brother? Then why this? We mean him no harm.' He held the gun openly, pointed casually in Thane's direction.

Liam made a noise which might have passed for a chuckle normally. 'So we gathered from the way you left these two policemen up on the ridge. They're all right, by the way—Margot is with them, but we can't do a thing till we get a key to their handcuffs. And both of them are still out to the wide. But, mister, there's one thing you don't know. I need Patrick. To even the account for our father, so to speak.' He shuffled another step forward, and as he did, Patrick moved a fraction closer to the wounded Thane.

'Stay where you are a minute,' advised Paxidena sharply. 'Don't be too hasty. You said yourself there is only one shot left in that gun of yours.'

Liam's eyes narrowed. 'Say what you want, but quickly,' he ordered.

Paxidena nodded. 'It is simple. Unfortunately, we cannot allow Patrick to be killed, though'—he gave a faint grimace of disgust—'I feel for you in my heart if I grasp this thing correctly.

'There are three of us. I have a gun. So has Patrick, even though he is shy to show it. And you have one shot left. If you shoot Patrick, I shoot you, then this policeman—or maybe the other way round, it doesn't matter. If you shoot me, then Patrick still has his gun, and will no doubt do the same. Even Grigor, the frightened one, has a little knife.' He paused, and gave a quiet little smile. 'So—it is difficult. None of us want to die, especially Mr Thane here. What are we going to do now?'

Liam Kilburn, whatever other attributes he possessed, was no great thinker. But, as slow seconds passed, bewilderment, anger, then something akin to disappointment appeared on his tanned face. But his hold on the gun remained tight as, obviously puzzled, he queried, 'Thane—what do I do?'

'You could shoot the ruddy lot as far as I'm concerned,

Liam,' groaned the policeman, one hand cautiously exploring his bleeding shoulder. 'The trouble is, I'd have to hang you afterwards. As it is, the fellow on the floor's going to take some explaining away. Ask Paxidena.'

'Speak up then, mister,' ordered Liam, jerking the shotgun a fraction higher and making Grigor's eyes show even more white.

Paxidena, careful not to point his automatic anywhere near the big Irishman, was ready with an answer. 'Simple. You will have to ignore this golden opportunity to blow a hole in Patrick. But you will have the satisfaction of saving both your own and this policeman's life. You have to let us go.'

'Wait.' Patrick Kilburn clutched the Greek's arm. 'What about my sister? If she's standing outside with another gun, she could blast the three of us down the moment we leave.'

'Nail you, anyway, you black-hearted carrion,' burst out his brother. 'Would to God I had killed you years ago, when we were still boys together. Yet I have to call you kin.' He began to tense again, knuckle whitening on the shotgun trigger.

'Mr Thane will be our safe-conduct,' shrugged Paxidena. 'It is simple. I will stay here with you, the policeman will go with Grigor and your brother. You will shout out the door to your sister not to fire, or the policeman dies. They will go down the road a little to the car, bring it up near the caravan. Then you get Mr Thane, and I leave here.'

The big Irishman looked questioningly at Colin Thane.

Thane sighed, and began to rise slowly. 'Best we can do,' he nodded.

Like a dog robbed of a juicy bone, Liam Kilburn gave a despondent growl. Then, never relaxing his watch, he backed to the still open door and shouted to his sister.

CHAPTER TWENTY

THE BARGAIN WAS KEPT—AS it had to be. Grigor at the wheel, Paxidena's big Sapphire backed noisily through the darkness to within a dozen yards of the caravan. The back door opened, and as Paxidena stepped down from the van, Thane was pushed out of the car.

The Greek murmured a polite 'good night' as he passed the CID man—then jumped lithely into the already moving car. Headlights blazing, it bucked and bounced across the rough surface towards the nearby track, then quickly increased speed.

As its taillights disappeared, Liam Kilburn walked slowly over from the caravan, methodically reloading his shotgun. For a moment he paused, closed the weapon's breech, then said, 'Let's get you back into the caravan, mister.'

Thane was honestly glad of the massive arm that the Irishman put round his waist to help him over the brief journey. The pain from his wound was getting worse.

They reached the door just as Margot Kilburn appeared, her smart leather boots caked with yellow mud, her face white and angry.

'I couldn't help it—' began her brother, almost apologetically.

She cut him short. 'You did the right thing. How were we to know we'd have to play nurses to the police?' Then, for the first time, she saw the wide-spreading stain on the shoulder of Thane's coat. Her voice changed abruptly. 'Was it Patrick?'

Thane clutched the caravan doorway for support, and shook his head. 'The one on the floor, I think,' he muttered.

The girl looked beyond him at the huddled, torn body of Paxidena's lieutenant, lying where it had fallen, shuddered, and closed her eyes for a moment. She went into the van, pulled a folded blanket from a shelf, and draped it over the limp figure.

'Bring him in, Liam,' she ordered. 'You'd better sit down for a spell, Inspector.'

As Thane sank down thankfully on the long couch, she asked him, 'Do you have a key that will fit the handcuffs on your two men? They're beginning to come round.'

He started to reach for his left-hand pocket, but the pain from his shoulder made him wince.

'I'll get it,' said the girl. She pulled out the key and handed it to her brother, standing patiently at her side. 'Bring them down here, Liam. One of them should be able to walk by himself, but the younger one may need some help.' Liam propped his gun against the caravan door, and disappeared out into the night.

Thane managed a smile. 'I feel happier now he's put that gun down,' he told the girl.

She tossed her dark hair. 'Liam? He wouldn't hurt a fly.' Then, realising the incongruity of what she had said, she flushed. 'I'll put a kettle on for some tea—then have a look at that shoulder of yours.'

'Wait...' Thane stopped her. 'I want to tell you something first. Right now, in theory, I should try to take you both into custody. But instead, I want you to promise something. And remember the man under that blanket before you answer. Give me a chance to talk to you both. Once we get this mess sorted out, there's a few things you must know. After that—' he paused, gnawing his lower lip. 'After that, I give my word that whatever you decide, I personally will do anything I can within the law to help put the record straight. Because now, whatever happens, the law itself can settle whatever account you have with Patrick.'

At first he thought she wasn't going to answer.

Then, unbuckling her raincoat, she agreed. 'We'll wait—and listen. I want to trust you. Believe me, I do, more than anything else. I only hope we can.'

CHAPTER TWENTY-ONE

THE NEXT HOUR was a daze of action from which Thane was mostly divorced.

The two freed uniform men, Constable Machrie, groggy but otherwise suffering only from an aching head, his sergeant apologetically furious at the way they had been overpowered, got busy on the radio. Their message had immediate results—roadblocks were set up over a wide radius, a fresh, top-priority warning was flashed to every police division within a hundred miles.

A naval doctor came up from the submarine depot not far along the road at Garelochhead. He unloaded his kit from the jeep which had brought him, then, while the seaman driver and the uniform sergeant took the dead man from the caravan, he got down to the job of patching up Thane's wound.

'First gunshot wound I've handled since Korea,' he confided. 'Makes a nice change.'

Gently, he removed the rough dressing Margot had placed to stop the bleeding, nodded approvingly, and, whistling a tune, opened his bag. 'Nothing much to it,' he remarked. 'I'll give you a "local" jag, and get the thing out.'

Within minutes, he grinned triumphantly, and held up the small, red-stained bullet between his forceps. 'That's the little fellow. You're a lucky man. Now, if we just strap you up a bit, that's the job done. No bones broken, arteries cut, or what have you,' he added almost regretfully.

He had helped Thane back into his clothes, left arm in a bandage sling, jacket sleeve flapping, when the sound of car engines and the glare of headlights heralded fresh arrivals.

Phil Moss, face strained with concern, bounded into the caravan.

He gave a sigh of relief as his friend rose to meet him. 'I told you I couldn't trust you on your own,' he complained in mock anger. 'See what happens... a couple of hours on the loose, and you let any Tom, Dick, or Harry use you as target practice.' Then, more seriously, 'How is he, Doc?'

'Fine,' replied the Navy man, closing up his bag with a snap. 'Dare I suggest that the proper procedure now is to get him into bed for a few days?'

He looked at Thane.

'I thought not. Ah, well, take it easy for a bit, anyway. You've lost quite a little bit of blood. I'll need to get back to work. There's a leading hand down in sick bay who's either got a gastric ulcer or is going to have a baby. From the fuss he's making, it could be either.'

Moss pursed his lips suddenly. 'I'm feeling a bit of pain myself, Doc. Wondering what shape Colin would be in has set my own duodenal throbbing. What's your advice?'

'Simple. Get it chopped out,' replied the medico. And departed still whistling.

Phil Moss gazed wrathfully after him. 'They're all the same. It's this National Health. We're just a lot of ruddy numbers.' He fumbled for his pill box. 'Think I'm going to let them poke around inside me?' He rolled two chalk extract tablets onto his palm, and swallowed them with a grimace. 'You have a lot to answer for, Colin, when my health finally breaks down.

'Now, what's been going on? We've got a general "special search" message about for Paxidena and company plus the fact they're armed and dangerous. And I see the Kilburns hanging around outside. Do we run them in?'

Thane shook his head. 'They're coming back with us, but peacefully,' he said. 'I probably owe my life to that big fellow and his shotgun, and so do the other two cops who were with me.'

They left the caravan. Outside, the scene was now bathed in the fight of car headlights. At the rear of the caravan, a plain-clothesman was carrying out the unpleasant task of going through the dead man's pockets, and already had a small, neat bundle gathered in a spread-out handkerchief.

'Scientific boys here yet?' asked Thane.

'They're on their way, Colin,' replied Phil Moss. 'I take it we leave searching the van until they've gone?'

Thane nodded. 'Better get a set of prints from that body, and run them through Records. Any identification on him?' he asked the kneeling policeman.

'Wallet here, and a letter addressed to John Quiller care of some London hotel,' said the officer. 'Haven't really gone through the stuff yet, sir.'

'Paxidena called him "Johnny,"' said Thane. 'Better send full details on all the prints and descriptions to Scotland Yard. They may have a line on them there. Who's out with you, Phil?'

'Well, there's some of the county men—and Superintendent Laurence is coming out from Glasgow with the laboratory stuff.'

Thane relaxed. Dan Laurence, head of the Scientific Bureau, knew more about mopping-up operations of this type than any other cop he knew.

'We'll take that bundle with us,' he said. 'And leave a message for Dan to take the caravan apart if need be.'

He eased his arm in the sling, and asked, 'Does my wife know about this yet?'

'Mary?' Phil shook his head. 'It's three in the morning, Colin. And when we left Millside I wasn't sure whether you'd be in a hospital bed or not. So— Well, maybe I was wrong, or just a plain coward, but I didn't phone her.' He glanced anxiously at his friend.

Thane was relieved. 'That's what I hoped. She'd be climbing the walls. But let's go—we'll take the Kilburns along. I'll phone home on the way, and tell her to put the kettle on.'

'You taking them to the house?' Moss was obviously surprised.

'Can you think of a better idea?' asked Thane. 'I've got to try and talk some sense into these two, and there's just a chance after this that we can manage it. By rights, we should shove them in a cell—but if we take them out to the house, well, it may make for a friendlier atmosphere. Mary won't mind, as long as we don't wake the kids, and you don't demand some exotic diet to keep that belly of yours quiet. How is it now, anyway?'

'Settling down to a quiet grumble,' was Moss's plaintive reply. 'Look, there's one thing I would like to know. Just how did the Kilburns know to come out here?'

His reply came from an unexpected quarter.

'I'll tell you,' volunteered Margot Kilburn, who had approached them silently from the rear. 'It's simple. We took a leaf from the police book, and followed you for a change.

'We had lost all track of Patrick. So, after we had dodged the men who were shadowing us, we doubled back, and began following you about. It was about the safest thing we could do.'

She smiled, an attractive, friendly smile that showed her fine, even teeth. 'Then, when Mr Thane left the house where that man Paxidena had been living, we knew we were on the right track.

'You probably never saw the little Ford driving behind you

on the road from the city—though, I'll admit, it took us all our time to keep up with you. It's only a rented car, and it has seen plenty of better days.

'We lost you when you took that side road up to here, and had to turn back again—otherwise we might have been close enough to warn your men when they were attacked. As it was, we almost tripped head-on over them!'

CHAPTER TWENTY-TWO

THEY TOOK the roomy police Humber in which Phil Moss had come out. Thane spread out on the front seat, beside the CID driver, and let himself doze off to sleep. Phil sat a trifle uncomfortably in the back, between Liam and Margot. Liam had somewhat unwillingly handed over his shotgun, and, unloaded, it lay on the window ledge behind them.

On the way down the road they met the Scientific Bureau's mobile lab—a high-sided van, packed with equipment. Dan Laurence was aboard. Careful not to waken Thane, Phil had the Humber stop alongside and quietly briefed the Bureau chief.

Back in the Humber again, Phil switched the two-way radio over to "headphone," cutting out the loudspeaker's persistent crackle of interference, and, after calling in control and telling headquarters they were returning, settled down again, the phone earpiece resting on his shoulder.

Margot Kilburn glanced at the still sleeping Thane, and, as the car drew quietly away again, murmured, 'You must think quite a lot of him.'

Phil Moss returned her gaze steadily. 'Colin Thane's as fine as they come,' he told her. 'And his word is his bond. There aren't many things I wouldn't do for him—though that's the last thing I want him to find out. Now supposing we all get in some rest. It's been quite a night.'

Thane was still out to the wide when the car began to purr through the first brightly lit suburbs of Glasgow an hour later. Phil let him sleep on, stopped the car by a phone kiosk, and, after a search through his pockets for pennies, dialled the chief inspector's home at Southwood. Mary Thane didn't take long to answer. Like most policemen's wives, she never really slept sound when her man was out on a job.

'He's all right, Mary,' reassured Phil, after briefly sketching what had happened. 'I just didn't want to wake him. But he wants to bring these two out to the house. Is it okay by you?'

'As long as Colin's more or less in one piece, you can bring the entire force out,' she told him, relief strong in her voice. 'Bacon and eggs suit, Phil?'

'Colin could probably use something like that,' he admitted wistfully.

'Don't worry, Phil,' said Mary. 'I haven't forgotten. Two eggs, nicely scrambled, for you?'

'I feel better already,' agreed Phil, and replaced the receiver.

CHAPTER TWENTY-THREE

THEY LET Thane sleep right up till the moment the Humber stopped outside his bungalow home, with its tiny garden and green-painted wooden gate.

He yawned, stretched, gave an "ouch" of recollection as a stab of pain reminded him sharply of his shoulder, blinked wider awake, then, dismissing the car, led the others up to the front door. Mary had it open before he could press the bell.

'Hey, gently, lass, gently,' he murmured as she held him close. 'I'm only slightly bent.' He kissed her, ruffled her hair with his free hand, then, eyes showing just a suspicion of moistness, said, 'There's some people I want you to meet.'

Neat in a dark-blue quilted housecoat, Mary Thane led them into the house, cautioning them against wakening the two young sleepers in the small back bedrooms, and showed them into the living-room.

Somehow, in the mere thirty minutes that had elapsed since she was phoned, she had caught the dying coal fire, now blazing brightly, had set the table for four, and had the coffee percolator burbling by the hearth.

The appetising smell of cooking came faintly from the kitchen.

I'm glad she isn't the fussing kind, thought Thane gratefully, as Mary gently but firmly stripped off his coat, inspected the bandage sling, then ordered him, 'Sit down by the fire for a moment. Phil, you know where we keep that whiskey bottle. I think a little drink wouldn't do any of you any harm—even you, for once.'

Then she turned to the girl, who was standing awkwardly, her boots still mud-caked, a large streak of dirt down one side of her face. 'Come with me, Margot,' she said firmly. 'You'll feel better after a wash and a tidy up. I'll get a pair of slippers—though,' she laughed, 'that's about all of my stuff that will fit you. I've put on a bit of weight these last few years.'

Liam Kilburn sat awkwardly, silently, on the edge of a chair sipping his whiskey until Margot returned. The wash, and some powder and lipstick, certainly had worked a transformation. And, despite Mary's rueful comment, she had managed to find the girl a soft pink wool sweater and dark skirt that completed the picture.

'Eat first,' said Mary Thane, appearing with a laden tray. 'Then Phil will help me with the dishes, and you can have a chance to talk.'

They were hungry, all right, even Thane, cursing at the unaccustomed handicap of eating one-handed.

He glanced up in surprise as Liam Kilburn suddenly grunted, 'Here...' and quickly sawed up the bacon strips on his plate into manageable portions.

The Irishman gave a shy grin, and Thane suddenly began to feel a little more sure of his chances of talking sense into the two Kilburns. But he waited, finished off the last piece of toast, took one of the cigarettes Margot produced from her handbag, split the last of the coffee in the percolator with Liam, and smoked quietly till Phil and Mary had disappeared with the dishes.

He took a last drag at the cigarette, stubbed it out in the ashtray at his elbow, and looked round.

'Now?' asked Margot.

'Now,' he agreed. 'Let's get one thing straight first. Whatever you say in here goes no further.'

He got up, and stood with his back to the fireplace, facing them both. 'Some things we know, some we can guess. You found out that your father confessed to murder he didn't commit in order to save your brother from the death sentence. Then, with your mother gone out of her mind over the whole business, things became pretty grim. And you decided there was only one way to avenge your father's death and your mother's condition—that was to kill Patrick.'

He stopped, fit a fresh cigarette, and went on. 'Now, I'll admit we can't prove it. But we know you made these attempts on his life at the open prison—when you heard he had been moved there, it must have seemed a golden opportunity. And we know that you persuaded another prisoner to smuggle in a note to him—though again, I'll admit he couldn't, or wouldn't, identify you. Patrick became so scared at the situation that he broke out.'

As he paused again, Liam Kilburn muttered quickly to his sister.

The girl shook her head. 'We said we would listen,' she told him. 'Go on, Mr Thane... the only comment I want to make, though I'm admitting nothing of what you say about the prison, is that Mother never knew why my father really died. She lost her reason within days of him dying.' Elbows on the table, she cupped her dark head in her hands, watching him steadily.

'Patrick breaks out,' Thane continued. 'He gets to Glasgow, and decides to go to a man whom he had had to trust, a man with whom, I believe, he had left certain papers and money. That was Jon Barlby. But for some reason they quarrelled, and Patrick killed him, then robbed him. It was a hanging job, and we can prove it now. The last thread we needed came tonight, in the caravan—when your brother, thinking I was just about to get my lot, said it would be easier than the way he snuffed out Barlby. When we catch him—and we will, sooner or later—he'll hang for that.'

Slowly, emphasising every word in his quiet, final sentence, he added, 'Why not let the law administer justice for you?'

Liam sat silent, eyes fixed on the wallpaper somewhere above Thane's head. It was Margot who answered him, fingers of one hand drumming nervously on the table.

'You make it sound simple, Mr Thane. But it isn't simple—not when you've gone through the kind of personal hell this family has experienced.'

'Tell me about it, if it makes it easier,' invited Thane, feeling a strong wave of sympathy for the girl despite his awareness of the willing eagerness with which, only hours before, she had been ready to see her brother shot down.

'We're here because of one thing only,' she said. 'That man Liam shot in the caravan. Oh, I know he had to do it, and probably saved your life too at the same time. But—' she frowned, struggling for words, 'but somehow it seems different now. Too many people are getting hurt. Maybe we're wrong—I don't know. But do you know what it is like to know your father is being tried for murder—and then to know he is going to hang?'

She was far away now, exploring dark, overpowering memories. 'It was five years ago, but I haven't forgotten a second of it. Maybe I never will.

'Once a week, every week before the trial, and while it was on, I went with my mother to visit the prison. We walked up that long tiring hill—then the formalities were always the same. I rang the little bell at one side of the big wooden gates, and a warder opened a small door set in the wall. Mum and I would step through, and hand him the "visit card," which Father had posted out to us.

'Then the warder would lead us farther into the prison, down a corridor and into a small room—not the normal visitors' room—maybe they don't like murderers or their families mixing with the rest. I remember there wasn't much furniture. Only a big table like a bank counter, with a peak in the middle. We sat at the chairs on one side, and waited. Then another warder would open the glass door at the other side of the room, and they would bring in my father.'

She sat silent for a moment, remembering the way her mother had always stiffened by her side at that moment, the strained smile with which her father always greeted them.

'Dad sat in another chair, on the other side of the table—at least five feet away. He was as near as that, yet we couldn't touch him, even hold his hand. The warders were always there, watching, listening. Oh, we could talk all right.'

A picture of her father, in his dark brown prison battledress and blue-striped prison shirt, without collar or tie, crossed her mind. Her voice was near to breaking as she went on.

'They gave us twenty minutes. And do you know something, Mr Thane? We didn't know what to talk about half the time. We'd stop short, and just sit looking at each other. How could my mother tell him the things in her heart, comfort him, how could he speak freely to us, with those two warders present?

'Even then, you know, he never mentioned Patrick. We thought he just didn't want to say anything about him, in case the warders reported it. And,' she smiled bitterly at the recollection, 'we thought then that the reason Patrick suddenly didn't want to see us anymore was because he was afraid Mother would be even more upset.'

Margot stopped again. Liam placed one giant hand over hers, in a comforting gesture, and, moistening her lips, she went on.

'We had twenty minutes, Mr Thane. Sometimes it passed

like a flash, sometimes, for no reason, it lasted like hours. Oh, Dad always tried to seem cheerful. But I knew that deep in his eyes there was a look that showed all the worry and tension he was going through.'

Then the prison officers would say, 'Time's up,' and the two women would leave, back down the hill again, walking automatically, only really becoming conscious of their surroundings again when they were back in the privacy of the hotel room they had taken in the city for the duration of the trial.

'Mum would break down afterwards,' said Margot. 'Just sit quietly crying for hours on end. She stopped the day they hanged my father. And then...' She shrugged. 'Somehow, it's the little things, too, you remember, Mr Thane. Like the way the prison rules said we couldn't take in sweets or cakes to Dad; the way the newspapers kept hounding us for pictures. The little smile Dad always gave to Mum, even that last time, just the day before he died.

'My father wasn't an angel, Mr Thane. Liam and I both know that. He had been in prison before; he had done things that were bad, some of them rotten. We found most of that out later—though we always knew he was a smuggler.

'Mum didn't like the idea but, well, you can get used to it. Patrick took to it like a duck to water—he used to boast he knew more about smuggling than Father ever would. But Liam had the farm, and my sister and I were never short of money for a new dress. Smuggling didn't seem so bad, when, as far as we were concerned, it just meant staying at home and hearing stories about how they fooled the English over some watches or cigarette lighters.'

'There was a lot more to it than that,' Thane reminded her quietly. 'Guns, explosives, helping criminals to escape—even some suspicion of drug trafficking.'

'Patrick began the drugs business,' protested Margot. 'We found that out from my father's papers afterwards. Father didn't know a thing about the first two loads they carried. I know my father was a crook, Mr Thane—but he wasn't a murderer. He had never carried a gun in his life. And yet Patrick let him hang. Can't you see, it's not so much our father we wanted to avenge, as our mother?'

Thane seized on her words. 'You said "wanted"—does that mean you've changed your mind?'

She shook her head helplessly, and glanced at Liam.

'Whatever you say, sis,' he told her. 'Right or wrong, we'll do what you say. I'm no thinker, you know that. I'm getting worried about a few things—it's getting complicated altogether. Not the way it seemed back home, when we just had to come and do the job, and to hell with the consequences, us with nothing to lose.'

She turned towards Thane again, still battling with herself. 'What happens to Liam—about shooting that man at the caravan, I mean—if we give up?'

Thane pulled his lower lip between finger and thumb. 'I'd call it self-defence. I think the Crown authorities would take the same view. That holds good whatever way you decide.'

The girl pressed again, 'If we refuse to stop, can we walk out of here? Or will we be under arrest?'

Thane had known the question would come sooner or later. 'I've been given the go-ahead to take you in,' he told her. 'But you came here of your own free will. I'll give you a fifteen-minute start—and then we'll come after you.'

Liam Kilburn half-rose from his chair. But his sister made him sit down again.

'If the law can really take care of Patrick, we'll stop,' she said. 'On one condition—that you accept our help. We know the Kilburn network.' She laughed bitterly. 'None better.'

He gave her a long, slow look. 'Officially, I must say no. But any policeman has to seek help now and again, and sometimes he needs quite a lot of help.

'I'd better warn you. Patrick isn't on his own now. He's with as vicious a group of men as I've ever come across. They would stop at nothing. And they're just as keen to hang on to him, and use the Kilburn network, as we are to find him.

'And another thing. Liam can't carry that shotgun of his around—not to mention a certain .300 rifle.'

'What about me?' smiled the girl. 'What if I have a gun in my handbag?'

Thane's eyes twinkled. 'You haven't. Mary took a quick peep while you were freshening up. Is it a deal?'

It was. Both Liam and Margot were emphatic.

'Phil,' called Thane. 'You can stop worrying over those dishes. They've seen sense, believe it or not.'

His thin figure covered in a large floral apron, Phil Moss came through to the room.

'Not before time,' he commented lugubriously. 'I've already dried the darned things twice over. Now, what are we going to do with them for the rest of the night, Colin?'

'We've got rooms in town,' frowned Margot. 'But the landlady would probably have a fit at this hour.'

'Supposing we fix you up at the same hotel as your dentist friend, Peter Angello?' suggested Thane. 'The night porter on duty can take care of it. And, unless we have a real break, you can have a few hours' sleep anyway.'

'You'll call us if anything happens?' asked Liam Kilburn.

Thane promised.

CHAPTER TWENTY-FOUR

FIRST ONE GIGGLE. Then another. Silence, a quick whisper, and more giggles. Phil Moss forced open one sleep-jammed eye, tried hard to engage his brain in at least bottom gear, and thought there was something wrong with the wallpaper. Then another spasm of giggles, and the feel of an unfamiliar quilt under his chin, reminded him where he was—on a made-up bed on Colin Thane's sofa. He carefully raised his head a couple of inches, to discover two grinning little faces staring at him.

'Hullo, Uncle Phil,' giggled Thane's small daughter Kate. 'It's time to get up.'

'Ugghr... hullo, youngsters. What's... aww... what's the joke?'

Young Tom, dressed for school, answered. 'You look awful funny when you're asleep. You've got a big bald patch and you make a funny noise breathing.'

With screams of laughter, they fled from the implied threat of the pillow Phil yanked from the bed. Yawning, he staggered over to the chair where his clothes were piled, and began to dress.

The 8 a.m. BBC news was just beginning as, shaved and now wide awake, he came into the kitchen to join the Thane family. The loch-side shooting merited a brief mention halfway through the bulletin, and there was also a fifteen-second piece about the continued search for Patrick Kilburn.

The newspapers were, however, neither so diplomatic nor so kind.

'This'll put you off your cornflakes,' said Colin Thane, tossing over the tabloid, Daily Disc.

The Disc crime squad—a bunch of young men with padded shoulders, American haircuts, and a woeful lack of shorthand—had excelled themselves. A full-scale battle, it appeared, had raged on the loch shore. Deprived of their favourite trio of heroes, 'young mum,' 'game grandad,' and 'pet pup,' they had still managed to play up the 'mystery beauty' who had, according to the Disc, braved the bullets to tend the wounded.

Like most of the other dailies, however, they had seized on the fact that Thane had been involved and that he was handling the Kilburn case. Theories ranged from the Disc's 'gang of Irish raiders' to the more sober 'alleged accomplices, possibly armed' put forward by the Glasgow Messenger, which seemed just a trifle embarrassed about having to feature a crime story on its front page.

'Can I tell the boys at school you've been shot, Daddy?' begged Tom. Ignoring his mother's warning glare, he persisted, 'Have you got the bullet, Daddy? They won't believe me unless I show them the bullet?'

'Bring them over here and I'll bleed for them,' growled Thane, glaring at one newspaper's editorial, yowling for immediate action.

'Time for school, children,' said his wife.

'But it's too early, Mum,' protested Kate. Then, as her mother repeated the instruction, she rose reluctantly, followed by her brother. They disappeared into the hall, still saying it wasn't time, and demanding what they were supposed to do, setting off before even the teachers arrived.

'Hard luck on the kids,' chuckled Phil. 'Still, I can appreciate Mary's point of

view. Well, we're getting our quota of headlines.'

'Can't do any harm now, except make the chief constable feel unhappy,' said Thane, pulling out his cigarettes. 'The car's coming for us in about ten minutes.'

'You going on duty like that?' asked Moss, nodding towards his companion's bandaged shoulder, now decently hidden under a clean shirt.

'I'll get by,' Thane told him. 'Doc Williams will be at the station when we get there. It'll make a nice change for him, too. The Navy bloke last night complained he didn't get enough gunshot wounds. Doc usually complains he never sees any live cases. Besides, I'm not feeling too bad, and I don't want to stiffen myself up just lying about.

'There's something big brewing, Phil. I gathered that much last night. If we find Paddy Kilburn, we find whatever Paxidena and his bunch are up to at the same time.'

'At least we've got the problem of the rest with the Kilburn family more or less sorted out,' mused Phil. 'Did you mean what you said about taking them along if anything happened?'

Thane struggled into his jacket before replying. 'Let's say we won't ignore them,' he compromised. 'I'm going to have a tough time justifying my actions to Headquarters as it is. General feeling there is that they should be chained hand and foot. I don't mind admitting I felt inclined that way myself, but last night seemed the only way I could stop both of them from ending up on a murder charge. And basically—'

'Basically, they're a pair of decent youngsters who just got caught up in circumstances, I know,' completed Phil. 'One of these days you're going to play one hunch too many, Colin, and land in a real jam. But this time, well,' he winked, 'well, I can't say I blame you.'

CHAPTER TWENTY-FIVE

DOC WILLIAMS WAS WAITING at Millside when they arrived. So were two others.

The big broad form of Chief Superintendent "Buddha" Ilford was settled firmly in one chair, his pipe billowing tobacco smoke.

Sitting beside him, a trifle self-conscious, brief case balanced neatly across his knees, was a stranger whose white stiff collar, striped trousers and grey spats rang a bell with Colin Thane immediately—Crown Office, Edinburgh.

Things must have been really happening to drag one of these characters out of bed in time to get through to the city at this hour of the morning.

'Morning, Colin,' grunted Ilford. 'Sit down, man. I'm not here to read the riot act—yet. Just came along to find out what the hell's happening now and to pass on a little information. I've read the rough report you phoned in early this morning, and I've been having a heart-to-heart telephone talk with Scotland Yard about Paxidena.'

Thane went round to his desk, eased back in his chair, and, just in time, remembered not to put his foot up on the desk edge.

'No trace of him at all, sir? I haven't had a chance to see through the reports.'

Ilford wrinkled a massive jowl. 'None.' He sucked the pipe again, then went on. 'He and your friend Kilburn can't be found. They abandoned Paxidena's car on the outskirts of the city—you'll see it in the reports. How's the shoulder?'

'Stiff, mainly,' replied Thane. 'Oh... Doc Williams is outside, waiting to have a look at it. Mind if he comes in, sir?'

As "Buddha" nodded consent, Phil Moss put his head outside the office door and said, 'Right, Doc... he's all yours.' Then, in an afterthought, he turned to the three men and asked, 'Like some tea? The brew here's foul, but warm.'

'Thanks,' Ilford beamed. He'd had to leave Headquarters before the kettle reached the boil, a bad start to any day. 'How about you, Mr Brixen?' he asked the man beside him. Then, as Doc Williams came in, growling a general welcome, "Buddha" apologised, 'Sorry... forgot to make the introductions. This is Mr Austin Brixen, from the Crown Office. He's going to be quite a help in this, Colin.'

They shook hands, then Phil Moss put his head outside the door again and bellowed for an orderly. 'Tea coming up,' he reported, and turned to Doc Williams, who was already unfastening his medical bag. 'Got all your plumbing kit, Doc?'

'All I need,' grunted the doctor. 'Still, I suppose this will give me a line or two for my autobiography.'

'Doc keeps threatening to write a book,' explained Thane. 'He's got a ready-made title too... Ouch, easy with that shirt,' he pleaded as the medical man began his examination. 'As I was saying, he's going to call it "Those we have lost" dedicated to... ouch... absent patients.'

'It's a pity they didn't kick you in the teeth while they were at it,' Williams replied sweetly. 'Seems a clean enough wound, Colin. Of course, the best thing to use on you would be a humane killer.'

'Fit for duty, Doc?' asked the chief superintendent.

'If you really need him,' said Williams more seriously. 'But he should be resting. That wound will take time to heal.'

Ilford frowned. 'It's up to you, Colin,' he declared. 'How do you feel?'

'I'll settle for a week's leave when it's over,' said Thane, fumbling one-handed with his tie.

'So much for my advice,' sighed Doc Williams, snapping his bag shut. 'I'd love to stay, but I promised to be along at the mortuary in half an hour to help in the post-mortem into that fellow who got shot last night.' He left the office, side-stepping the orderly entering with a tin tray crammed with cups.

Ilford waited until the man had gone, then said, 'Let's get down to business. Mr Brixen, suppose you lead off?'

The Crown Office man cleared his throat. 'Well, it's a trifle unusual, to put it mildly, but after hearing the situation that has presented itself, we—the Department, that is—made a number of telephone calls this morning. As a policeman, Mr Thane, you're familiar with the position in law regarding county boundaries?'

Thane knew, all right—it was one of the basic rules drummed into every cop even before he went on the beat.

The highest-ranking officer in any Scottish force became automatically classed as a civilian, without powers of arrest or inquiry, the moment he stepped outside the boundaries of his own county or city. If he was in "active pursuit" of a man, he could physically chase him over the boundary all right—but beyond that, a cop going outside his own territory had either to be accompanied by a local officer, whose authority would cover them both, or to have obtained a "temporary" warrant card from the chief constable into whose territory he was moving.

'Hruumph.' The Crown official took his answer as read. 'This case is obviously a particularly worrying one. Naturally, you'd be able to operate more freely if we relieved you of boundary difficulties.'

'It would help,' Thane admitted. 'It isn't a major difficulty, but sometimes we're really taking a chance when time doesn't let us go through channels.'

'Exactly.' Mr Brixen beamed. 'Well, we—the Department, that is—have managed to secure complete freedom of operation, with full powers, for yourself and Inspector Moss. You can call on any county forces for whatever help you need, of course, but,' He plunged into his briefcase and handed over two envelopes, 'this is a general warrant, for the period of this particular case. And... ah... good hunting.'

'We're also arming you, Colin,' said Ilford, who had been absorbed in an apparent contemplative study, a habit from which he had long since acquired his odd nickname. 'These characters are obviously playing for keeps. Mr Brixen has been quite a help in that, too. The only thing now is—where the devil are they?'

Phil balanced his now-empty cup on the windowsill, and queried, 'How about this character Johnny who was shot? Did Records have anything on him?'

'The Yard supplied plenty. He escaped from an army detention camp in West Germany while awaiting court-martial after shooting an NCO he didn't take to. After that, he was believed responsible for two armed hold-ups in the Rhine area, turned up in France, then disappeared again. But we didn't know he was anywhere in Britain till now.

'I'll lose no tears over that character,' said Ilford grimly. We came pretty close to losing Thane last night, he thought, noting the pallor still present under the surface tan of his skin.

Once again he wondered whether he shouldn't pull the Millside man off the case... but Thane at that moment was the only officer who could control the Kilburns, had a unique inside knowledge of Paxidena, and, most important of all, could identify Grigor, his companion. For Grigor was a complete blank as far as the files were concerned.

The Crown Office man gave a delicate cough, 'Er... Mr Thane...'

'Sir?'

'I must say we feel a trifle perturbed at the suggestions you have made regarding—er—' he consulted his papers—'Liam Kilburn and his sister Margot. To let them go absolutely free, well... you do appreciate there are serious charges that could be brought against them?'

Ilford and Phil waited, faces expressionless.

'Maybe there are,' agreed Thane softly. 'We know they did several things, including taking potshots at their brother. But you're the expert in law, Mr Brixen. You should know that the only thing we can prove in a court is that Liam Kilburn shot a man last night—and that by shooting him he saved the lives of three policemen, myself included.

'Do you want to charge him with that? Right now, we've talked them out of their half-crazy idea for revenge. They'll leave it to the hangman. That family's gone through hell. We've got them on our side now. In a way, I'd say we were just squaring the books.' Thane waited, tense and earnest.

Suddenly, Brixen smiled. 'I can get a train back in fifteen minutes, I think.' He rose, pushing the bundle of papers back into the brown leather briefcase.

'And the Kilburns?' asked Phil.

'You heard what Mr Thane said,' retorted the Crown Office man. 'And my department always likes our books to be... ah... square.'

CHAPTER TWENTY-SIX

THE BARN-LIKE BUILDING, sole remains of a small factory which had failed long before World War Two, could be reached from the main road only by a weed-grown ash-surfaced track, liberally sprinkled with potholes.

Easing the swaying van along in bottom gear, the driver halted outside the building's wide double doors, where only flakes of weather-beaten paint hid the time-darkened wood.

He got out, looked around, then, satisfied, turned a key in the heavy lock and slid the doors back with an ease that told of well-oiled hinges. He drove the van into the gloom of the building, closed and locked the outer doors, then rapped confidently on the rear of the van.

Giore Paxidena was the first to emerge. He jumped down, strode confidently through the gloom to the nearest wall, and snapped on a light switch. As two bare bulbs sprang to life, he called, 'Come out now, Kilburn, it's time to get down to business.'

Patrick Kilburn scrambled out, followed by the small, stout figure of Grigor. The Irishman blinked in the glare of the lights —they had been travelling for nearly an hour in the back of the van, squatting uncomfortably on its floor, sealed off from the driver.

He glanced at his watch. Just after 9 a.m. Time had flicked past since they had made that dash from the caravan. Grigor had driven the Sapphire like a madman, twisting and turning along the worst of side roads in what was, obviously, a well-planned escape route, kept for just such an emergency.

Then they had abandoned the car, and walked for nearly a mile through the outskirts of the city, dodging into shelter more than once to avoid the footsteps of a beat cop on night patrol. Finally, they reached their goal, a ground-floor house in a red sandstone tenement block.

Arthur Lagen was the name on the door. And Lagen, obviously at ease with his visitors, had fed them, let them clean up, then, after they had snatched a few hours' sleep, had led them through streets busy with shipyard "black squad" men heading for work, to where the van was lying on a bombsite lot. They had piled in the rear, Lagen had taken the wheel... and that was the last clue Kilburn had had to his whereabouts. Giore Paxidena had kept a nerve-wracking silence throughout the journey.

He suddenly realised there was another vehicle in the "garage"—a dark blue Bedford lorry with canvas side covers. The scent of still-new paint was faintly present, and Kilburn puzzled over the obvious but mysterious significance of the "RN" number plate and other service markings on its wings and body.

Lagen, the driver, had disappeared into some small store-room at the rear. Grigor was leaning against the van, obviously amused at his bewilderment, and picking his teeth with an old matchstick.

'Over here,' commanded Paxidena, and the Irishman followed the swarthy restaurant owner past the lorry to a long workbench beyond.

'Straighten your tie... and put these on,' he was ordered.

Puzzled, Kilburn put on the horn-rimmed glasses, and allowed himself to be pushed into position against the white-washed wall. Paxidena snapped on a powerful inspection lamp lying on the bench, turned its focussed beam on the other man's face, then, taking out a pocket comb, gave Kilburn a new central hair parting.

'What's the idea?' demanded Kilburn.

'Shut up,' said Paxidena, picking up a small camera. The shutter clicked twice. 'All right, relax. You must have a proper picture for your passport, my friend. It will be a poor likeness—but then, most passport photographs are, and in this case there's something to be said for it.'

'Passport?'

'Of course.' The Greek's voice was tinged with amusement. 'You can't leave the country without a passport. We've got one ready, except for the picture, which will have to be changed. But that's a simple matter.'

Grigor shambled over, picked up the camera, and went off again, whistling.

Paxidena turned, obviously enjoying his role. 'Take a look at these crates, Kilburn. Well made, eh?'

They seemed ordinary enough... roughly finished wooden boxes, about a foot wide by five feet long. They were empty, and their waiting lids lay alongside.

Kilburn bent down to examine the labels already attached to their sides. 'Machinery—urgent,' he read. And his eyes widened as the rest of the wording sank home. 'Don't tell me you're in the engineering business, Paxidena,' he sneered.

'Just for this once,' the man replied. 'These boxes are to be your very particular care; in fact, now that we have lost Johnny you must be their sole guardian, for part of the way anyway.'

'You're taking a pretty long chance trying to smuggle anything out like that,' Kilburn told him. 'Even if you've got the red-tape and form-filling organised'— Paxidena gave him an ironic little bow—'I wouldn't give a hoot for the idea. What's going in them—and come to that, where the hell are we?'

'Patience,' chided Paxidena, grinning again. 'Didn't you learn the art of waiting when you were in prison? First of all, we have come far back along the road we travelled last night. This'—He waved his arm around the building, two high-set skylight windows the only break in the structure—'is on the outskirts of Helensburgh, about ten miles from the caravan, to which, unhappily, we cannot return.'

'We're where?' Kilburn was almost speechless. 'Are you off your bloody loaf? They'll be turning the place upside down looking for us.'

'Why should they, here?' questioned Paxidena. 'They will have found the car by now, in Glasgow. They will believe we are far away from the entire area by now. And, whatever that nosy policeman may have heard, he has no idea what we plan—no more than you have. Calm down. Your nerves disappoint me—though thinking of that brother you have, and his shotgun' —he grimaced—'perhaps I can understand.'

His whole personality seemed to harden. 'Listen now, and listen closely. Then see if my ideas are so foolish.'

Still shaken, Kilburn lit a cigarette with trembling care.

With boyish energy, Paxidena hoisted himself up into a sitting position on the bench-top. Lagen walked over, and craned forward, as if waiting to hear a favourite story.

'Four hours from now, these boxes will be filled, and will be on their way,' began Paxidena. 'They will contain over fifty thousand pounds in the most negotiable currency in the world—gold.'

'You're crazy.' Kilburn could hardly believe his ears. 'You've been reading too many comic books, Paxidena. What're you going to do—nip down to the Bank of England and slip the stuff in your pocket while no one's watching?'

Paxidena didn't like it, didn't like it at all. 'I have stood a lot from you, Kilburn. But any more, and maybe I will decide we have made a mistake, that you belong back in prison—or, better still, at home in the happy bosom of your family. The gold exists all right. All three of us have seen it, within thirty miles of here.'

Lagen nodded silent agreement.

Eyes bright and hard, the man went on, words tumbling out in a torrent of quick, excited explanation.

The golden hoard lay at Lochhead Castle—Kilburn started at the name. Even he had heard about the Lochhead plate—the fabulous seventeenth-century collection owned and guarded by Lord Lochhead, as it had been by his forebears for generations.

Royalty had supped from its dishes, and compared them favourably with their own Palace treasures. From salt cellars to exquisitely worked centre bowls, from heavy ornate spoons to the smallest napkin-ring, only one material had been used—solid, pure, glittering gold. It had been sent to America before the war to keep it safe.

Now, it was home again—and, though the Lochheads might still have to open their castle to half-a-crown-a-head visitors, the plate remained intact—displayed behind armoured glass, bristling with burglar alarms, two burly ex-policemen always in attendance.

'Old Lochhead gifted it to the National Trust, or somebody like that, four years ago,' said Paxidena. 'It was a clever move—preserving a treasure for the nation, he called it. In fact, he still has the right to its use on banquet occasions, it must remain under the family's control—yet he doesn't have to worry about it being valued for death duties and maybe sold from under the family. It is the kind of wonderful scheme only a race like the British could conjure up.'

Lagen was growing impatient. He shuffled his feet, looked around, and brightened as Grigor came from the back room, carrying a large, shapeless bundle wrapped in cloth. The man dumped the bundle on the bench, opened a small cupboard, and fished out a bottle and some well-worn cups. As he slopped beer from the bottle into them, Paxidena went on.

'So, when we take Lord Lochhead's plate, we are, I suppose, robbing this Trust—but they will be well insured, and that is hardly our worry.'

Kilburn impatiently waved aside the beer. 'But you admit yourself that stuff's guarded as tight as the Tower of London. How do we get it out of there, short of starting a war?'

Grigor spluttered and almost choked on his beer. Lagen, grinning broadly, thumped the swarthy little man on the back to help him recover.

'They are going to give it to us!' Paxidena, too, was close to laughter. 'In fact, they will help us carry it out. I cannot blame you if you find that ridiculous—but it is true!'

Kilburn was speechless, his mouth half open. For a moment, he wondered if Paxidena was deliberately making a fool of him. But the Greek's next words showed the truth in dazzling simplicity.

'Lord Lochhead spent many years in the Navy—when he retired he was some kind of minor admiral. He still loves the sea, and his Service.'

A month ago, the story had appeared in the papers. Britain's newest aircraft carrier, just completed and commissioned, was to be visited by a group of top-ranking NATO politicians and service chiefs... as she lay at moorings in the Gareloch.

The giant carrier bore the same proud name as the cruiser Lord Lochhead had once commanded. And when he heard that a banquet was planned aboard to celebrate the unique occasion he had immediately offered—insisted—that the Lochhead plate should be there to give glittering service.

'When I read that story, I knew this was the chance of which I had always dreamed,' said Paxidena softly. 'Do you know there is over two hundred pounds weight of gold in that collection? And do you know that a tiny sovereign, little bigger than a farthing, is worth over three pounds today—because it is gold!'

Kilburn leaned forward in a fever of impatience. 'But how, man, how?'

'I have contacts. Some officers who come to my restaurant—though that is all finished now. After last night, I can never go back. I, too, must quit this country—but with this treasure, that is no worry.

'What is more natural than that a restaurateur should ask about the preparations for such a glorious meal? And Johnny, too—poor Johnny—learned much, drinking in the right hotels.

'The entire collection of plate leaves the castle today, bound for the ship. That is why, when I heard of your escape, it seemed as if Providence had come to my aid in the last problem, disposing of the gold abroad.' He turned, and ripped open the cloth-covered bundle lying beside. 'There...' he paused dramatically. 'There is our key.'

A collection of overalls, blue jerseys, and sailor caps spilled onto the floor. 'Just after eleven o'clock, the Navy are sending a lorry from the carrier base to Lochhead Castle. A driver, a lieutenant, and two of an escort, armed—you can't take chances with an ex-admiral's property!'

Kilburn turned suddenly, staring at the lorry a few feet away.

'You're catching on at last,' nodded Paxidena approvingly. 'We take the lorry, drive along the route that the real naval vehicle has to travel, and wait at a quiet little spot we've picked out. Lochhead Castle's in the middle of nowhere. If half a dozen cars drive up and down that road a day, it amounts to a traffic jam. We'll be in uniform, of course—and there's a slight complication. With poor Johnny gone, we are only four. Lagen has to get the Navy lorry and its crew out of sight—then he's got other things to do.'

'What about the escort?'

'Listen to the boss,' drawled Lagen. 'Everything's worked out, Mac—but everything.'

Paxidena was brisk, 'Patrick is right.' His tone was warmer than it had been. 'He wants to make sure we have dropped no little bricks. I didn't place my caravan up on that hillside for the view—or Maria. Poor Maria—I wonder if she is missing me.' He sighed. Then, crisply, he continued. 'We have this place on the road—nothing but mountains on either side. Not even sheep to see what is going on.

'When the Navy come along, they see some sailors working round a lorry—a breakdown. The officer on the Navy lorry sees a fellow-officer waving to him for help. He stops—he has to, the way this truck will be placed. And *our* officer—that will be you, Patrick, now that Johnny isn't here, Grigor and I aren't the type who get commissions—asks the Navy to help push his poor, broken-down lorry out of the road. The escort come out and—poof.'

It was Kilburn's turn to grin. 'You'll need a shave first, Grigor.'

'Eh?'

'The moustache—it's a beard or nothing in the British Navy.' Grigor stroked his upper lip sadly. 'A sacrifice—but it will grow,' he agreed.

'What happens to the sailors—the real ones, I mean?'

'A bump on the head. Then Lagen drives them away, gagged and bound, in their own lorry. He has a nice quiet track in mind, that goes to an old forestry camp. When he gets there, he abandons the lorry, changes into ordinary clothes, and heads back here—I forgot—we take a little motor-scooter along for him,' said Paxidena.

Kilburn frowned. 'Then we go on, pose as the real naval party, and collect the plate. But there's two sticky questions. What if Lochhead knows the officer who's supposed to be coming out? And why not simply whip the real Navy lorry—why use this one?'

Paxidena placed one of the seamen's caps low on his forehead and gave a little dance of glee before replying.

'Lochhead knows only a few of the senior officers. And we'll use our own truck because the Navy lorry, like all the others, is governed to thirty miles an hour. We may want to go faster, much faster. Besides, we don't want the real truck seen driving around the wrong part of the world before the alarm starts up—anyone from the camp might see it, and wonder.'

He patted the side of the Bedford affectionately. It had been bought at a Government surplus auction in Nottingham two weeks previous by a "Mr Brown." Arthur Lagen had been working on it ever since.

They hadn't much time left. Grigor went back to faking Kilburn's passport. Lagen made a last check of the Bedford, and loaded the little Vespa scooter aboard.

And Paxidena, nervously talkative as his hour drew nearer, showed his guest the final stage of his fantastic plan. A small oil-fired furnace, not much bigger than a console TV set, was already burning quietly in a corner at the back of the building.

'Lagen took over the rent of this place. He's told anyone interested that he's planning to start a small agricultural engineering business—it's a good cover story. He got the furnace delivered and laid in a stock of fuel.

'Gold is nearly as soft as lead—and softer than silver. It melts easily,' explained the Greek. 'That's what we'll do with the plate. Then we'll run it into these moulds...' He pointed. 'Within a couple of hours we have two long metal shafts, urgently needed to repair machinery of a small motor yacht lying on the south coast, not far from Dover. The owner has been waiting there for days now, complaining to the locals he can't start his holiday until they arrive.

'The gold gets a coat of grey paint, goes in the boxes.'

And from there, Kilburn heard, the van would drive them into the city.

'We let British Railways take care of the rest. You'll get a porter at the station to help you load the "shafts" on to the London train, and then travel down with them—alone. You change trains there, deliver the "shafts"—and the boat can sail.'

'The cops will pick me up the moment I go near the station,' protested Kilburn, grinding out his cigarette stub under heel.

'Why? You've got an overnight bag with you, you're wearing spectacles, walk with a limp—a stone in one shoe—and you arrive at the last minute, shouting and making a tremendous fuss. Drawing attention to yourself, in fact, getting two big packing-cases on the train. Would anyone in his right mind act like that if he was trying to get away from the police?'

'And you three?'

Paxidena gave a soft, dangerous smile. 'We'll be on the yacht when it sails, don't worry. I hadn't planned to move right away—but that can't be avoided now. Grigor has a car waiting in the city.

'And, Patrick— Don't think you can do it alone. I have many friends.'

CHAPTER TWENTY-SEVEN

THE NAVY DIDN'T HAVE a chance. Their truck swept round the bend of the road, then slowed as the driver sighted the blue-painted lorry ahead. The lieutenant at his side tensed for a moment, then relaxed as he saw the overalled figures grouped round the opened bonnet, and an officer standing beside them, waving.

'Looks like they need some help,' he remarked. 'Pull up, driver.'

'They're blocking the road as it is, sir,' nodded the seaman, foot already on the brake pedal. As they stopped, a few yards away, the officer left the group round the stranded Bedford and came across.

'Lend a hand, old boy,' said Patrick Kilburn, conscious of the fact that his white collar was two sizes too small.

'We're completely lost—and now the ruddy engine has packed up.'

The young lieutenant looked concerned. 'My driver can have a look if you like,' he said. 'But we're in a bit of a rush. Where are you from, anyway? Didn't expect to meet any of our chaps up here.'

'One of these delivery jobs from up north,' said Kilburn smoothly. 'Someone thought he knew a shortcut—and it didn't work out. Look, I think a good push might do the trick—you know, all together, heave—and once she starts rolling the driver lets in the clutch.'

The lieutenant brightened. 'Fair enough, though it'll cost you a gin if we meet again.' He turned. 'Everybody out.'

Unsuspecting, the four seamen moved across, exchanging friendly nods with the strangers.

'How's tricks, mate?' grinned one.

Face smeared with grease and oil, Giore Paxidena shook his head.

'Where do you want us, then?' asked the lieutenant.

'In a neat line, faces against the side of that truck,' snapped Patrick Kilburn harshly, and the sailors found themselves looking at the steady muzzles of four automatics. A lanky torpedo-man growled and moved forward and Kilburn squeezed the trigger with the casual unconcern of a fairground marksman hitting a cardboard target. The sailor buckled and fell, a bullet in his chest.

'We mean it,' said Kilburn, gun dangling carelessly.

The other three Navy men lined up—and crumpled in a neat row as gun-butts thudded against their heads.

Minutes later, gagged and bound, they were in the back of their lorry. Paxidena fastened a guard's white-blancoed webbing belt, with holstered service revolver, round his middle and nodded approvingly as Kilburn did the same with the lieutenant's weapon.

The Irishman thumbed through the papers from the unconscious officer's pockets.

'Here it is,' he confirmed. 'Letter of authorisation—made out to a Lieutenant Edwin Churchman—collect plate from Rear-Admiral Lord Lochhead and convey under escort.'

'We'd better do that, eh?' smiled Paxidena. 'Lead on, sir,' and he gave a mock salute.

CHAPTER TWENTY-EIGHT

POUNDING waves seemed to be jarring right through the rolling ship. God, he felt ill. The lieutenant came to slowly. Another bumping toss, and his head banged against something hard, sending a bright violet flash of pain through his skull. He couldn't move his arms or legs; for a moment, panic swept him. His mouth too... then, as the lorry lurched again, he remembered, and groaned again, this time in anguish.

There was going to be hell to pay for this. The old joke about the Admiralty records 'This man should go far—China.' Old Charnel-guts, the CO, would chew him to pieces for this. He could still see, anyway—facing the side of the truck.

With an effort, he rolled over. Hands tied behind his back, feet secured, he noted automatically.

Oh, my poor head. He closed his eyes a moment, and became conscious of another sound, a curious gobbling grunt. With another groan, he looked again—into the staring eyes of his driver, now also gagged and bound, lying beside him. His two other men seemed to be still out, their bodies jarring with every heave of the truck's platform. One of them would be the torpedo-man... poor devil, he might be dead by now.

The driver's eyes seemed to be signalling. The lieutenant turned his head, trying to interpret, and saw the scooter.

Almost at the same moment, the bumping and rolling died away, the truck's engine stopped, and there was a silence broken only by the slam of the driver's door.

With a quick shake of his head, the lieutenant gave a lead to his companion. Both fell back, shutting their eyes, lying still. There was a thud as the tailboard was lowered.

A voice growled, 'All still out,' and then there were other sounds as, grunting at the effort, Lagen heaved the motor scooter to the ground.

The lieutenant risked a quick glance. The man was stripping off his overalls, changing back into civvies. He could just see the scooter's rear number plate. Then he quickly shut his eyes again as Lagen turned.

The scooter pop-popped to life, then it drove away with a familiar low-pitched whine. The lieutenant wriggled against the side of the truck, and, falling back only once, raised himself into a sitting position. Slowly, he began sawing his bonds against the edge of one of the metal struts.

CHAPTER TWENTY-NINE

COLIN THANE HAD a steady stream of callers for the hour after Chief Superintendent Ilford's visit.

There were about twenty pressmen waiting outside, and at Moss's signal, they poured into the room. Cameramen, their heavy leather bags dumped along the wall, Rollies, and Speed Graphics poised hungrily, occupied one sector, reporters moving in on his desk from the other two fronts.

Thane noted Jock Mills of the Bugle among their mass, and gave him a private, welcoming nod.

First, he let the photographers have their turn, a blinding splutter of electronic flashes.

'Keep the public relations side of things happy, Colin,' "Buddha" Ilford had counselled. 'The more they write about what's happening, the less space they've got left to slang us.'

Then it was the reporters' turn. There was not a notebook visible—standard drill for delicate interviews. But Thane knew not a word exchanged would be missed, and that ballpoints would positively steam the moment they got outside.

'Just psychology,' Jock Mills had called it once. 'Show a notebook, and people start to dry up—choose every word with care, and then don't say even half of that. Any self-respecting news editor would tear a strip off a man who fouled things up the notebook way.'

'Look, boys,' Thane told them, 'I'm going to give you what I can, but that's not very much—for obvious reasons.'

He sketched to them the Crown Office's help in obtaining an all-counties warrant—avoiding the other points involving Liam and Margot, or the fact that a small, flat suitcase left by Ilford contained two Webley automatics.

'As far as last night is concerned, well, most of the mornings guessed right that we had a tangle with Kilburn. He linked up with some pals, and we were in a pretty tight spot for a time.'

'How about the dead man?' queried one reporter.

'He's identified,' nodded Thane, and told them Johnny's background. 'We can't and won't tell you who shot him—it was someone helping the police, someone we want to protect for a spell. You'll get the full story later—once we've got Kilburn and his associates under lock and key.'

'Who does the caravan belong to?' probed another pressman.

'Sorry.' Thane shook his head. He gave the same reply to the next half-dozen questions. Then he added, 'You can say this. We regard Kilburn as highly dangerous. He's armed, and the gang he's with won't hesitate to shoot—I know.'

They grinned sympathetically as he eased his injured shoulder.

'If anyone thinks they spot him, the best thing to do is to act as if nothing's wrong—then phone the police as soon as they can.'

That was all. They filed out. Only Jock Mills hung back. 'I heard about Paxidena,' he said quietly. 'Through a friend of a friend. But I'll keep quiet about that, and the earlier stuff, till you're ready.'

'I'll remember it,' said Thane. 'And I promise you'll get the go-ahead on your story the moment it's safe.'

He had fifteen minutes clear with Phil, studying the flow of reports that had come in. Then the duty officer downstairs came through on the telephone. Liam and Margot Kilburn had arrived with Angello. Thane ordered them shown upstairs, and waited until they were seated.

'Feel better now?' he asked the girl.

'Like two people who've just had a ton weight lifted from their shoulders,' her brother answered for her. 'We've told Peter Angello what happened.'

'I call it a miracle,' chimed in the Italian. 'It is a very good—a wonderful thing you have done, Signor Thane. In my heart I hardly dared believe it could be possible.'

'Have you— Have you found him yet?' asked the girl.

Thane shook his head. 'They've disappeared. The car was abandoned, covered with fingerprints. As far as the caravan is concerned, the laboratory crew are still going over it, but the results tell us nothing more than we knew already. We'll be going out there in an hour or so, for another look around.'

'Can we come?' asked Margot.

Thane hesitated, then remembered his words earlier. 'All right,' he agreed. 'No harm in taking witnesses back to the scene —besides, that car of yours is still lying out there. But if you see any pressmen about, you say nothing.' He glanced at his watch, and told them, 'Come back here at eleven.'

When they had gone, he pressed the buzzer button at the side of his desk. 'Bring Paxidena's girlfriend up,' he told the plainclothesman who answered.

Maria Colante's outfit of velvet slacks and white sweater didn't seem so appropriate at that hour of the morning as they had the previous evening. Her face was pale, and devoid of make-up. Her eyes widened as she took in his wounded shoulder, and she seemed empty, dispirited, as she went to the chair Phil Moss drew forward.

'We found Paxidena last night,' Thane told her in a flat, deliberately toneless voice. 'And Kilburn. And a couple of others.'

One hand went involuntarily to her mouth. 'Where are they?' she asked. 'Is... is Giore all right?'

'Johnny's dead. He gave me this.' Thane pointed to his shoulder.

'Johnny?' The girl was genuinely puzzled. 'Johnny who? Where is Giore?'

'You don't know Johnny?' Thane picked up a small Records Office file card from his desk, and showed the girl the picture on it. She shook her head.

'How about someone called Grigor?'

'I don't know... please, I don't know them.' She was trembling, hands clasping and unclasping. 'I lied last night—this man Kilburn came to see Giore. Then Giore went away with him. I was to say nothing; but these others, I have never heard of them.'

Thane waited till she dried her eyes and blew her nose. 'Let's try again,' he suggested.

Behind the girl, Phil Moss got his pencil and book ready.

'You help us, and we'll help you,' said Thane. 'If you weren't too deeply involved in this, and can prove it, then you've nothing much to worry about.'

'And Giore—is he all right?' Obviously she believed the restaurant owner was under arrest. Thane saw no reason to disillusion her.

'Seems to be,' he answered. 'How long have you known him?'

Once the girl had started her story, the rest wasn't difficult. She was obviously only too anxious to steer her course clear of the trouble which had enveloped Paxidena.

She'd met Paxidena six months before in London, when he came along to the club where she was working. He had plenty of money—he came from the part of the Mediterranean the Stepney-born girl still regarded as home—and his harsh, demanding love-making appealed to her instincts.

He had gone—and come back again. Then he had taken her north with him. For two months now she had lived at the flat.

'And the caravan?' prompted Thane.

'For a holiday, just a week or two ago,' said the girl. 'A long weekend—Giore said that was all the time he could spare from the business. And even then, he had to go and meet people nearly every day.'

'Did you go along?'

She shook her head. 'I don't want to go to jail. I'm telling you all I know—but Giore never took me with him. He said it was private business, that I wouldn't understand anyway. I used to sunbathe until he came back in the car.'

'How about his friends?' probed Phil. 'Do you know many of them?'

The girl swung round to answer him.

'A few—at the restaurant, that sort of thing. He said he preferred to be alone with me.'

Thane smothered a grin. 'Did you know he was on the crook?'

She was slow in answering. 'I—I knew he had been in trouble in Europe. He told me he could never go back home, that he'd been in prison once, too. Then he got drunk one night, and told me no one knew his real name—that he'd left that behind him. Next morning, he hit me when I asked him about it, and told me to forget he'd ever mentioned the subject.'

Obviously, Paxidena believed in keeping life in neat little watertight compartments.

The girl had known about the smuggled lace. And she had

guessed there were other things—from the strange telephone calls that often came in, calls she wasn't allowed to overhear.

'Did you know he was planning a big job?'

Yes, she'd known—for weeks he'd been talking about a fortune to be won. Afterwards, they would go abroad, and live in luxury. And he had plans for the future, big plans. But he always point-blank refused to answer her questions—she had learned not to ask.

'How about the caravan holiday?' pressed Thane. 'Was that part of his plans for the job?'

Maria frowned. Perhaps—it was difficult to say what had happened in his long absences. She could remember one strange thing.

'We were out for a drive one morning. Giore stopped the car at a garage, and bought some oil—two or three big gallon cans. I remember, because the garage man gave him car oil at first, and it was the kind you use for central heating he wanted. The garage man said it wasn't sold that way, but finally he opened a big drum, and gave Giore what he wanted.

'Giore went off on his own that afternoon, and when he came back, the oil had gone from the car boot. He told me he'd got it to help a friend try out a new heater—and then he was angry when I asked him where he'd got a paint stain on the sleeve of his jacket.'

That was all. Maria went back to the station cells, and, while Phil went off to dictate her statement to a police typist, Thane paced his room in frustrated energy.

Was he to simply wait and hope till Kilburn and Paxidena pulled whatever they had planned? The county force were already on their toes in Dunbartonshire— at "Buddha" Ilford's suggestion, all banks in the area had been warned about the possibility of raids, and every spare off-duty cop had been hauled in to reinforce patrols at every likely target area.

There was still the restaurant—Thane crammed his grey

trilby on his head, hesitated, then, working awkwardly, cursing his bandage-strapped left arm, opened the gun case and took out one of the Webleys. He checked the magazine, thrust the automatic into his trouser waistband, and pressed the buzzer.

'Take that case down to Mr Moss,' he told the orderly. 'I'm going out to Paxidena's restaurant.'

CHAPTER THIRTY

THE POLICE CAR took only a few minutes for the journey. The restaurant was neon-tubed and chromium-plated, with a red and black umbrella awning and menu-card prices that made the sausage-and-mash trade steer well clear. Inside, two fashionably dressed women were having coffee at one table, and a handful of waitresses were moving about under the direction of a man in waiter's dress.

The waiter's eyebrows rose questioningly as he took in Thane's figure. But he was polite enough.

'Police,' said Thane briefly, showing his warrant card. 'I'd like to see the manager.'

He was led through the long, narrow restaurant. The waiter tapped on the office door, and waved him through.

The manager was unhappy about it at first. But finally he agreed, and took the big detective into the small inner room behind his own—Paxidena's private office.

'The police have already been here,' he complained. 'They came early this morning—in fact, they got me out of bed to open the place up. It is bad for trade, all this. The boss is in some sort of trouble, that's all I know. You can maybe tell me about it?'

'Not today,' said Thane briefly. 'Got the keys?'

The manager handed them over.

'I'll get on all right by myself,' said Thane pointedly, and the man left.

He wasn't sure what he was looking for. He took the safe first—a bundle of papers referring to the restaurant, a cash box, some odds and ends. Then the desk. Files and records in the left-hand drawers, a cupboard to the right containing some bottles and glasses. The shallow centre drawer was more personal—chequebook, a clean white collar, some more pictures of Maria, at the flat this time, by the look of them. Then he came across it: a small, brightly coloured leaflet, almost lost in the back of the drawer, having slipped over the edge. Only its tip showed.

What the heck did the restaurateur want with a leaflet on an oil-fired furnace plant? It had obviously been used—there were pencilled price figures jotted down in the margin.

Thane turned the leaflet over—no, nothing to show it had come from any local firm. He strode out into the main office.

The manager looked up from his desk.

'What's the heating arrangements in this place?' asked Thane.

'All electric—one of the first things Mr Paxidena had done when he took over was to have a completely new plant installed,' the man replied.

Thane shrugged his shoulders. 'You'd know most of the people who came to visit the boss. Were there any visitors during the last few months who were—unusual?' He pulled a selection of photographs from his wallet pocket, and laid them squarely before the manager. 'Any of these men, for instance?'

The man flicked through the pictures disinterestedly, frowned, went over the "rogues' gallery" selection again, and slid one photograph aside.

'His face seems familiar—I've a feeling he has been to see Mr Paxidena a couple of times. But then, in the restaurant business, people are so often just casual customers, passing trade—do you know where this man is now?'

Thane nodded. 'In the mortuary.' He replaced Johnny's photograph in the pile, and lifted them from the desk. 'Anyone else—anyone you've wondered about?'

The manager shook his head. 'Mr Paxidena is a pretty quiet type. He has the usual business acquaintances—all in the trade, you know. But apart from Miss Maria, he has few friends who come to call.' He glanced impatiently at his watch. 'Do you need me much longer? It's time I was in the kitchens, getting ahead with drawing up today's menu.'

'I'm finished for the moment.' Thane turned towards the door. With it half open, he told the man, 'If Paxidena should show up, or telephone, don't waste any time contacting us—though it's pretty unlikely he will.'

For the first time, the manager showed real concern. 'Do you mean he won't be coming back? What—what about the business?'

Thane settled his arm more comfortably in its sling. 'Let's just say a change of job every now and again does no harm,' he replied. 'Better luck next time.' And he was on his way before the manager had recovered.

CHAPTER THIRTY-ONE

IT WAS STARTING to rain as the police car headed back to Millside. The downpour grew heavier and the skies darker every second that passed. Shoppers crowded every street doorway, sheltering from the sudden September storm, and the drumming rain swirled down the windscreen of the car in solid waves.

Whistling softly, the driver turned off the road, splashed the Humber through two giant puddles inside the police station courtyard, and halted at the foot of the steps leading to the CID offices.

Thane threw the car door open, and dived for shelter, ploughing through the swing doors of the building. Two plainclothesmen were busy "booking in" a leather-jacketed, tight-trousered youngster of about sixteen.

One of them broke off long enough to report, 'Stripping lead from the roof of a church, sir—usual thing.'

Upstairs, the Kilburns were already waiting, accompanied by Peter Angello and Phil.

'Nothing fresh, Colin,' reported Phil. 'Interpol have been asked to investigate Paxidena's native background, and the Yard are also passing on to them the description you gave of his pal Grigor. And Liam here has just remembered that he saw what looked like a rifle lying hidden in the bushes not far from Perth.'

'That's right, Mr Thane,' the big Irishman gave an engaging grin. 'Now it would be doing no good at all to let a thing like that lie around where some foolish person with the wrong ideas might find it.'

'They might even pull the trigger to see if it worked,' commented Phil Moss in tones of heavy sarcasm. 'Will I pass it on to the local force, Colin?'

Thane agreed. 'Tell them to preserve it for possible fingerprints—but not to act until they hear from me,' he added, as sudden alarm welled in the Kilburns' faces. In an almost whimsical vein he told them, 'It would never do if people were to change their minds, and the poor, puzzled police had thrown away all their evidence. We're happy as it is, but we'd be silly to take chances.'

The Kilburns settled back.

'We still want to see Patrick get all that's due him, Mr Thane,' said Margot Kilburn quietly, hands clasped lightly on the lap of her simple, yet attractive, grey linen dress. 'But we've given our word to leave it to the law. We'll stick by that.'

Phil was busy counting heads. 'Three, four—five of us, six, including the driver. It'll be a tight squeeze in the car,' he told Thane.

'Only in the one direction, Phil,' said his friend. 'Our guests will be driving back in their own car, remember. Ready?'

Phil glanced out the office window at the steady downpour outside, and groaned. 'Why didn't I do what my mother wanted, and get a job in a bank?'

'Because you'd feel unhappy among all that money,' retorted Thane. 'And think what would happen when the books didn't balance.'

CHAPTER THIRTY-TWO

ONCE THE TRAFFIC thinned on the outskirts of the city, the police Humber made good time on the road to the Gareloch.

The weather brightened, too, and, speeding along the broad highway, Thane let the uniform driver worry about the road, and gave their passengers a running commentary on the broad panorama of the Clyde spread below them on their left.

He loved the river, as he loved the city. For him, together, they added up to home—a place for deep-down roots, that drew nourishment equally from the soot and grime behind them and the broad, muddy, casually beautiful riverbanks.

They listened politely, but obviously failing to grasp how a mixture of monotonous scenery and dull, factory-speckled townships could add up to heaven. The car purred on, into the more pleasant, tree-fringed country along the side of the Gareloch. The water was calm and blue, and deserted.

Then, as the car swung round a bend on the road, Angello gasped. 'Look at the ships.'

Row upon row they lay at their moorings, tankers and tenders, the grey low silhouettes of destroyers, the bulkier, higher shapes of cruisers and supply ships.

'Part of the reserve fleet,' explained Phil Moss. 'Some of them have been lying here for years—most of them probably won't leave again, except to be towed to the shipbreakers.'

A pinnace, tiny from their distance, was heading up the loch, her wake cream-white, a flag fluttering from her stern. She disappeared round a headland, then, as the car rounded another bend, reappeared again, striking still farther towards mid-channel.

'Well...' Thane drew in a deep breath of pleasure at the sight.

There was nothing dead or decaying about the ships now visible. Soft plumes of smoke floated from the single funnels of two destroyers at anchor, decks busy with men.

Around them, small boats buzzed. And astern, dwarfing them with her bulk, lay the carrier—her long, flat-topped deck broken only by the island bridge, a small lighter lying alongside her, transferring supplies from her hold into the huge cargo-entry opened in the carrier's hull.

'Must be the *Axehead*, sir,' said the driver, taking his eyes off the winding road for brief seconds. 'I read she was coming up this way before she goes off on a settling-down cruise.'

A few miles more, and the driver flicked his trafficator switch before they left the main road and headed up the narrow track leading to the caravan site. Twenty yards up, a uniform cop waved them down, then, as he recognised the car, stood back and saluted. The Humber bumped and lurched on, past the Kilburns' small saloon, lying to one side of the rough road, and finally stopped a few yards short of the level grassland and the caravan.

It was cream and blue in colour, Thane noted idly as, seeing the area in daylight for the first time, he stepped out of the car and looked around.

Paxidena hadn't been joking about the drop that lay beyond, he thought grimly. The slope where he'd crouched the night before levelled out only for these few yards—then plunged sharply downwards on the far side, terminating in a sheer fall of —call it sixty feet into a tangle of deep-water rocks. He shivered, and turned towards the caravan again, the others following. The door was open, and another uniform man, hurriedly nipping a cigarette, emerged from the interior to meet them.

'The last of the CID left about two hours ago, sir,' he reported. 'They said they'd be back after lunch.'

Thane stepped into the van, and whistled. A very, very thorough job had been done on it—cushions slit open in the search for hidden papers, even some of the wall-panelling unscrewed. Drawers and cupboards had been turned upside-down. The white smudge of fingerprint powder was visible everywhere.

Margot followed him in, her eyes involuntarily avoiding the small, stained area of carpet where Johnny had died a few hours before.

'Were there any results, do you know?' he asked, gesturing around the search-scarred van.

'Well, they didn't tell me much, naturally,' said the uniform man good-naturedly. 'I think they've gone to do up their report now, actually—pity you missed them, sir, they'd no idea you were coming.

'Still, I did hear them say that it looked as if that bloke who was shot and his mate had been sleeping up here for a day or two. And they found a strange set of prints they couldn't account for. But this mob were pretty careful—didn't leave many traces, apart from a mound of beer bottles round the back of the van. They had a good stock of food laid in too—mostly tinned stuff.'

A sudden shrill whistle made them jump.

The constable dived back into the caravan kitchen, the whistling stopped, and he emerged with a sheepish look.

'I was just making a cup of tea, sir,' he confessed. 'Seemed no harm in it—and my mate and I have been up here since pretty well daybreak.'

'Sounds a good idea to me,' cut in Phil Moss from the doorway. 'Got any spare cups handy?'

The uniform man relaxed. 'Manage that soon enough,' he grinned.

Thane turned his attention to the two heaps of clothing lying beside the opened wardrobe. He turned them over casually, then stopped, frowned, and lifted up a pair of flannel trousers for a closer examination at the window.

'Found something?' asked the girl, close to his side, her faint perfume for a moment almost blanking out another, more pungent odour.

Thane squeezed the cloth in his hand, and sniffed it closely.

'Paint remover,' he said. 'You can still see the stain.' Awkwardly, one-handed, he spread the cloth out. 'Down this one leg. There's still some specks of the paint visible just above the turn-up.'

'Yes, I see,' the girl agreed. 'It's a dark bluish shade, I think. Is it important?'

He shook his head. 'I don't know—half the job is filing away little bits and pieces that don't add up—' He stopped, as the blare of the car horn sounded from inside.

'Our driver's waving,' said Phil Moss from the doorway. 'Must be a message coming over.' The two detectives hurried across the grass to the waiting Humber.

'They're calling us on the county frequency,' reported the driver. 'I've acknowledged the call, and they're on standby.'

Thane picked up the hand-microphone. 'Glasgow car 46,' he reported. 'Thane here. Go ahead with your message.'

The buzz of static was broken by the control room operator's metallic voice.

'Hello, 46. Urgent message. Will you telephone in immediately? Major robbery reported, suspects believed to include men you are after. Please phone in immediately. Over.'

'Roger, out.' Thane threw the microphone through the car window into the driver's lap, then turned and shouted to the trio standing beside the caravan. 'We've got to go—something's turned up. You've got your own car—we'll see you later.'

He didn't wait to gauge their reaction, but piled into the rear of the car beside Phil Moss, who was already pale-faced with excitement.

The Humber's clutch jarred home, and the wheels screamed round in the mud and grass, and then they were off, in a tight U-turn, bucking and jumping down the track, the driver's hands gripping the steering wheel rock-hard, his two passengers being tossed around in the back seat like corks in a stormy bathtub.

The first phone box was a mile down the road. Thane jumped out and entered it, cursing as the closing glass door banged against his wounded shoulder, expanding on his language as he thumbed the phone bridge to arouse the operator. He got through to the control room in just under two minutes, but it seemed immeasurably longer.

Outside, waiting in the Humber, Phil and the driver could only gauge the conversation from Thane's intent expression, the fact that he seemed to be listening most of the time. Then he kicked the phone box door open, and jumped back into the car.

'Down the road two miles, then fork left, and straight on,' he ordered, fumbling for his cigarettes as the car took off.

Phil Moss helped him open the packet, fished out another two cigarettes for himself and the driver without invitation, lit up, then waited.

'They've done it all right,' said Thane bitterly. 'A dream of a job, just as Paxidena boasted—so big a job that we literally drove past the biggest pointer to it.'

'What do you... mean?' asked Phil Moss, breaking his words

as the Humber dropped a gear and swung savagely to overtake a slow-moving farm lorry.

'The *Axehead*,' gritted Thane. 'A hundred thousand quids' worth of gold plate being taken from Lochhead Castle to the carrier for a banquet—and they've nobbled the lot.'

Phil whistled wryly. 'I read about that. How'd they do it?'

'We're heading for the castle now. Lord Lochhead can go into the fine detail when we get there. They stuck up the naval truck heading for the castle, dumped it and its crew, and went on in its place—Navy uniforms, Navy-style truck, the lot. One of the sailors got free, found himself in the middle of nowhere, and had the sense to light a bonfire.

'Some forestry lookouts saw the smoke, thought some of the trees were ablaze, and rushed over a fire-fighting squad. They found the Navy men, and radioed in—one of the sailors is critically ill with a bullet in his chest.

'The police phoned the castle, but it was too late—Kilburn and Paxidena had left half an hour before. Kilburn shot the sailor.'

Moss fumbled in his raincoat pocket and pulled out his Webley. He slid out the butt clip, checked the mechanism, and slammed the clip home again.

'These Kilburns seem to make a habit of going gun-crazy,' he commented. 'Looks like we may need these after all.'

Thane was silent. The plate—that was why Paxidena had needed Kilburn, to provide an easy way of disposing of the gold abroad. But how could they hope to get it out, and how could they hope to sell the collection, every item of it known in minute detail by jewellers and collectors throughout the world, and photographed almost as frequently as the Crown Jewels?

Phil answered his unspoken question. 'They'd have to melt stuff like that down—here or abroad,' he declared. 'What colour was their truck? Same as the paint stains on the flannels back at the caravan?'

Thane nodded. 'So they said.' He was piecing together other things now—the fuel oil Paxidena had bought on the car run with Maria, the furnace plant leaflet, the snatch of conversation he'd overheard at the caravan, when the restaurateur had boasted to Kilburn he'd 'be on his way within twenty-four hours.'

'You'd expect them to get as far away as possible from the area, then, once they were really clear, get down to the problem of disposing of the plate,' he began.

Moss nodded silently. He knew Thane's habit of theorising aloud—thoughts form better in actual wording, the big man often declared.

'I found a furnace plant brochure at Paxidena's restaurant, Phil—no trace of origin, but plenty of pencilled prices. Then you'll remember his girlfriend's story about the fuel oil.

'This whole affair has been planned to a hairsbreadth, we can take that for granted. And Paxidena is likely to be deliberately unorthodox. He knows we'll have roadblocks out, that the whole place is already swarming with cops looking for him and Kilburn. So, supposing he doesn't run—not far, anyway. Supposing he melts the lot down before he makes his break?'

He paused, concentrating on lighting another cigarette, then let it smoulder between his fingers. 'He cuts the value of the plate by almost half—but he's left with a fortune in pure gold that Kilburn can feed out through a dozen different sources abroad.'

'If he gets it out of the country,' Phil interrupted dryly. 'That amount of metal will take some moving.'

'He'll have all that planned,' said Thane grimly. 'We've got to move fast, Phil, faster than ever. My guess is we've got a few hours at the most—and that even then, we don't stand a dog's chance of getting old Lochhead's plate back intact.

'First thing we do, is get on the radio and have Headquarters start working up a list of any furnace plant sold by firms to customers in the last few weeks, over a fifty-mile radius around Glasgow, but more especially around this part of the world. Then get the county police checking every garage and supplier within a twenty-mile circle of the caravan, finding out whether any strangers have been ordering fuel oil in the last fortnight.'

Phil shook his head. 'That's a king-sized job,' he protested. 'It may take days—and you said yourself, we've only got a few hours. Obviously, you're banking on the caravan's siting being the clue to them operating from a hideout not too far away. But that doesn't cut down the job—they could have picked up supplies any number of miles away, and the same applies to the furnace plant.'

Thane bit his lower lip. 'I know—I know. But these furnaces are pretty hefty weights—the chances are they would have to be delivered by lorry. And if Paxidena had a good enough cover story, there's no reason why he shouldn't have ordered fuel locally—in fact, it would be more suspicious, he'd probably feel, if he didn't go shopping for it around the local suppliers.'

Phil shrugged, and stubbed out his cigarette on the ashtray. 'Keep your fingers crossed,' he cautioned, and stretched over to the front seat for the radio microphone.

CHAPTER THIRTY-THREE

LOCHHEAD CASTLE WAS LISTED in the guidebooks as: 'Originally built in the seventeenth century on the site of a still earlier fortification. Now extensively modernised, with a new wing in similar architectural style having been added at the beginning of the century.'

It lay at the mouth of the glen, a great, jutting pile of locally hewn granite, a broad driveway a full half-mile long winding from the lodge gates through shrubs and lawns to the broad semi-circular sweep of the courtyard.

Three police cars were already parked outside the main doorway when Thane's Humber pulled up.

A liveried manservant ushered the two Glasgow detectives down a deep-carpeted hallway into the morning room, where Lord Lochhead was deep in agitated conversation with a county police inspector.

The local man nodded to Thane, made the necessary introductions, and told him, 'There's no doubt about it—the descriptions tally with your men. I've already asked for an immediate rundown on all theatrical costumiers and naval outfitters to try to trace the source of the uniforms they wore. And there's a general alert out for the motor-scooter used by the man who dumped the naval truck up that forestry track. We've got the number of the bike.'

'And the lorry?' asked Thane.

The policeman shook his head. 'No joy, I'm afraid. Nobody took its number—the sailors because things happened too quickly and the castle staff because—'

'Because we'd absolutely no reason to,' finished Lord Lochhead. He was a small, slim man, with a ginger red beard and a rough tweed suit to match. 'How were we to even guess anything would be wrong? We expected a lieutenant and escort, and they arrived in a normal service vehicle. He had a letter of authority, the plate was already waiting and crated—why, he even had a glass of sherry with me while his men helped some of my staff load the crates.'

'Didn't he say anything to you that might have'—Thane corrected himself—'might now appear suspicious?'

Lord Lochhead's beard twitched with rage. 'No. The villain sat there, sipping my sherry, hardly saying a word. I thought he was perhaps a little overawed. Can happen, you know—youngster meeting a senior officer, all that sort of thing. Said he'd not long been posted up here, and had been in some shore station for the last few years. Had the audacity to tell me it was secret, classified, what he'd been doing.'

'He's been in a shore station, all right,' grinned Phil Moss. 'Complete with a classified number. But it was one with iron bars over the portholes.'

The little man didn't appreciate Phil's humour. 'Damn it, what are you going to do?' he demanded, almost dancing with rage. 'What's happening to my plate? This is a Government matter, man—the collection belongs to the nation. And what about my butler?'

'Butler?' Thane gave an inquiring glance at the county officer.

'Lord Lochhead's butler went off with the truck. It was an arrangement his Lordship had made with the Navy,' nodded the man. 'He was to supervise the unpacking of the crates, and keep count of the pieces. I don't think he's in on it—he's nearly sixty, and has been in the family's service since he was a boy.'

'Of course he has nothing to do with it,' snapped Lord Lochhead. 'Damn it, man, do you think I run a thieves' kitchen here?'

'Can you tell me the approximate weight of plate taken?' asked Thane.

'Oh—somewhere under two hundred-weights,' he was told.

'Pure gold, easy enough to melt down?'

'Absolutely—' his Lordship's mouth fell open, his voice died away to a whisper. 'You—you—the vandals couldn't possibly destroy the collection?'

Thane pursed his lips. 'That's what I would do,' he replied. Then, turning to the county man, he asked, 'Where are the original members of the truck crew?'

'The wounded seaman is in hospital; the others are probably back at their shore station by now,' he was told. 'Thinking of going there?'

'It seems as good a place as any at the moment,' said Thane. 'I know where it is—we passed it on the way up to the caravan site just after noon.'

It was just under eighteen miles to the shore station—one of the many installations in the area run by and for the Admiralty. Ten-foot-high unclimbable metal fences encircled its landward width, and within were grouped a variety of buildings, large and small, leading to a series of pierheads.

As the Humber headed towards the camp's main gates, he suddenly recognised the small saloon car parked at the road's edge.

'Pull up,' he ordered. And as the Humber slowed, Liam and

Margot Kilburn left their car and walked towards him, faces grave and impassive.

'What are you doing here?' asked Thane.

'Waiting for you,' said Liam. 'Not long after you left, another police car arrived at the caravan. We heard what had happened. It was too late to follow you, but we made up our minds that sooner or later you would come here, and when you did, we would be waiting. We left Angello at a bus stop.'

'Look, I know what I said before,' Thane began impatiently. 'But you can't help here—you can only get in the road.'

'We won't take "no" for an answer, Mr Thane,' said Margot Kilburn softly. 'The only way you can stop us is to lock us up, and that would lead to all kinds of complications and explanations. We won't interfere—but we want to be somewhere in the background.'

Thane temporarily capitulated. His shoulder was aching more than a little, his mind was a buzz of urgency. He turned away without another word, and got back in the Humber. As it passed through the camp gates, he took a last backward glance. The little Ford was still there, its occupants once more back aboard, patiently waiting.

Commander Speedwell was the senior naval officer ashore. At that moment, he was a very unhappy SNO. In addition to his obvious acute concern over the condition of his wounded matelot, there was also the little problem of exactly what their Lords of the Admiralty were going to make of this whole business, aggravated ten times over by the imminent arrival of the NATO chiefs and the already present bulk of the carrier. He had already explained in microscopic detail to the young lieutenant exactly how he felt about the whole business.

In consequence, the lieutenant was by now at the stage where he was in his own mind convinced that the commander was right—he really should still be back home sailing toy boats in a purple-pencilled boating pond.

The youngster went over his story again with Thane, while Commander Speedwell huffed and grumphed at regular intervals. When it was the rest of the lorry crew's turn—one by one they told their stories.

As the last one left, Thane sat down with a sigh, and was thankful for the two fingers of gin handed him by the senior naval officer. Phil declined a similar offer with thanks, and the commander raised a distinct eyebrow as the thin, wiry detective settled for a plain lime-and-soda.

'Stomach,' explained Phil.

The commander relaxed immediately. His brother had a stomach, he exclaimed. He knew exactly what the position was.

'Well, Mr Thane,' he turned towards Colin. 'Learned anything fresh?'

Colin took another sip from his glass. 'I've managed to build up a pretty full description of the fourth man,' he nodded. 'We hadn't a thing on him before—just some fingerprints at the caravan. By the way, can Inspector Moss use your telephone? I'd like to check with Headquarters on that fingerprint report—they may have had some results by now.'

'Any chance of our getting the plate back in time for the banquet, Mr Thane?' asked the commander. 'The position doesn't seem so hopeless, now that I know you have the names of three of the men off pat.'

'I wouldn't hope too much.' Thane drained his glass, and waved away a proffered refill. 'If we don't get a clear lead soon, well, we may get the gold back, but Lord Lochhead wouldn't recognise it.'

The commander shook his head. There was a pretty nasty liaison officer job just about to become vacant in one of the hottest, most unpopular small republics in South America. There was a horrible feeling in his bones that he knew who might draw it next.

'Have you any idea how many of your people knew the arrangements for collecting the plate?' asked Thane.

'Too many.' Commander Speedwell came back from South America with an effort. 'Most of my officers, and quite a few men—we thought our precautions were completely adequate, of course.

'There didn't seem any real need for secrecy. And, after all, the Admiralty Press Office released the first story that the damn stuff was going to be aboard the carrier for this blessed banquet. I don't think anyone here would be in league with those thugs, do you?'

'Probably not—but remember the slogan during the war: "careless talk,"' Thane told him quietly. 'This gang have been in the area for some weeks, perhaps cultivating acquaintances in pubs or hotels. It wouldn't take them long to get a pretty concise idea of your plans. Next time, I'd be a little more inclined to leave arrangements to the last minute.'

Phil, who had been using the telephone in the far corner of the emptied wardroom, replaced the receiver and returned.

'Some progress,' he reported. 'Fingerprints at the caravan are those of a man, Arthur Lagen, previous convictions for robbery with violence, serious assault, and housebreaking while in possession of explosives. He came out of Brixton Prison about three years ago, and nobody knew he was back up here.'

'How about the checklists?'

'There's a squad working on it nonstop. The job isn't as difficult as they thought it might be—there are only really five wholesalers for the entire West area on the oil-furnace side. Fuel oil is a different matter—but they're trying hard on that too. They hope to ring back within the half-hour.'

The marine steward who was on sentry-go at the wardroom door poked his head round its corner, and coughed discreetly. 'Sir—Sub-Lieutenant Michaels would like a word with you. Says it may be important.'

'Show him in,' growled Speedwell. 'Officer of the watch at the main gate,' he explained to Thane. 'Can't think what the deuce he wants, though.'

Michaels was somewhat nervous—word had got around that Old Charnel-guts was in no mood for frivolity. But the young officer was quick with his story.

'We had a complaint from a woman about a dog, sir.'

'A dog?' The commander's face darkened.

'Yes—but it's peculiar, sir, because we couldn't have done it.'

'Done what? Speak English, damn it.'

'Yes, sir.' Michaels gulped. 'Run over her dog, sir.'

'Are you trying to be funny, Michaels?'

Thane stopped the commander from bursting a boiler. 'What about the dog that was run over, Lieutenant?'

Michaels threw him a glance of pure gratitude. 'This woman telephoned, complaining that one of our trucks ran over her dog and didn't stop. She was making an awful stink about it. But I've checked every truck that's come in, and not one man knows a thing about it. We've only another two trucks out just now, and neither of them should be anywhere near where this dog was killed.'

'She's sure it was a naval truck?' Thane's eyes were glistening.

'Positive, sir. But none of our trucks should have been up that way, and I thought—' he hesitated. 'Mind you, sir, it could have been from some other unit. We can't be sure.'

'Sure... of course we're sure,' boomed Speedwell, South America suddenly receding. 'Damn good deductive reasoning, young fellow—here, help yourself to a gin.'

Phil Moss was already busy spreading a large-scale road map on the wardroom table.

'Whereabouts did this woman report the lorry?' he asked.

Michaels came over, and pointed—a small hamlet two miles

north-east of Helensburgh, little more than seven miles from where they were at that moment.

'Heading?' Thane peered closely at the map.

'North-east again, sir,' said the officer.

The big detective traced one large finger along the thin red road lines on the map.

'Pretty strange direction to take if they're trying to make a complete break from the area,' he commented. 'When was the dog run over?'

'Nearly two hours ago, sir,' he was told.

Perhaps he was right after all, Thane mused. The gang could have counted on a good hour's clear run out of the area. Why instead they had chosen to head up into that maze of country roads—unless, as he guessed, they were planning to melt down the plate locally and then split up.

He made up his mind.

'Commander, I'm going to have a look at this place where the lorry was reported. We'll leave right now. Can you contact Police Headquarters, and ask them to have the local bobby and a carload of men meet me at' —his finger stabbed down on the map—'just here, these crossroads?'

The commander agreed. 'Some of my men would rate it a pleasure to help you in this,' he volunteered. 'That torpedo-man who was shot was an extremely popular fellow. Would you like a truckload of ratings—armed—to come along with you? They may come in handy. These fellows seem to have no scruples about using firearms.'

Thane declined the offer with thanks. 'We'll try to tackle them on our own first,' he declared. 'That's our job. If they really show fight, then I hope your offer will still be open.'

As the Humber headed out of the shore station, Thane settled back to rest on the seat cushions—then remembered the Kilburns. As he sat upright, Phil pointed ahead. The Ford car was there, engine ticking over. The Humber turned right—and the Kilburns' car began moving after them, keeping a discreet hundred to hundred and fifty yards back.

'How about stopping and giving them another bawling out?' suggested Phil, far from happy at their strange shadows.

'Let them be,' said Thane wearily. 'But, driver, if you can lose them, so much the better.'

The uniform man at the wheel growled in understanding. His right foot thudded down on the accelerator pedal, and the Humber speedometer began climbing swiftly. For a while the Ford kept up, gamely trying to maintain the short distance between them. Then, slowly, it began to fall back, and finally disappeared from view. The police driver didn't let up until he reached a road junction where the Humber forked left, onto the minor highway. Then he eased the accelerator, and began driving once more with a speed that showed respect for the road.

Commander Speedwell had been busy on his telephone. Two police cars—not just the one Thane had asked for—were waiting at the crossroads, the village bobby standing beside them, holding his bicycle.

Every hint of tiredness had vanished from Thane's manner as he began questioning the local constable.

'Do you know the woman who complained her dog was run over?'

'I certainly do, sir,' grinned the man. 'She's been telephoning me at ten-minute intervals since it happened. Mind you, she's no crank or anything like that. If she says a naval truck hit the dog, then that's what happened.'

'Take your time over the next one,' said Thane. 'Do you know anyone around here—either a house owner or a farmer, or —in fact, anyone at all—who might have a furnace plant?'

The uniform man was ahead of Thane. 'You mean some kind of furnace that could be used to melt down this gold that was stolen?'

Phil Moss made a mental note. This man shouldn't be on the beat much longer.

Now the village bobby took his time, thinking carefully. A full two minutes passed before he spoke again.

'There's the old Forgings building, about three miles from here. Started off as a factory in a small way, then lay empty for years. I heard somebody from the city was planning to reopen it as a tractor repair centre—good area for it too, mind you.'

'Ever seen the man?' probed Thane.

The constable shook his head. 'Isn't really in my area, sir—last time anything happened that way was three years past, when there was some trouble with poachers. But I've heard there's been some sort of equipment taken out to the Forgings in the last couple of weeks.'

There was an AA telephone box less than a hundred yards away. Phil got through to the CID detail at Headquarters who were still busy on the round-up of oil suppliers and furnace plant equipment concerns. He had to hang on while they ran through their lists.

There was nothing useful listed under the returns of new fuel oil users—but the customer sheet supplied by the third firm of heating engineers contacted had the information they wanted.

Lochrich Engineering—Phil gave a wry, appreciative grin—had paid cash for a small furnace unit, despatched to the Forgings ten days previously.

The village constable abandoned his bike, after carefully padlocking the rear wheel, climbed into one of the patrol cars, and guided the three police cars towards their target. The lead car slowed as the road curved through a thick belt of trees, and the other two drew behind it, engines ticking over.

'Another three hundred yards along, sir,' said their guide. 'Then you'll see an old track going off to the left. The building is set back from the road a little way, but I thought we'd best stop here in case they've got a man on guard.'

Thane nodded appreciatively. The next stage must obviously be a cautious reconnaissance.

Leaving the three police drivers by their vehicles, he waved the rest of the party—seven men not counting Phil and himself—forward. Using every scrap of cover the woodland and bushes afforded, they advanced in a strung-out line.

The earth was dry, hard, and warm beneath their feet, the bright sun high in a now cloudless sky. A rabbit, flushed from hiding by their advance, dashed off at a wild tangent, white tail bobbing madly. The occasional crackle as a dried twig snapped beneath a regulation boot was the only noise they made.

Then the uniform sergeant on the extreme left of their miniature dragnet gave an urgent hand signal, and dropped to the shelter of a small patch of scrub.

The rest of the line followed his example, Thane and Moss wriggling rapidly over to where the sergeant waited. The man pointed ahead, finger to his lips in an exaggerated warning. Thane moved to the edge of the bushes, seeking a clear view, and cautiously raised his head.

The building called the Forgings lay dead ahead. They were almost on the edge of the woodland now, and their target was only about seventy yards off.

From their vantage point, they had an angled view of the building's front. One of the big vehicle-sized doors was open a few inches—and Thane suddenly threw himself flat, ignoring the stab of pain that came from his shoulder. There was no mistaking the man who had stepped out of the building.

Grigor, one hand deep in his jacket pocket in an unmistakable attitude, cigarette burning in the corner of his mouth, looked carefully around then, satisfied, leaned back against the wood of the doorway, obviously enjoying the sunshine.

Phil Moss nudged Thane gently, and murmured, 'Chimney.'

He followed his gaze. A thin, but steady, column of smoke was coming from the short smokestack at the rear of the building, dissipating in the light breeze after only a few feet.

Thane moved closer to his companion and, lips only inches from Phil's ear, told him, 'If we try to take them from here, it means a dive across the open, giving them a wonderful chance to knock some of us off. See what the back of the place looks like, Phil—take the sergeant with you, and make a pretty wide sweep so that there's no chance of your being spotted. Luckily, there don't appear to be any windows apart from those big skylights.'

Phil slid away. A tap on the shoulder and a gesture was sufficient for the sergeant, who followed him, and within seconds they had disappeared among the greenery.

At the doorway, Grigor finished his cigarette, and gave the glowing end a finger-and-thumb flick that carried it several yards in the direction of the watching police. Then he dragged his gun from his jacket pocket, and gave it a cursory inspection. Satisfied, he stepped back inside the doorway, which remained a few inches open. Thane had no illusions. The small fat man would not be far away.

Phil and the sergeant returned a few minutes later, and Thane retired a few yards back into the woodland to hear their report.

'There's only one other door, a small one at the back,' said Phil. 'There are a couple of windows to that side, but they have frosted glass fitted, so we can pretty well forget them. The back door is closed, and there's no sign of anyone on watch there.'

'How close can we get to it under cover?'

The sergeant answered, 'To within twenty feet, sir.'

The plan formulated swiftly in Thane's mind. 'Pull back your men, Sergeant, all but one to maintain a watch. We'll take them from the rear. Oh, and send a man back to the cars. Tell the drivers to stand by, and the moment they hear a whistle blast, to bring their cars up as fast as they can and block that pathway.'

A flash of grim humour crossed his lined face. 'Now listen—here's how we're going to get them to open the back door for us.'

CHAPTER THIRTY-FOUR

PATRICK KILBURN GLOATED over the glistening haul piled carelessly on the workbench before him, then plunged elbow-deep into the straw and paper of the opened packing-case at his side and pulled out another linen-wrapped bundle. He ripped the cloth away, and hefted the strangely shaped golden dish—must be a good half pound and more in it.

For a moment he puzzled over the niceties of its design, then turned and demanded, 'Here, you—what do you put in this one?'

'Thick pouring sauce—it's one of the oldest pieces in the collection.'

Tied hand and foot, and dumped on the floor beside the packing-cases, Lord Lochhead's butler had already felt the weight of Kilburn's foot against his ribs. Add to that the fact that he was still recovering from the smashing blow on the head that had sent him into a black-velvet oblivion within minutes of the truck leaving Lochhead Castle, and he could hardly be blamed for caring little about the fate of his master's plate but a lot about his own immediate personal safety.

Tie loosened, shirt sleeves rolled up, beads of sweat glistening on his forehead, Giore Paxidena reappeared from the rear of the building.

'Beautiful, beautiful,' he murmured, surveying the glittering array. 'It seems almost sacrilege to melt down such beautiful things, eh, Patrick?'

'Gold's gold, whatever way it's decked out,' shrugged Kilburn. 'How's it going? We're way behind schedule.'

'Only by about fifteen minutes,' protested Paxidena. 'Just because that feed pipe seized up—Lagen had to make quite a few improvisations to adapt the furnace for this job. It's going beautifully now—want to see for yourself?' he invited.

Kilburn shook his head. 'Just get on with it,' he said harshly. 'I'll get the rest of this last packing-case unwrapped—the other two are completely emptied.'

Paxidena's eyes hardened for a fraction of a second before he turned away.

Kilburn's confidence—and arrogance—was growing by the hour. It had positively spurted on when he had been play-acting in his role of officer at the castle. Perhaps it was better, having him thus, with the task that lay ahead for the Irishman—Though certainly, he had been easier to handle in the early hours of their meeting than he was now.

The restaurateur saw a clash of wills ahead—but he was going to do his damnedest to postpone it for two good reasons, the eagerness with which Kilburn used his gun, and the thought of the first small trial batch of gold plate, now stewed down to a fluid mass in the steel bowl which fitted tight over the roaring pink-white heat of the furnace jets. He scooped up an armful of spoons and small plate, stuffed a couple of salt cellars into his trouser pocket, and strode back.

Also down to his shirtsleeves, face red and glistening in the heat, Arthur Lagen looked up as Paxidena entered the back room.

'First batch ready, boss,' he reported. 'I've got the mould

opened out, waiting. Want to start pouring?'

'Let's go,' agreed Paxidena.

Each man pulled on a pair of rough leather gauntlets, then they picked up the two carrier bars lying beside the mould, ready to thread them through the eyeholes set in the stub arms protruding from the bowl, where the temperature was now above the 1,000 degrees Centigrade mark.

At that precise moment, the stove gave a sudden muffled hiccup. A dense cloud of smoke and soot forced its way out of every joint in the chimney's metal vent, and even flashed-back through the air control opening.

Paxidena dropped his carrier bar, and stood open-mouthed. Lagen was quicker to recover.

'Chimney—something's happened to the chimney. Must be blocked.' With one swift move he turned the furnace control to minimum feed.

'I'll check outside,' volunteered Paxidena, rushing to the rear door. He freed the heavy bolt, turned the lock handle, and then the door seemed to fly inwards. He caught a jumbled glimpse of blue sky, a man scrambling down from a tree—uniforms—then the door panels, propelled by the weight of two hefty uniform men, smashed him backwards.

In the background, a whistle was shrilling. Thane's men boiled into the building through the wide-open back door—all except the man who had climbed the tree, and balanced perilously on a branch while he used a long pole to drop a car-blanket over the chimney-pot. He was the whistle-blower now.

Paxidena, still staggering backwards from the blow he had received, made a dazed, desperate attempt to reach the gun in his shoulder holster.

Before he could, the uniform sergeant's sixteen-stone weight took him square on the chest. Air whooshed from his lungs under the blow.

The sergeant had no time for fancy stuff. As Paxidena hit

the floor, a fist the size of a half-brick thumped him under the ear—and the following police jumped over his sprawled, unconscious form. The sergeant turned him over, pocketed the gun, then, after a quick frisk for other weapons, handcuffed Paxidena's right wrist and left ankle together.

It took seconds—seconds in which Arthur Lagen, spinning round from the furnace at the sudden clamour, shouted a warning to Kilburn, scooped up the iron bar from the floor, and brought it smashing down with two-handed force as the leading uniform man charged him.

The policeman's arm, thrown upwards in a sudden protective movement, took the full force. There was a sound like a stick snapping, and the young cop went down with a moan of pain.

Lagen swept the bar up again—at the same time as Patrick Kilburn began firing, the flat boom of the shots echoing above all else in the confines of the building. With a roar of triumph, Lagen jumped forward, swung the bar—and missed as Phil Moss flung himself to one side.

Before the driver could recover his balance, a baton smashed on the side of his head. He grunted and swayed for a moment—long enough for the bar to be wrested from his grip. He heaved himself upright, drew back his gloved fist, then as half a dozen hands seized him, the last of the colour drained from his face, he dropped his arms and quietly allowed himself to be handcuffed.

Outside, three automatics were now firing.

Crouched just within the doorway leading to the main building, Thane triggered two shots from his Webley into the brightly lit interior, then ducked back as Kilburn, sheltering behind one of the plate packing-cases, sent two bullets screaming off the brickwork inches from his head. From the big double doors, Grigor was also firing—in two directions alternately, down towards Thane and out the gap between the doors towards the wood.

'Up here,' bellowed Kilburn.

'No—there's a cop in the wood, and cars heading up the drive,' yelled back Grigor.

Gun in hand, Phil Moss materialised beside Thane, and then dived for the other side of the doorway.

Kilburn sent a bullet screaming inches from his heels, then yelled, 'Grigor—get ready.'

Thane stuck his head out—and jerked back again as Kilburn, switching to the heavier naval revolver he still had with him, began a sudden blast of shots.

'He's running for the lorry.' Phil had begun firing, but Kilburn made the safety of the vehicle's side, and joined Grigor in another pinning burst. Suddenly, the truck's door slammed, and the engine came to life with a high-revved bellow.

'Now—quick.' Thane jumped from his cover, and, Phil at his side, the uniform men at their heels, they dashed forward, with no time to spare, for the butler, still lying in the corner tied hand and foot.

Grigor smacked two final shots into the mass of blue, and a uniform man spun, then grabbed the wall for support as one of the bullets raked his side.

Kilburn ground the truck into reverse gear, jarred the clutch, and the vehicle roared back, towards the still-closed doors.

Grigor, already running to meet it, raised his gun arm for a last shot—but Phil, aiming along the barrel, triggered first. Grigor gave an animal-like squeal as his knee-cap shattered, and he rolled along the ground. The lorry didn't slacken. One rear wheel bumped over the wounded man—then the truck hit the wooden doors, bursting through them like matchwood.

In the open Kilburn sweated over the heavy steering wheel to change the lock, ground into first gear, and roared off again, ducking as a shot from Thane's gun starred the windscreen.

Thane reached the doorway as the truck got going, snarling through the gears, 'Get the tyres,' he shouted.

He and Phil hammered off the remaining rounds in their Webleys, but the Bedford, its naval insignia bright in the sunlight, kept on.

'The cars will get him,' said Phil.

But Kilburn had other ideas.

The truck was doing over forty now, jumping and bucking over the track towards the spot where two of the three police cars were slewed across its width in a hasty roadblock.

Then, with a howl of defiance, lost in the engine-roar, he swung the wheel. The Bedford shot off the track, dropped a clear foot as it took the dip to the grassland, then, springs heaving, charged between two trees.

Frantically, muscles straining, Kilburn swung the wheel again, accelerator foot pressed hard to the boards. The truck heaved round and, tyres screaming and spinning, raced back onto the track.

The third police car was swinging to intercept it—but the Bedford's solid steel bumper bar tore a gaping rent into the Jaguar's radiator and wing, and the truck kept going.

Colin Thane sprinted down to where the two "road-block" cars were busily turning, and jumped into the nearest. There was no need to order the driver—he was already in gear—Thane was hurled back in his seat as they took off.

The Bedford reached the road, and turned right without pausing, and Thane's car hammered after it.

'Making for town,' shouted the police driver. 'Will I try to take him?'

Thane shook his head. 'We could stop him—but there wouldn't be much left. Keep on his tail. I'll radio for a block ahead—maybe it'll work this time.'

The second police car, the Humber, was only feet behind them now, siren wailing. Thane picked up the radio-mike, and was about to flip down the transmitter switch, when suddenly his driver gasped in horror.

He looked up. Ahead, the road swooped down into a hollow, crossed a narrow bridge over a stream, then rose on again over the rising ground.

The Bedford was speeding for the bridge—and heading for the same bridge, from the opposite direction, was a small saloon.

'The Ford.' Thane recognised Liam and Margot Kilburn's car at a glance.

Even as he watched, the little car increased speed, deliberately racing for the bridge. Above the continued shriek of the police siren, he could hear the non-stop wail of the small saloon's horn.

'They're crazy,' said his driver despairingly, while the Jaguar's needle reached the seventy mark. 'They'll meet the truck square on the bridge.'

Patrick Kilburn realised it, too, as the truck hammered on. And like a flash, he knew that only two people in the world would throw themselves head-on at him in this lunatic to-hell-with-it test of nerve.

Head on—at that speed, nobody could survive, either in the truck or car.

The Ford zipped onto the far-away end of the bridge—and with a scream of fear, Kilburn swung the steering wheel for the last time.

The Bedford slew, tyres smoking—at seventy mph it hit the parapet, overturned, and, ripping yards of masonry down, plunged off the bridge.

The Ford, never faltering, swept arrow-like past the spot, lurched frantically as it hit a piece of stonework thrown onto the road, smacked down again with a spring-snapping bang, then, off-side drooping, Liam sawing at the wheel, brakes screaming, halted only feet away from Thane's car, which had also come to an emergency stop.

Behind them, the Bedford's petrol tank went up with a booming roar, an orange ball of flame shot skywards, sending out a shockwave of heat.

Conscious of Phil and other officers running past him and down the side of the bridge towards the wreck, Thane climbed shakily out of the police car and walked slowly across to the Ford.

Margot Kilburn got out to meet him. Liam stayed where he was, behind the wheel, face white as a sheet, hands fumbling blindly with a cigarette packet. The girl moved her lips twice before the words came.

'I'm—I'm sorry,' she whispered. 'Is he—?' She broke off, trembling, tears in her eyes, and Thane gave her a steadying hand.

They waited there long minutes until Phil returned.

'He'll live,' he reported laconically. 'Till after the trial, anyway.'

Margot gave a long, shuddering sigh of relief. 'You were right,' she told Thane. 'It would have been still worse for us to have his blood on our hands.'

Liam heaved his bulk out of the Ford, and placed his arm round his sister's shoulder.

'We can go home, now,' he said.

'In peace,' Thane told them. 'The rest is our business.'

He watched them being driven away a short time later, and a tired, yet satisfied, feeling came over him as the car disappeared over the rise.

'Another job done, Phil,' he mused.

'Are you kidding?' grunted his friend. 'This lot's going to need a pile of statements feet high to explain.'

It did.

PRAISE FOR BILL KNOX

'Bill Knox writes with the factual accuracy of a good reporter. He does his homework thoroughly.'

Evening Times, Glasgow

'His plotting is impeccable... and he can build his books to a relentless climax.'

New York Times Book Review

'The expertise is interesting, the invention good and the writing literate and lively.'

Sunday Times

'Always a thoroughly reliable, good read.'

The Times

'Sound technical details... thrills without frills.'

Sunday Telegraph

'The only practitioner who writes with complete authority and accuracy about the police procedures of Scotland.'

Glasgow Herald

'Bill Knox is a highly skilled professional ... he stamps his books with his own brand of authenticity and accuracy and compelling plotting.'

Irish Times

Printed and bound by CPI Group (UK) Ltd, Croydon, CR0 4YY
24/03/2025
01836028-0002